Inevitable

A Novel by Bella Black

INEVITABLE

Inevitable

Copyright © 2018 by Bella Black

All rights reserved. No part of this book may be reproduced or transmitted in any form or by any means without written permission from the author.

CREDITS:

Cover Concept and Manuscript Editor: N. Renee McFadden
Cover Design: Antonio Marshall (Tiggio)
Song: "He Loves Me" by Jill Scott from the album *Who Is Jill Scott: Words and Sounds, Volume 1* (released July 18, 2000)

INEVITABLE

To the one who makes it all possible, our Creator.

Reflections

INEVITABLE

1

Giselle Mosely reclined on her grey, leather chaise as she reveled in the magnificent views of downtown Atlanta. The focal point of her living room was a floor-to-ceiling panoramic window that eventually sold her on the $870,000 investment. She felt on top of the world whenever she looked out upon the bustling city of zealous professionals ranging from actors to musicians to politicians. Here is where childhood dreams could become reality – but only if you possessed the irrefutable grit to outperform your competition. She sniffed her glass of Egon Muller Riesling and breathed deeply. After rolling the wine around her palette, she swallowed slowly. The $2,000 libation was her favorite and she didn't plan on sharing for the occasion. The weather was seemingly not going to cooperate with the day that lie ahead as scattered showers were in the forecast. She tossed a throw over her swollen, aching feet and massaged her right ankle as she closed her eyes. It was hard to believe that 18 years ago she was stuck in her small hometown going nowhere fast. She smiled a confident smile as she glanced around the two-level penthouse. She remembered her realtor having to convince her that she not only could afford the hefty mortgage payment, but would also be able to completely decorate the 3,200-square-foot space to her liking. Giselle was so used to saving money that she'd forgotten how to spend it. But as she looked around, in awe of her second biggest accomplishment, a sense of pride arose within her. Basquiat's "Horn Players" gave her living room immense flavor. It was her beloved oil stick canvas that spanned the wall adjacent to her kitchen. Its colors spoke volumes while telling a quiet story of triumph and progression. She loved jazz and this particular piece paid tribute to those who Giselle deemed as the greats - Charlie Parker and Dizzy Gillespie. While she didn't have much growing up, she could vividly remember her mother playing old jazz records to cheer her up whenever she had experienced a rough day at school.

Giselle would constantly be teased for her second-hand clothing and worn shoes that she seemed to outgrow every three months. Because her mother and father had both dropped out of high school, they struggled more often than not. Despite the hardships, they managed to stay together. When her mother, Grace, found out that their family of two would soon become four, she threw herself into work, securing odd jobs here and there throughout the city. But with only one post office and two grocery stores within a twenty-mile radius, she couldn't find much. She volunteered at the local church and accepted offerings when the pastor felt like giving. She was also a local seamstress, altering clothes for neighbors and church members. Her father, Gerald, worked on and off at the Black Diamond coal mine and supported his family the best way he could. The nearest school was ten miles away. Giselle would walk nearly half a mile every morning just to catch the bus. She hated it but pressed forward as she knew that her parents didn't want her to experience life the way they had. *"Learn the value of hard work by working hard"*, her mother would often say.

To escape her dismal life, Giselle visited her aunt in Atlanta during the summers. And while she wasn't rich, Aunt Gigi lived a much better life than her sister Grace. She was successful, intelligent, and everything that Giselle aspired to be. Except in the "men" department.

Giselle picked up a picture of the last memory of her and Aunt Gigi. Her health noticeably started to deteriorate when Giselle began the juris doctorate program at Emory University. She rubbed the outline of the silver frame and wiped her tears as they began to fall. She died in January - four months before her graduation. Giselle wished she had been able to show her how much she was appreciated. Her aunt had inspired her to become a lawyer. Gigi used to joke that she would one day need Giselle to rescue her from her crazy boyfriends. One late summer day, when she was about 11 years old, Giselle remembered returning to find her aunt's then boyfriend, William, hovering over her with a hammer. Even though she was young, Gigi's frightened eyes somehow warned Giselle of the untold truths that could change a person's life forever.

Giselle continued to fumble through the pictures on her leaning bookcase. She smirked as she picked up the picture of her two best friends, Elicia and Marley. Even then, the three of them looked like they were ready to run the world in their sexy bikinis and lean beach bodies. She'd met them during Black Beach Weekend seven years ago. She hadn't planned to go but was persuaded by a few of her co-workers who hadn't missed a year since they were in college. Once she arrived, her associates ditched her for some guys they'd met in the hotel elevator and

INEVITABLE

she found herself sitting at a bar on the beach alone. Elicia came and sat next to her. She cackled at the thought of how pitiful she must have looked.

"I'm Giselle," she said as she extended her hand.

"What a pretty name. I'm Elicia and this is my girl, Marley. We came down from Atlanta for the weekend."

"To have some fun!" said Marley "And of course, to meet my future husband." Elicia smirked as she pulled out a blunt.

"You two smoke regularly?" she inquired as Marley handed her the lighter. "I don't smoke at all," said Elicia. "But this weekend we've decided to channel our inner "bad gal Ri-Ri" and make a few exceptions to the rules. After all, you only live once, right?!"

After partaking in marijuana use for the first time, Giselle felt carefree and blissful. She explained the mess she was in and was invited to stay with Elicia and Marley for the remainder of the trip. From that day on, the three were inseparable. Needless to say, there was never a dull moment. Over the years they were able to master some of life's greatest challenges while building an impeccable bond. It was only fitting that they were there to celebrate tomorrow's most momentous occasion.

Giselle stopped reminiscing long enough to check her phone. She had six text messages from Elicia. She quickly dialed her.

"Girrrrrrrlllllllll, what are you doing? Why are you not answering the phone and you know people are coming through in less than twenty-four hours? Wassup with that?"

"I apologize. I've been having those random headaches and exhaustion again."

"That's because you're overworking yourself. You need to slow down."

"Well, obviously, all this work is working for me, isn't it?"

INEVITABLE

Elicia sighed. "Yes, but you really do need to relax more…this is coming from your friend. I'm serious."

Giselle was quiet.

"Anyways, you didn't send me a list of the things you need me to pick up for tomorrow. And, when are you going to go to the doctor?"

"You know my memory is shot. I'll send the list once we hang up. And you also know that I don't do doctors."

"Well, please expedite the list. I still gotta pull my 'fit together."

Giselle sucked her teeth. "Why do you always do this, Elicia? Why would you wait until the last minute to find something to wear?"

"I didn't intentionally wait until the last minute. I just haven't been able to find anything that's purple and sexy. And plus, I'm trying to snag Mr. Right so you know ah gotta be da baddest ting in da building," she sang in a very convincing Jamaican accent.

"Well, you better get it together because that is the color scheme!"

"Why must everything be purple with you, Giselle, why!?" Elicia said with an exaggerated tone.

"For two reasons. Number 1, Prince is my man and we will all pay homage to him and Number 2, because we represent royalty over here, boo. You already know this."

"The royalty concept I get, but I think you need to go see a professional about your obsession with Prince," huffed Elicia. "Send me the list, please. I'm heading out in twenty."

"Yes, ma'am. Don't forget to bring samples of your makeup." Giselle heard her other line beep.

"That's tacky, G. It's your day."

"Elicia, you've been working on this makeup line for months. This would be the perfect crowd to test it on."

INEVITABLE

Elicia sighed. "I suppose you're right. FaceIt is ready for the world to see!"

Giselle ended the call and clicked over to answer her brother.

"Sis!" he yelled playfully.

"Did you get the drink list?"

"Well, hello to you, too. Yep, I got the list. Purple-Rita, Pomegranate Martini, Purple Haze, and Z Violet. I told you I got this."

"Remember that you will be here to bartend. Not flirt with my friends and guests."

"Whatever, G. I have my queen already."

"Yea, whatever. Just don't be late, Gerrod. You damn near missed my graduation, remember?"

"I won't, sis, and Eva is not going to allow it. A'ight?! I'll holla at you at 7:00."

"Gerrod!"

"Just kidding, see you at 6:00. And I just want you to know that you are being disrespectful by asking me to wear all purple."

"It's just for one night."

"I'll try, but don't be surprised if I show up in Big Bird yellow." He hung up.

Giselle smirked and made her way back to the leaning book shelf. She picked up a picture of her brother, Gerrod, when he was younger. They were very close siblings - growing up he was practically her shadow. Now he was a Morehouse graduate working in real estate. Giselle cracked up at his missing front teeth. She was proud of him.

A hint of sadness came over her as she was reminded that she didn't have that special someone to share this moment with. She had been praying to

INEVITABLE

God to send her a man who would be her everything. While her patience was getting the best of her, she knew that the next guy to come into her life would be worth the wait. He would have to be 'the one'."

She walked onto the rooftop terrace and began tidying up. The cool autumn breeze made her shiver a little. After moving around furniture and plants, Giselle swept the wooden floor and made sure the glass firepit was stocked. She polished her metallic leather sectional and arranged the solar light planters to her liking. Stepping back, she admired her Property Brothers-inspired layout and grinned from ear to ear.

After following up with her makeup artist, Djane, and photographer, Giselle opted for a short nap before doing anything more. As she dozed in and out of sleep, a special kind of excitement came over her. She was elated about sharing this moment with her loved ones.

Not every day does an African-American woman from Adger, Alabama make partner.

INEVITABLE

Unmasking

INEVITABLE

2

"No!" she said firmly. "I can't go out like that again!"

"Come on, so you want to be single for the rest of your life?"

Giselle shot her the look of death.

"I would rather be single than to date any more of the sorry-ass-excuses-for-men that you try to hook me up with."

"How was I supposed to know that he was going to be an asshole? He was a friend of Nasir's and he thought you was cute. I didn't put a gun to your head and make you go out with him!"

Giselle and over forty of her closest colleagues, family, and friends gathered Friday night to celebrate her long overdue partnership with Simon and Franklin Law Firm. Elicia and Giselle stood in a corner in her L-shaped kitchen trying to converse without anyone noticing. Her granite countertops were hidden by an assortment of entrees for her guests to indulge. Merlot, Riesling, Sauvignon Blanc, Chardonnay, Shiraz, and Petrus were chilled on ice. Trays adorned with gouda, provolone, goat, and sharp cheddar cheeses were being replenished for those who enjoyed a good wine and cheese combo. Giselle was pleased with the turnout and enjoyed the admiration and praise she received from those who had been there for her throughout the years. She allowed Elicia to arrange the all-purple affair and was ecstatic about showing off her girl's event planning skills. The impressive selection of hors d'oeuvres ranged from everything including filet mignon, smoked salmon, crab cakes, bacon wrapped scallops, stuffed mushrooms, and caviar. She didn't know that Elicia could pull together such a delectable menu, especially considering the fact that she didn't cook. As the late Ronny Jordan's *Brighter Day* echoed throughout the penthouse, visitors entertained each other by playing Taboo, Jenga, and other popular trivia games. Others danced the night away while hoping to make new connections.

Giselle sucked her teeth. "I should have known not to go out with him once you said he was friends with Nasir."

INEVITABLE

Giselle regretted making a statement like that about her best friend's husband, but she'd already let it slip. She had had enough of being hooked up with losers.

"So, what exactly are you trying to say?" retorted Elicia as she sat her wine glass down on the counter.

"I'm saying that Nasir isn't the most upstanding guy, so why should his friend be?"

"Don't bring Nasir into this. We've had our troubles, but every couple does. What you need to do is worry less about him, and more about your damn self," she whispered angrily.

"I thought this was supposed to be a victory celebration," interrupted Marley as she entered the kitchen area with an empty tray. "You've finally made partner at Simon and Franklin - the firm that you have been busting your ass at **for six LONG years** - and you two are standing here arguing over a guy who isn't even in the picture anymore…unbelievable."

Marley refilled the sushi tray and went to amuse the guests.

"Marley's right. This is petty. Let's get back out there."

Giselle sighed. "I guess it's not your fault. All of the men in Atlanta are pretty much unqualified in my book."

They both headed to the rooftop terrace where seemingly all the couples had decided to retreat. Giselle sighed as she again thought about when she would meet her Mr. Right. When everyone left tonight, she would be alone. She was 36 years old with no prospects, potentials, or time-fillers. She thought about all the so–called relationships she'd been involved in since she relocated from Alabama. Besides her ex Sidney, there were only three other less serious relationships and she could write a book on all of them.

"Black women don't know what they want," shouted Dwayne, her assistant. She had walked right into the middle of a lively discussion. "Women are always talking about what they want, but when they get a good brother they don't know how to hold him down."

"Not true," snapped her co-worker Samantha. "Black men just ain't worth a damn. They want someone to be their mama, and I'm not here for all that." She rolled her mink-lashed eyes while tugging at her too tight one-piece to avoid exposing her unmentionables.

Giselle sometimes admired Samantha's boldness and authenticity. She could always count on her to keep it real…drama-filled and all. Samantha confided in Giselle on numerous occasions about her own nonexistent love life. She was currently having an affair with the lawyer she worked beside and walked around the firm acting oblivious to the fact.

"Prime example," Dwayne continued, "I had a woman tell me that I didn't look like I made enough money to even take her out, and **she** worked at Wal-Mart. Now, what is that about?"

Everyone howled.

Yasmin, a paralegal for the firm, chimed in. "Well, explain this, I dated a man for three straight months and had an instant connection with him. I saw him every day and as soon as we embarked upon month four he tells me that he thinks that he's in love with another woman and that he isn't ready to make a decision."

"How long did you wait before you gave him some?" asked Dwayne.

Yasmin scratched her head while looking into the sky. "I don't know, maybe a month…maybe a couple of weeks. Anyway, what's so wrong with that?"

"**That** is what's wrong!" yelled Dwayne. "And the only reason he told you was to see if you would be foolish enough to stick around and watch him have his cake and eat it too."

Marley interrupted. "Aren't we all consenting adults?"

"Yes," Gerrod injected. "But once you give a man a reason to stop working for the prize, he will. It's like you are giving him permission to act a fucking fool. If he can get it right away, you're just letting him know that whatever else he wants he'll receive with no work as well."

Giselle noticed the heads nodding in agreement and thought about what he said. Was he telling the truth? Or, could it be the other way around? What about the women who didn't give it up and maybe held out for too long?

INEVITABLE

Gerrod's wife took a seat by him and grabbed his hand. "My baby is right," she said as she kissed the top of his head. "I made Gerrod wait seven months before we were intimate."

All the men looked at him like he was crazy but Gerrod didn't seem to care.

"Ay-ay-ay, I know what you all are thinking. I'm dumb, I'm stupid, I'm this, I'm that - but honestly - it was the best thing any woman could have ever done for me. I was so used to catering to women until they gave me what I wanted - which was usually within two weeks - that I never took the time to be their friend first. And by friends, I mean active communicators, with each other, and most importantly with God. If you all are not clear about what you want from each other you will go nowhere fast."

Throngs began to form around the outspoken man on the Italian leather sectional. He saw the strange looks that overcame all of the women in the room and knew he'd hit a soft spot.

"A man likes a challenge, and if you aren't challenging enough, he will move on to the next one." He looked up at Eva. "She was the greatest challenge I've ever come up against." Eva kissed Gerrod softly on the lips and smiled.

Giselle began to wonder if he was genuine in his revelation. She remembered all the times she lied to females to cover for her brother, but with Eva it was different. It was as if she made him want to be a better man. They met three years ago at Eva's first book signing. She was a new author on a promotional tour and he was on the prowl for his next victim. Instead of the typical club scene, Gerrod frequented bookstores in hopes of scoring a friend with benefits, but on that particular night he just so happened to find love. He knew that there was something special about her. They dated for ten months and on her birthday, he proposed. The rest was history. Even though Giselle was happy for Eva and her brother, a hint of jealousy always came over her when they were around. She longed for what they had and was tired of waiting on it. After a couple of more hours of fellowship, Giselle packed a few to-go containers and said goodnight to her guests. She was too tired to do a thorough cleaning and headed upstairs. Sipping her wine, she undressed in the mirror.

"36 ain't old," she said caressing herself. "I still got it." Giselle combed her fingers through her shoulder length hair. After removing her makeup, she examined the splotchy red patches on her skin. The flare-ups had been occurring more often and had even spread to her thighs. She rubbed the back of her right leg and a sharp tingle came over her. Giselle suddenly lost her balance and sat on the edge of the tub. *I've had way too much to drink,* she thought. While the water was running, she lit vanilla-scented candles and placed them around her quartz espree jacuzzi. She ran her hands through the soft bubbles and imagined someone massaging her tight shoulders and removing her robe while carefully placing her into the lukewarm water. She felt strong, phantom hands washing her most delicate parts and then drying her off before placing her on the white goose down comforter in the master suite. Giselle smiled when he whispered to her that she was the most beautiful woman in the world and how proud he was of her prodigious accomplishment and what they had built, together.

Tears streamed down her face as she wearily helped herself into the tub and consumed the entire glass of wine in two gulps.

Two hours later, Giselle fumbled around for her cell phone as she squinted at the clock. *Who in the HELL is calling me at 5 in the morning?* she thought.

"Hello," she muttered.

"Yes, I am trying to reach Giselle Mosely."

"Speaking." She didn't recognize the voice.

"Yes, this is Hill Stokes calling from Stokes & Associates law firm in California. I have been trying to get in contact with you for quite some time regarding a position we have open at my practice."

Giselle remembered applying for several jobs at various law firms once she passed the bar exam over a decade ago. She had only worked for two other firms before finally settling down at Simon and Franklin. She had no plans to leave them unless the position came with respect, an outstanding compensation package, and perks.

INEVITABLE

Giselle cleared her throat as she sat up. "I apologize," she said in her most professional tone, "but I honestly don't remember applying for a position there."

"You wouldn't remember because I found you."

Giselle didn't know what to say. "I'm flattered," she mumbled, "but I just made partner at Simon & Franklin."

Hill paused for a few moments. "Yes, I know. Congratulations. There is no rush Mrs. - I'm sorry- Ms. Mosely. I just wanted to inform you of the research we've been doing on you. Is it true that you have not lost a case? And that you are only 36 years of age?"

"Yes, that's correct," she responded.

"Well, here at Stokes & Associates we pride ourselves on making sure that anyone who represents our firm comes first and we know that you will be best suited partnering up with the most professional law firm in the world."

Silence flooded the line. She had never thought about leaving Atlanta. She had made it her home and worked too damn hard to get to this point. But maybe this was a sign. Maybe God had something greater in store.

"Um, is it okay for me to get back to you at a more convenient hour? You do know it's 5 in the morning, right?"

"Yes," said Hill, "and I do apologize but I wanted to make sure I reached you. I will be in contact soon. Enjoy the rest of your day."

The line went dead. Giselle glanced at the clock to make sure she wasn't going crazy. *Was this a joke? Who, in their right mind, calls at 5 in the morning to propose a career move?* She rolled over and went back to sleep. She had a busy morning ahead of her.

INEVITABLE

***

"Make sure you know all there is to know about your man. Let him know what you will and will not tolerate up front and, trust me, he *will* get the picture. If he doesn't, kick him to the curb. It's important that you know your worth, ladies. A man will ONLY do what you allow him to do. Always remember that your self-worth is key to navigating relationships."

All of the young women in the room nodded their heads in agreement. Some even took notes.

"Make certain that the man you decide to invest your energy possesses the qualities that you would want your husband or even your son to possess. Otherwise, you will simply be wasting your time."

Giselle took a sip of her herbal tea as several hands flew in the air. She pointed to a young sister wearing too much makeup, blue contacts, and a blonde weave. "Hey, Ms. Mosely," she shrieked, "First, I wanted to thank you for coming down to the YMCA to speak with us. You are truly my role model." Giselle smiled. "I personally come to all of your seminars and you give such great advice. But I, and several other sisters, have been wondering if *you* have a man."

This question caught Giselle off guard. She cleared her throat. "Yes, I do, and he is wonderful," she lied. "He is one of my main motivations for speaking with you all today. I want to let you beautiful ladies know that you, too, can experience the love that I share if you know your self-worth and are sure about what you want in life." Everyone in the room applauded.

Giselle took time out of her demanding schedule to give back to the community at least once a month and she loved every minute of it. She would come down to the YMCA on Campbellton Road to speak with young women whose ages ranged from 18-25 on various personal development topics. Speaking engagements would be held in hopes of enlightening the young women about relevant issues that weren't being discussed in their homes, romantic relationships, and constituent circles. Today's topic was about building generational wealth. But no matter

INEVITABLE

what topic she opened with someone would always inject a question about relationships. Most of the women were single parents attempting to make a better life for their children and themselves and when she thought about it – most of them had shared with her their experiences with unhealthy relationships. Giselle did not want to see the cycle of broken homes and broken dreams continue in the lives of others and took matters into her own hands. She began a mentoring program at the firm, when she started there six years ago, and then branched out by initiating community service through speaking engagements. Giselle anxiously watched everyone leave the seminar and was relieved when the room cleared. She hurried to the comfort of her E-class Mercedes Benz and quickly lit a cigarette.

She took a puff and sunk down into her leather magenta bucket seats. The nicotine consumed her body and she closed her eyes. "Shit," she grumbled as she brushed the ashes off her lap.

This wasn't something that Giselle was proud of and so far she had gone two weeks without succumbing to one, but had no other way to relieve her stress. She needed someone to talk to.

INEVITABLE

3

Elicia jumped in the car with an attitude and Giselle already knew why.

"*Now* what did he do?" she asked with a look of disgust.

Elicia sucked her teeth. "I deserve better and I know it."

"So why are you still with him?" asked Marley as she consoled her.

The three friends were headed to the Apache Café in downtown Atlanta. Sunday nights were reserved for spoken word and open mic performances and they attended whenever their weekends were open at once – which was rare. Live jazz, funk, hip-hop, soul and more was featured. The Apache Café had become a favorite of all three. The atmosphere was sexy but classy, and relaxing. This was one of the few places in Atlanta where you could let your hair down and really be yourself.

They sped up 75 South as Elicia spilled the drama once again. She sighed. "What do you do when the man you love doesn't believe in the God you serve?"

"That again? You two have been arguing about that shit for the past month. Build a bridge and get over it. I can't comprehend why a beautiful woman like you is with a man who should be one of your clients. Everything in your life is consistent, but **him**." Giselle didn't mean to sound harsh, but she felt like she had to. "Let him go if you're not being fulfilled in the relationship."

"Pull the car over. That's why I don't tell you anything!" Elicia was irritated by her friend's bluntness.

Giselle realized she was being a little too insensitive. "I apologize, but you know I don't care for Nasir. You know you deserve better but yet you stick around for the bullshit and for the life of me I cannot understand why."

INEVITABLE

Marley chimed in. "Maybe it's not meant for *you* to understand, Giselle. We are her best friends. Stop the judgement. Besides, marriage is a deep commitment. It might not be that easy to just walk away."

"I have been praying for the last few months for God to give Nasir clarity. If I gave my life over to God, in order to build up *our* marriage, I don't know why he can't do the same. He doesn't realize how much this hurts me. I thought we were in this shit together, but obviously that's not the case. ***He*** changed, not me."

Giselle shook her head. "Well maybe it's time for *you* to change. Besides how are you growing if you're not changing?"

If you asked Elicia why she married Nasir in the first place she would tell you it was because she was in love…in the beginning. The two met at the Velvet Room Nightclub and immediately began dating. Nasir explained to her that he had a criminal past (one that he still hadn't fully disclosed to Elicia) and that he was trying to change his life around. Elicia saw the potential and made him hers. The fact that he only had an 11th grade education and no steady employment didn't bother her outright. It did, however, bother Giselle.

"Why does he even deserve to be with you?" she hammered.

Elicia shook her head in disbelief. "He ***deserves*** me because I say so."

Giselle pulled out a compact mirror. "Look at yourself."

"You look like you're mixed with Indian and I don't know, Haitian or something. You rock the baddest short cut I've ever seen. Your makeup is always on point. Your body is from the gods…especially those hips. And for whatever reason you're always smelling like berries and shit."

Elicia burst into laughter.

"Not to mention you are the only Black developmental psychologist I know! How many sisters you know doing that?"

"My accomplishments have nothing to do with whom I choose to be with," said Elicia with exasperation.

INEVITABLE

"But they should. He's not on your level. ***You*** intimidate him. ***You*** remind him of how much of a fuck up he really is."

Elicia often found herself replaying this same conversation over and over again in her head.

In the beginning, Nasir was handy around her one-bedroom apartment and made her feel like a queen. During their courtship, he would come by her job and surprise her with chocolates, flowers, and other inexpensive tokens of appreciation. After a year of serious dating the two went to the justice of the peace and got hitched. The first six months of their marriage was great, but as time went by, Elicia realized she didn't even know the man she'd married. He became somewhat controlling and his mood was sporadic. He would lash out for no reason even sometimes starting fights with her out of the blue. Elicia knew that the death of his best friend affected him, but didn't know that it would change who he was and how he treated her. She wanted their marriage to work and didn't want to give up without salvaging what they had left. Nasir on the other hand, didn't. Out of the blue he developed habits that Elicia wasn't familiar with. He smoked weed and drank every chance he got. He recently quit his job, using the excuse that he wasn't being recognized for his talent, and would stay out all times of the night. Elicia didn't have any physical proof of cheating, but deep down knew that he was.

"I asked him to attend one Sunday service with me and what do you think this negro did? He gave me a million excuses as to why he couldn't go." *"God ain't got nothing to do with us,"* he said. *"There is no such thing as God anyway."*

Marley shook her head.

"He went on to say that if there was a God, He wouldn't have taken his mother and father from him at the same time." She teared up. "I don't understand. He was raised in the church. I have talked to my pastor, friends…everybody, and everyone tells me the same thing. Let God handle it."

Giselle finally found a place to park. "Well I suggest you do that," she said. "God will get his attention in due time. Trust me. Stop crying, you're messing up your pretty face. Let's go in and have a good time…and find *me* a husband." They all laughed.

The Apache was jumping and people were everywhere. It was definitely a place for the grown and sexy. Marley fumbled through her oversized Louis Vuitton bucket bag for her ID and cover fee. Once they made their grand entrance all eyes were on them.

As the live band serenaded the audience with a Jill Scott medley, the three lucked up and found seats right in front. The venue was packed. Intellectuals. Dreads. Party-Goers. Liberalists. Sophisticated business men and women. You name it, the Apache had it. Giselle's eyes surveyed the place before taking off her Burberry shawl. The all crimson brick venue was covered with timeless creations by some of Atlanta's most renowned fine artists. The lighting was very dim and everyone felt free to express themselves. The café smelled of incense and pleasant Jamaican cuisines. There was even a distinctive aroma of Black 'n Mild in the air. Janelle Monae was the feature act scheduled later that night and Giselle was excited as she was one of her favorite artists. Elicia relaxed a little bit and was finally enjoying herself. The entire crowd sang in unison with the thick red-bone bellowing out notes on stage:

Woke up this morning, with a smile on my face
Jumped out of bed, took a shower dressed, cleaned up my place
Made me some breakfast, toast, two scrambled eggs,
Gggggrrrrrrrrrrrrrrrriiiiiiiiiiiiiiiiiiiiiittttttttttttttttssssssssssssssss
Grabbed my keys, grabbed my jacket, off to work
Beaming, all the way down 3rd
Is it the waaaaaaaaaaaaaaayyyyyyyyy
You love, me baaaaaaaaaaaabbbbbbbbbbbbyyyyyyyyyy

Everyone in the building sang along as if the ballad evoked some type of personal memory. Giselle motioned for a waiter to take their food orders. She selected her favorite - the jerk chicken wings, and Marley and Elicia both settled on shrimp and grits.

"This place is the shit!" yelled Marley over the loud music. She stood up and swayed from side to side allowing her Ultimate Apple Martini to take over her mind, body, and soul. As she threw her head back and closed her eyes she felt someone grab her hand. Marley was reluctant to peek. She knew that it would be a man and based on past experiences, she also knew that he would be repulsive. As she silently prayed, she slowly opened her eyes only to discover that the brother was *fine*. He grabbed her waist and led her to the makeshift dance floor. As soon as they took center stage other couples began to join, too. This super-sexy, chocolate brother moved gracefully across the deck and turned and twirled her so much that she thought she was dreaming. He was definitely smooth. He stood about 6'2", which she found complimentary to her 5'8" stature. He smelled of Usher cologne (she recognized the scent because her ex Ethan wore it all the time) and had a fade that showed off his deep ocean-like waves. His goatee was full, just the right length, and trimmed to perfection. He wore a Polo button down, army fatigues, and Timberlands. *He* was perfection.

He stared into her eyes and caressed his goatee. "Please tell me you're here with your girls and not your man," he whispered in her ear as they moved around the crowded space. She grinned. His breath smelled of Dentyne and alcohol that sent chills down her spine.

"Maybe I am, maybe I'm not," she teased.

"Well let's just say that you are. What are the chances of a brother like me getting to know a sister like you?"

She acted as if she didn't hear him prompting him to speak a bit louder. "You're looking real good tonight too, might I add. I can tell you don't play no games."

"I'm glad that you can recognize a real woman when you see one." She gyrated her hips and pressed against his body. Elicia watched her from her seat.

"She ain't slick. She trying to see how big his dick is!" Giselle laughed. No one knew her better than her girls.

As the band wrapped up their set, the emcee of the night announced for all poets to come to the stage. Giselle stood and rushed to the front. Spoken word was therapy for her. She didn't do it often, but when she did, she rocked the mic! She had been approached by other club owners willing to pay her to perform in various spots in Atlanta, but refused. This was simply a leisure pursuit.

The mysterious brother led Marley to an intimate corner in the back of the café. She noticed he had a band on his ring finger and decided not to acknowledge it.

"So, what's your name?" he asked showing his pearly whites and dimples.

"Marley," she said as she sipped the Merlot he'd purchased for her at bar.

"Marley? As in Bob Marley?" he guessed.

"Yes!" She giggled to herself. "My Mom loved that man…she still does. And she also loves herself some Supremes."

He raised a brow.

"My middle name is Diana as in Diana Ross." She wanted to get the full history lesson behind her name out of the way so that they could focus on more important topics.

"Marley Diana. I think it suits you very well. So, what do you do for a living, Ms. Marley Diana?" He moved in closer to the bar stool she sat on.

"It's actually Dr. Marley Diana," she winked. "I'm an African American studies professor at Clark Atlanta. I'm also the host of Dynamic Discourse. It's a web-based talk show that's filmed on campus - I'm not sure if you've heard of it."

"Actually, I think I have heard of it. Wow, I can't say that I'm not impressed. Are you originally from Atlanta?"

Marley felt like she was on a job interview. "Enough about me. What do you do for a living, Mr. Um-"

INEVITABLE

He laughed. "I apologize. Let's try this again." He extended his hand. "I'm Trey Roberts." The way he said it gave Marley goose bumps.

He stroked his goatee once again. Marley was so immersed that she didn't hear Giselle being introduced to the stage.

"Greetings, my Apache fam. I'm Giselle and I wanted to share this piece I've been working on entitled "Never See Him Coming."

"Is that your girl?" asked Trey.

"Yes, that's my girl!" Marley beamed.

Giselle cleared her throat and motioned for the band to give her a few strings.

(singing) *And I never felt this way about……..you*
Ooooo it has to be the things that you do
Melodically stimulating my euphoria's sensation, strumming my pain, my sweet sensation
Did I mention that this man also has intellectual conversation?
Yes yall…he glided into my heart…my perfect imperfection of Barack Obama
Did I also mention that he loves his mama?
Damn…you're my beautiful nightmare, except I'm not dreaming
You keep me pulsating and screaming…and did I mention steady creaming?
He's my Spanish fly…I'm his Bey, he's my Jay….my hearts on a rollercoaster ride…going every which-a-way
He's my pen to my paper and my cover to my book, bounded together…this man got me shook
And keeps me shaking, character needs no re-evaluation because he got his shit together
Financially stable, my subliminal aphrodisiac and also very clever…
Just like Anita, I'm caught up in the rapture…Cuz I never thought in a million years my heart he would capture
Respects my thoughts, my body, soul, & mind
Has a Bachelor's, Masters & PhD in pleasing me all the time
So, don't be jealous, just be patient, drop your baggage and don't take off running
Because when you least expect it, you will never see him coming

INEVITABLE

Elicia and several other spectators in the crowd stood to their feet. Most of them yelled and snapped their fingers. Performing always gave Giselle a new swag. She felt free and in control. She removed her dangling curls from her eyes and threw up the peace sign as she shook hands and made her way back to her table. The emcee introduced the next act.

Trey settled back down in his seat. "Wow, she was good but I'll give her props later." He grabbed Marley's chin. "Now back to you." Marley felt her lovebox starting to pulsate. *The man has a hold on me already*, she thought.

She changed subjects. "So, what do you do for a living Trey Roberts?"

He cleared his throat. "Well, right now I run a construction company with a few guys I've known since college. It's fairly new but we're rapidly growing. On the flip side, I also do video production." *Owns his own business? A second source of income? In Atlanta, Georgia? This one is definitely a keeper,* she thought to herself.

"So, what kind of videos do you produce?"

"Um, you know, videos."

"Please don't tell me those BET-like, all girls have to be light-skinned with excessive fake booty and titty videos," said Marley as she rolled her eyes and flicked her jet black bob. "The women in those videos are such a poor representation of what a beautiful Black woman, like myself, is comprised of. These are the women that our youth look up to. Fake everything…it's just a fallacy. And the men are no better, glorifying the ignorance." She felt the wine kicking in.

"Something like that, but I have to make a living too, right?" They both chuckled.

"I apologize. Issues like that in the Black community need to be addressed. As you can see it is something that I am very passionate about. We discuss it on the show at least twice a month. I'm off my soapbox now."

Trey's phone rang. "Excuse me while I take this."

INEVITABLE

Marley watched him stride across the packed room and outside the café. *It's probably his damn wife* she thought. *A man that fine couldn't possibly be single.*

He returned wearing a NY fitted cap. "I apologize, but I have to go. I have some business to take care of. It was very nice meeting you and I hope to hear from you soon." He handed Marley a card and kissed her hand. She inhaled his delectable scent as he walked away.

Marley was all smiles when she joined Elicia and Giselle back at their table. "Who in the hell was that, whore?" teased Elicia as she finished up her shrimp and grits.

"Oh, that was no one," Marley said innocently.

Giselle snatched his card out of her hand. "Well, if that was no one why are you cheesing from ear to ear?"

Marley rolled her eyes.

"*Con-struc-tion?*" Giselle said with playful exaggeration. Looks like Marley found herself a blue-collar man!" Everyone at the table cackled. Marley snatched the card back and placed it in her bag. She had decided to give him a call later.

The trio locked arms as they walked back to the car. Giselle didn't realize how tipsy she was until she got behind the wheel. After dropping Marley off she decided to stay the night with Elicia. "Trey's sexy ass seemed all into Marley," said Elicia as they rode home. "And that beard...sexy as hell!"

"He is a nice-looking brother. I don't know if I care for the beard though."

"Well, he seems pretty stand up. But you never know."

"I just hope Marley's insecurities don't get in the way. She is notorious for fucking shit up with her attitude," Giselle said as she pulled her car into the driveway.

INEVITABLE

"Yeah, let's just pray that she doesn't." Elicia said as she noticed that the porch light was on. *Nas must be home tonight*, she thought to herself.

"Ooooh…your landscaping looks fabulous – even at night!" she blurted changing subjects. "I can't wait to see the inside."

"Yes, I must admit. It is the bomb!" agreed Elicia. She'd purchased the 2004 construction about a year earlier and completely rehabbed it in eight short months. The mature landscaping was what attracted her to the sought-after property, so she was happy that Giselle took notice as she hadn't been by her home since it was completed.

They walked into her fully-furnished living room to find Nasir sitting on his chocolate leather recliner. He rolled his eyes once he saw Giselle. She was too exhausted for the drama and decided to be cordial.

"Hey Nas, How are you?"

He ignored her.

"Elicia can I speak to you in the bedroom for a minute?" he huffed.

"Giselle, you know where the guest room is. There's fresh linen in the bathroom closet." Giselle trudged between the both of them and headed upstairs.

Elicia slammed the door and folded her arms as Nasir took a seat on the edge of the bed. He had been drinking. "What the fuck was that all about, Nasir? You couldn't even acknowledge her?"

"Why in the hell are you coming in at three in the morning?"

"Are you kidding me? You come in every other night around this time and then when I do it, it's a problem? Are you fucking serious?"

"A woman with any decency should not be out this late. I was worried about you. You don't respect me or our relationship. You just want to party all the time with them hoes you call your friends."

"Hoes?!" she yelled. "**Your** friends are hoes. You have me hook my girl up with a man that you know damn well has a **wife**. Not to mention that he lives with his mama. Makes me wonder what the fuck you are up to when you are not here with me and out with them."

"Darnell going through some things right now and for the record, he's separated, and his Mom is just helping him out. Don't talk about him. Let's talk about how you're a whore and why you have whores for friends."

Elicia slapped him as hard as she could. "Don't ever talk to me like that again. I am not a whore. I am your wife. I am a good woman to you and I put up with shit that I don't have to. You are sorry. You can't even take care of home because you're so busy running the streets doing God knows what."

"What does God have to do with this?"

Nasir ducked just in time to watch the vase she threw towards his head shatter into pieces.

"God has everything to do with this!" she screamed. "When are you going to realize that?"

He jumped up and tried to leave but Elicia blocked the door. "Do you see what is happening to us, Nas?" she muttered in tears as she pleaded with her husband. "You are not the same person I married two years ago."

She started to pace the floor.

"Fuck that Elicia! Why do you feel like I am supposed to kiss the ground you walk on because you finally found religion? It's not happening. All I want to know is why you didn't call?"

"If it was such a big deal why didn't you call?" she snapped.

He didn't respond.

"You know what, this is stupid. I thought that I could do this. I thought that if I hung in here a little bit longer you would change and get your shit together, but I see that I can't and you won't. This is obviously not what either of us wants. But what I do want - and I never thought I would say it - is a divorce."

"Good!" he yelled. "*I've* wanted to say that shit for the longest. This ain't no real marriage anyway."

Elicia felt her heart drop. Something had come over him. She could see it in his eyes that she'd somehow lost her best friend. He went to the closet and angrily stuffed as many of his belongings that he could into a duffel bag.

"You can have all this shit. Don't call me."

Elicia grabbed a suitcase and began to help. "That's where you are mistaken. All of this *is my* shit." He snatched up his things and Elicia escorted him to the door. Nasir looked at her and whispered, "You really messed up this time."

"No, you fucked up! Give me my damn key."

Elicia slammed the door. She wanted to cry but didn't have any tears left.

INEVITABLE

4

Giselle awoke to the smell of blueberry pancakes, omelets, turkey bacon, and grits. She hurried and dressed so she could satisfy her hunger. "Mornin' Elicia," she hummed as she sat at the breakfast table.

"Mornin', G," Elicia responded while pouring them both a cup of freshly-brewed Illy coffee.

"Where's Nas? I know he's not at work."

Elicia sucked her teeth. "Don't start, Giselle. I am not in the mood." Giselle noticed her tone change.

"My bad. What happened?"

"I kicked him out. I'm tired of his shit and I did what I had to do." Giselle was speechless. She always teased Giselle about moving on, but never thought she could ever bring herself to do it. Nasir and Elicia always had drama.

"Wow," she responded. "Well, are you okay?"

"I'm fine. Do you mind if we just talk about this later?"

Honestly, Giselle didn't care if they ever talked about it at all. Nasir caused more confusion than contentment. He didn't appreciate Elicia and it was time she found someone who did. After Giselle finished breakfast, she swung by her house to dress and headed straight to the office. She had to finish up paperwork for a case she'd won two months prior.

"Afternoon, Giselle," said Dwayne, her assistant. Giselle smiled as he handed her a fresh cup of coffee and a notepad scribbled with messages.

"So, who's the lucky guy?" he asked. "You know I need to be informed about any and every man who enters your life." Giselle hired Dwayne to assist her over a year ago. At first, she was hesitant due to the fact that an African American woman in a position of power intimidated some men, but Dwayne wasn't bothered by this. He found it attractive and plus he needed employment. "I'm all man," he said during his third interview.

INEVITABLE

"I know who I am and who I am destined to be." Over the 14-month period, Giselle and Dwayne had developed a brother/sister relationship. He even cursed people out on her account. He was one of the few people she considered a good friend. All the other males that were in her life always tried to pursue a relationship, but Dwayne simply enjoyed her company.

"What are you talking about?" she asked as she skimmed over the messages. He took the notepad back. "I'm talking about Hill Stokes."

"Who?" She then recognized the name from the other morning.

She sighed. "He's not my man, Dwayne. He owns a firm in California and wants me to work for him." Dwayne looked puzzled.

"Does he know you just made partner at one of the most preeminent firms in Atlanta?"

"Yes, he knows, but it's not stopping him." She playfully snatched the notepad from him and went into her office.

Giselle didn't want to admit it but Hill intrigued her. She decided to further explore his offer and looked up the firm online. "Impressive...*Law Firm of the Year* award over five times," she mumbled after examining the company's steady accomplishments and national recognition.

Samantha knocked on her door and Giselle motioned for her to come in. "You have a Mr. Stokes waiting in the reception area for you."

"Are you freaking serious? Is this man stalking me now?"

"If you don't want him, I'll take him," she said as she pushed up her 38DD's and swung her freshly installed bundles from side to side.

She rolled her eyes. "Thanks, Sam. You can leave now."

Giselle refreshed her lipstick and smoothed her mane. Lights. Camera. Action. She stepped into the quiet lobby outside her office.

INEVITABLE

"Mr. Stokes, I'm Giselle Mosely." Hill turned around in what appeared to be slow motion. Dressed in a well-tailored olive green suit and sandy brown leather moccasins, Hill extended his right hand while locking eyes with Giselle. For a moment, time seemed to stop, and she absolutely didn't mind. This man was exquisite and easy on the eyes. His perfectly symmetrical hairline and cropped waves did something to her spirit. His scent was tantalizing and reminded her of a woody floral musk. Giselle took it all in as she felt sweat puddles forming under her silk blouse. This man effortlessly made her hot and bothered.

"It's nice to finally put a name with a face. I must say that your headshot on the website does you no justice."

Giselle blushed.

"I apologize for showing up unannounced like this. I was going to tell you that I would be in the Atlanta area on business this week but you rushed me off the phone before I had a chance to inform you."

"Don't forget that it was 5am, not pm. I didn't know what the hell was going on!"

They both laughed.

Giselle's throat felt dry. She normally performed well under pressure but this was a totally different ball game.

"Follow me." She offered Hill a seat in her 900-square-foot executive retreat overlooking Woodruff Park. "It's actually weird that you would show up right now. I was just doing research on your firm."

She poured him a glass of water.

"That's good to hear. I can assume that means you're considering my offer." Giselle didn't hear a word he said as she handed him the crystal goblet. She was too mesmerized by how amazing he looked. His russet brown eyes were big and mysterious and his gleaming smile turned Giselle on. The man's eyelashes were even attractive. They were the perfect long and curly compliment to his almond-shaped eyes. She didn't really care too much for the diamond stud earrings but was willing to make an exception. His full, juicy lips were enticing too.

"Ms. Mosely, are you alright? Ms. Mosely?" He reached over and grabbed her hand. Giselle snapped back to reality.

"Oh, I apologize." She crossed her legs.

"I have a lot going on at the firm right now," she lied. "With me finally making partner, my duties have become endless."

Hill nodded his head in agreement. "Yes, I definitely understand. Look, I was wondering if you would like to grab something to eat so we can chat more about your future."

Giselle stared at her watch. She was hungry, but didn't know how she felt about going out with a persistent stranger.

"I won't bite," he smirked. "I promise."

But what if I want you to? thought Giselle. It was something about him that eased her spirit.

"Look, you can even follow me if it would make you more comfortable."

Giselle declined. "We can take your car."

"Let's go," he smiled.

Giselle instinctively knew that the white Maserati coupe next to the meter outside the office entrance belonged to Hill. His sense of style was just as attractive as he was. He opened her door, made sure she was buckled in and jumped into the driver's seat. Giselle felt like a star. As Kem blasted from the custom speakers she tried not to seem too impressed. She reached into her Hermes tote and grabbed her shades.

"So where are we headed?" she asked nonchalantly. "Two Urban Licks," he responded. "The vibe there is real chill." Giselle was familiar with the place.

INEVITABLE

After arriving at the restaurant and placing their orders, Hill unloosened his tie and rubbed his hands together. "So, have you thought about my offer?" Giselle sipped her water and sighed.

"Actually, I am going to have to decline. I have never considered moving outside of Atlanta and right now that would simply be too much."

Hill started to taste his wine. "I never said you had to move to California. I simply asked you to come and work at my practice."

Giselle was confused.

"What do you mean?" Hill sat down the glass and made his way next to Giselle in the cozy booth. "I mean that I am relocating my firm to Atlanta in roughly six weeks and I know that we could use someone like you on our team. You are the best criminal defense attorney in Atlanta- within *and* outside the entertainment industry. I want you."

"Is that right?" Giselle retorted.

Hill flashed his pearly whites and nervously scratched his eyebrow. "What I meant to say is that I want you to come and work with me."

Giselle felt a warmth between her legs and excused herself to the restroom. She began to experience a shortness of breath. She splashed water on her face as her chest heaved up and down. This had been happening a lot to Giselle as of late. She slapped herself. *Come on Giselle. Get your shit together. Tell this man no and keep it moving.* She hated to admit it but his offer did sound tempting. She wasn't so sure about working so close to a man she found attractive though. That could be dangerous.

She returned to their table and was relieved to see that her food had arrived. With her mouth stuffed with grilled lamb chops, she wouldn't say the wrong thing. Hill, however, was insistent on an answer. Giselle watched him take a piece of paper from his notepad and slide it across the table. She almost choked on her food. "What is this?"

"That, is how much I am willing to offer you to join my firm." Giselle felt her heart stop. She didn't expect to be making that kind of money for at least the next three years or so. This would definitely be an upgrade to her already fabulous lifestyle.

"At what cost?" she asked.

He grinned. "What do you mean?"

"Look, I've been in the game for a minute. I know that when something sounds too good to be true that it usually is. It's called *bribery*. Now, at what cost?"

Hill shook his head. "You've got it all wrong, young lady. It's called a business opportunity of a lifetime!"

She slid the paper back across the table.

"I'm sorry Mr. Stokes, but you couldn't possibly expect me to make a decision based off of what you *say*. I don't know you from Adam. For all I know you could be a contracted serial killer."

Hill's deep voice bawled with laughter. "Damn, you can mess a brother up that bad? I mean you fine, but you ain't that fine." Giselle found herself laughing as well. As much as she wanted to say yes, she also knew that jumping from firm to firm wasn't reputable. She hadn't even made a year at Simon and Franklin as partner. To leave now would be dishonorable.

She pushed her plate away and folded her arms.

"I see this is going to be tougher than I thought," he said.

INEVITABLE

5

"What exactly do you want to speak to me about, Mr. Lawrence?" asked Marley as she packed up her briefcase. She looked at her watch. It was 8:52. "Well," said Kahmin, "this is more of a personal matter." Marley was exhausted after receiving a night of complaints from students about their exam grades. She removed her glasses.

"Concerning?"

Kahmin cleared his throat. "I don't mean to sound too forward, but I think that you are phenomenal." *Great*, thought Marley. She had been approached numerous times in the past by students who waited until the semester was over to profess their love to her and it was starting to become quite irritating.

"Thanks," she said as she tried to make her way out of Warren Hall, "but this is a conversation that I will not have, especially with one of my students."

"Look," he said as he grabbed her hand, "I know that you think that I'm young, immature, and childish, but I'm not. I'm a grown ass man. I am 26 years old. My decision to come back to school was solely on me. I'm not who you think I am."

Marley snatched her hand away from Kahmin. "This is inappropriate. I am flattered, honestly, but as a scholar I have a code of ethics that I must follow. I am not interested. See you next Monday in class."

Marley hastily made her way to her car. Something about him worried her. When she finally got settled in her silver Range Rover, she let out a sigh of relief. *Damn*, she thought. *My students really are obsessed.* She nearly jumped out of her skin when she turned to find Kahmin standing at her window.

"What do you want, Kahmin? You have no right to follow me to my car!" She shrieked at him through the slightly tinted window.

"I apologize. If you would just hear me out I will be on my way. Please roll your window down."

INEVITABLE

Kahmin seemed harmless, but Marley wanted no drama. She cracked it just enough for him to see her eyes.

"Our last session for class is next Monday. We are all meeting at Benihana's downtown at 6:00pm. I will speak with you then." She backed her car out of the parking lot and sped off. Marley arrived at her home off of Clifton Springs Road in Decatur to find Elicia in her driveway. *More drama* she muttered to herself. She didn't mind being there for her friend but tonight she had her own problems to deal with.

"Hey babe," she said while grabbing her briefcase and laptop out of her car.

"Hey," uttered Elicia. "I apologize for just showing up unannounced. I really just needed to get away. Everything in the house reminds me of Nas."

Marley smiled. "No worries." Once inside, she headed to her Keurig to make a cup of tea then ran upstairs to change into something more comfortable. She returned with an oversized t-shirt and slippers for Elicia to put on.

"You might as well stay," she said as she tossed her the items. "We can have a sleepover like old times." Elicia smiled at Marley's comforting spirit.

"Guess what I have?" Elicia asked as she grabbed her purse. "I was washing up some of Nasir's pants and found a sack of weed in one of his pockets. "So, we", she said while grabbing the marijuana, "are going to have a night to remember!" Elicia cheesed as she sniffed the loosely rolled joint. Marley shook her head. "Woman, are you crazy?" She snatched the blunt out of her hand.

Elicia stared at the floor.

"I can't believe that Nasir has got you trippin' like this. You are one of the top developmental psychologists in Georgia and you are telling me this man – who isn't even present at the moment - is going to have you give it all up on the account of a night of high?"

INEVITABLE

Elicia burst into tears. "Well what else am I supposed to do?!" she screamed. "I miss my husband."

Marley sat next to her on the caramel-colored sofa. "You are also going to miss your career and everything else that you have worked for if you choose to make dumb decisions over a man. We aren't in college anymore, Elicia." She grabbed her chin. "Look, I know it's hard, but *you* made that choice. Now you have to live with it. If you know you can't handle it, go and get your husband back." She handed her a tissue.

"You are not in a position to be making mistakes that could potentially end your career. You are better than that. You deserve better than that. You have worked too hard to give up everything so easily."

"I just don't understand how you do it, Marley. You are 38 and have no desire to get married or prospects."

"Not true," interrupted Marley. "I do want a husband and a home with a picket fence…but I am also waiting until God wants me to have it as well. Maybe you need to take this time to figure out who you are and what you really want. Settling is not an option for me. I have worked too damn hard to get to this point in my life and no man or anyone else is going to change that."

Elicia threw her head back in despair. "He hasn't called, texted, or anything. I just never thought my marriage would end this way." She blew her nose as she continued to wail.

"Maybe you just need time. Everything happens for a reason. And no one said it was over. You have to stand your ground so that he can understand how seriously you take your marriage and how serious he should take marriage period. If he does not come back, and I'm not saying he won't, understand that it will be his loss, not yours."

For the rest of the night Elicia and Marley pigged out on ice cream, read passages from the Bible, and watched old movies. By the time Elicia fell asleep it was four in the morning. After that eventful night, Marley was sure of one thing…marriage was definitely not on her "to do" list.

***

INEVITABLE

Over the next couple of months, Giselle found herself swamped in paperwork, endless phone calls, and countless meetings. *I guess this is what making partner is all about,* she told herself to keep from complaining. Mr. Stokes had officially relocated his office to Atlanta and was having a gathering that evening to celebrate. Giselle didn't know if she wanted to go. Hill had been sending roses to her office, gourmet candies, and invitations to various venues around Atlanta all in an attempt to persuade her to work for him. Nevertheless, Giselle declined. They talked on the phone a couple of times and Giselle made it her business to keep the conversation short. She did not want to destroy their professional rapport on the account of a possible disastrous encounter. She found herself surfing his company's website again and was interposed by Samantha knocking on her door. Giselle waved for her to enter and noticed tears in her eyes.

"What in the world is wrong with you?" she asked while closing her blinds. She handed Samantha a tissue and motioned for her to sit.

"His wife found out about us and now we are done!" she sobbed.

"Well, what did you expect to happen, Sam? He *is* a married man. Eventually you were going to get caught. How did she find out?"

Samantha shrugged her shoulders. "I don't know. He called me into his office about a week ago and told me that whatever we had or whatever I thought we had was over." Giselle sat down to comfort her.

"So, that's why you've been moping around here? I'm sorry, but you *have* to pull it together. You are acting very unprofessional right now. You can't do dirt and think that it's never going to catch up with you. Now stop crying."

Giselle often warned Samantha of her extracurricular activities interfering with her professional life, but she refused to listen. She knew in her heart that Justin wasn't going to leave his wife and start a family with her. Their affair had been going on two years too long.

Samantha wiped her face and suddenly pulled herself together. "You're right, Ms. Mosely. I knew. He has been giving me signs all along. He

INEVITABLE

never took me out in public. We always met at the office or hotel. I was never introduced to any of his friends or family although he promised me a million times. *I was nothing to him*…nothing. I guess White men ain't shit either."

Giselle maintained her composure. "Race has nothing to do with it, Sam. You made the decision and now you have to deal with the consequences. Now let's go, we have a meeting in five minutes."

As all seven members of the staff, both executive and non-executive, formed around the oakwood table, Giselle suddenly felt uneasy. Justin Keitel stood up and welcomed everyone while Samantha distributed portfolios and read the minutes from the last meeting.

"I want to begin by showing a video from a potential client interested in having representation from our firm." Everyone turned to the 50-inch flat screen on the wall.

Giselle, sitting farthest away from the screen, noticed Samantha smirk as she took a sip of her water. Giselle couldn't quite process what she saw next.

There they were, Samantha and Justin handling business on Mr. Keitel's desk. Samantha was positioned doggy style and Mr. Keitel was stroking like a German Shepard in heat. Samantha looked as if she was in complete ecstasy as she moaned and groaned every few seconds.

Justin's face turned beet red while whispers surfaced in the room. "Umm….umm, I apologize," he stuttered as he tried to hit stop on the remote. Samantha chuckled because she had purposely removed the batteries. Justin knocked the entire system over while trying to eject the disk.

"What in the hell is going on?" asked Jordan Franklin, partner in the firm.

"This has got to be some kind of mistake!" yelled Justin. "She is trying to blackmail me!"

"NO bitch," intervened Samantha, "you blackmailed yourself." She stood up and headed to the front of the board room.

INEVITABLE

"Yes, everyone," she announced. "The rumors are true. I have been fucking Justin Keitel for two years in the hopes of marriage and last week he finally dumped the lonely Black woman." She gave a menacing laugh. "YES, HE FINALLY GREW SOME BALLS!" Everyone in the room gasped. Giselle shook her head in disbelief.

"Both of you, in my office, NOW!" yelled Jordan.

"I can't do that, Mr. Franklin," Samantha said curtly, "because I quit!" She threw a portfolio at Justin's head, grabbed her purse, and made her way out the door.

"Keitel, in my office…NOW!"

"This meeting is adjourned until further notice."

As everyone cleared the room as though a fire alarm was sounding, Giselle thought about Mr. Stokes. This is why she could not work for a man that she might be interested in. She loved her life too much to destroy it. She decided to go to his celebration and inform him of her final decision to not join his firm.

***

Giselle wanted to appear sexy, yet professional and chose a Nicole Miller strapless foil print dress to wear. She sported a ballerina bun with heavy bangs and diamond studs. She topped it off with a red lip and bangles. Marley was her "plus one" and wore a Phoebe Couture evening gown. She swept her hair into a braided ponytail and wore her favorite purple lip.

"So, what's up with Bob the Builder from New York?" Giselle asked nonchalantly as Melanie Fiona blared from her car speakers.

"Oh, you got jokes now?" Marley gave Giselle the side eye. "Nothing, I haven't called him."

"And why not?"

"I don't know. He seems too good to be true, which means he probably is, which means that I am not going to waste my time. Besides, he had a wedding band on his finger."

"How are you ever going to get a man with that attitude? You haven't even taken the time to get to know him. Even if he is married, you could use a friend right now."

Marley turned the radio down. "Married men don't make good friends, Giselle and you know this. It's too risky. First, you find yourself just talking about your goals in life and then they wanna fall in love and start acting a fool. Anyway, how are you giving advice that you don't take?"

"What do you mean?"

"I mean you're telling me shit that you need to do. You haven't taken two seconds out of your high-profile life to get to know Hill, so why in the hell are you coming down on me?"

"I have been getting to know Hill, just not in the way that he might want to get to know me. I want to remain professional."

"And you feel like you can't get to know him and still remain professional? You are a trip. Stop making excuses. No one is telling you to fuck him on the first date. You know you are interested in that fine ass Black man. You better jump on that train before someone else does."

Giselle sighed as she paid for parking. "Well, that's the real reason I'm here tonight. I am going to let him know that I am not leaving the firm. We will see what happens from there."

INEVITABLE

***

Hill stood at the front entrance of the Biltmore Ballroom as they walked up. He looked stellar in his Brooks Brothers tuxedo and Armani loafers. "I'm so glad that you could make it." He kissed Giselle's hand as she introduced him to Marley.

The event was well-attended and the most prestigious people from all over the state came to support. Hill led them both across the crowded room and picked up two glasses of celebratory champagne. The gold and ivory chandeliers were monumental and the view was breathtaking. Giselle felt like a princess in a fairy tale. Opera-infused jazz blared from the overhead sound system and Giselle couldn't help but examine the spectators. She saw a man pointing over in Marley's direction and nudged her.

"I think that guy is staring at you," said Giselle.

Marley gasped. "What in the hell is Trey doing here? I'm going over to speak."

Giselle snatched her arm. "Don't seem so desperate. Play it cool. Let him come to you."

Giselle and Marley continued to involve themselves in meaningless conversation until Trey approached them.

"Well, well, well," he grinned. "If it isn't *Ms. Catch Me If You Can.*" Marley laughed. "Excuse us Giselle," said Marley as she guided Trey to a corner by the bar.

"How are you?" she asked as she inhaled his cologne.

"I'm good," he responded. "It's a small world. What are you doing here?"

"Well, I'm Giselle's plus one. And you?"

INEVITABLE

Trey looked Marley up and down and licked his lips. "I'm the man around Atlanta... ask anybody in here...they'll tell you. You look damn good by the way."

Marley blushed while cheesing on the inside. He had successfully piqued her curiosity. "Thanks," she said. "You clean up pretty nice yourself." Marley glimpsed at him while he took a sip of his gin and tonic. *Damn,* she thought. *He looks even better in a suit.*

"This old thing," he said, "I've had it for years." He winked at her and she immediately became aroused.

"So, tell me something. Why haven't you called?"

"I don't know. I've just been um, real busy."

"I don't understand. I thought we had a good time at the Apache."

"We did, but-"

"But...what? Never mind. Let's get out of here...now."

"Now?" she asked.

"Right now."

"I can't leave Giselle. We came here together. It's our girlfriend code. You wouldn't understand." Her eyes pleaded with him.

Trey took Marley's glass out of her hand and sat it on the bar. "Look ma, what I do understand is that this is the perfect opportunity for us to become better acquainted. My business consumes so much of my time. I mean who knows when this opportunity will present itself again. Who would have thought that I would even see you **here** tonight?"

Marley felt bad. She knew it was wrong to leave Giselle but wanted to spend time with Trey. He was right. Who knew when she would get to see him again? She glanced over at Giselle. She seemed to be under the hypnotic spell of Hill Stokes. Maybe she wouldn't be too mad at her for breaking the code this one time. She walked over to her while Trey anxiously waited at the bar.

INEVITABLE

"Giselle, I'm going to get outta here. Trey and I want to move to a cozier setting so we can get to know each other better."

Giselle sucked her teeth and rolled her eyes.

"I tell you to talk to the man and now you're leaving with him? But I ain't mad at cha'!" She half smiled. "You better be careful. Do you have your mace?"

"Of course!" said Marley as she patted her clutch. She kissed her friend on the cheek and disappeared.

Hill returned with another glass of wine for Giselle.

She declined.

"Would you care to dance?" he asked. Giselle took his hand and they glided to the dance floor.

As the instrumental to Ascension by Maxwell rang throughout the ballroom, Giselle sashayed and dipped, never missing a beat. All of the female guests watched her and Hill with envy. A photographer scuttled by and took a snapshot of the two. *Let them hate*, thought Giselle as she dipped. *This night is about me.* As the evening progressed Hill and Giselle engaged in harmless flirting and stimulating conversation.

"Let's take a break," suggested Giselle. "We've been dancing all night and I need some fresh air."

They headed out to the terrace where the wind was breezy but comforting. "It's beautiful out here," said Hill as he placed his jacket on Giselle's shoulder. "But not as beautiful as you."

Giselle blushed as she moved around the deck looking for a place to relax. She settled on a wrought iron bench away from a group of men conversing several feet away. "Let's sit."

"Look, before you speak, I have something to say...."

Hill placed his finger against her lips. "I know you don't want to work for me. I also know that you feel like you can't let down the firm that has invested so much into you. I understand why you don't want to leave Simon & Franklin."

"Simon, Franklin, & Mosely thank you."

Hill chuckled. "Yes. Simon, Franklin, & Mosely. Please forgive me." Giselle smiled.

"I just can't leave the firm that has stood behind me for years, you know. I feel like I owe this service to them."

"Believe me when I say that there is no explanation needed. Your loyalty to that firm definitely comes first." Giselle finally felt relief come over her.

"You know, my mother always told me that closed mouths don't get fed and that if you have something to say, say it."

"What do you mean?"

He grabbed both of her hands. "What I mean is that I would like to get to know you on a more personal level. You are a beautiful woman, Giselle. Sexy, intelligent, classy…everything I want in a lady. I peeped your demeanor during our lunch date and I know why you behave the way you do. It's evident that you've been hurt before, but I am not here to hurt you. I want to change your life...for the better."

Giselle was speechless.

"I…I don't know what to say."

"Say you will give me a try. I have been sending you roses, candy, and grade school letters…for over a month. While I did want you to work for my firm, I want you to walk by my side even more. Gimme a chance. A brotha's been putting in overtime trying to get with you."

Hill took his hand and placed it on Giselle's cheek. She closed her eyes and allowed his warm tongue to dance around in her mouth. Giselle felt like a teenager. She grabbed Hill and pulled him closer to her. The kiss seemed eternal and she didn't want it to end. She finally decided to pull away.

"I am flattered, but right now at this point in my life, I don't know if I even have the patience to do this. I'm not going to lie, I find you very attractive, but I don't know." He stared into Giselle's eyes and gently kissed her forehead. "You seem nice and everything, and men always do at first, but I think I'm better off being by myself for a while." She felt that her defense was solid.

Hill shook his head. "Shot down again. What do I have to do, Ms. Mosely? So, you mean to tell me that you don't have any spare time to allow me to show you that I am different than most men? Let me take you out on one date and then if you decide at that time that you don't want to move further then I will leave you be. Nothing ventured, nothing gained."

Giselle rolled her eyes. "Okay, one date and that's it."

Hill beamed from ear to ear. "Great! I'll pick you up tomorrow night around 7. Is that fine?"

"Actually, I was hoping we could meet at my office and then go from there. After all, I still don't know you."

Hill shook his head. "Will do, sunshine. Will do."

***

"So, this is your spot?" asked Marley as they pulled up to the luxurious condo. "Looks like your business has done more than just take off. Apparently, you're the connoisseur of construction in Atlanta."

Trey laughed. "I do alright."

Marley was surprised to find his home meticulously decorated. It smelled of jasmine incense. Along the cherry walls were framed pictures of various blues artists. Etta James, B.B. King, Muddy Waters, Ray

Charles...the list was endless. The portraits accented his charcoal and white living room and were the perfect contrast to the array of russet colored vases and abstract figurines strategically placed throughout the main floor.

"This is really nice...especially for a man. A woman helped you decorate?"

Trey smiled. "Yea, something like that," he responded.

Marley continued to tour his home and was shocked to find pictures of Trey and a tall, slender woman in his home office. While Trey retrieved the beverages, Marley took a closer look. One of the photos was from a maternity shoot. The woman looked to be seven or eight months pregnant. *He not only has a wife, he has an entire family,* she said to herself. She hurried and sat on the living room sofa before he returned.

Marley tried to control her attitude but couldn't. "So, what am I supposed to be?"

Trey looked caught off guard. "Marley, what are you talking about?"

"I wanna know why in the hell you brought me here knowing that you have a wife *and* a child?! So, is this what you do when she's out of town? You fucking sleaze bag! You actually brought me into your wife's home for a booty call?!" Marley was hurt and confused.

"Yo, ma, calm down. Why don't you let me explain before you persecute a brother?"

"No! Don't say shit to me. Just take me home." She grabbed her clutch and headed to the door.

"I should have known you were full of shit when I saw that wedding band on your finger. I didn't want to make any assumptions, but now that I *see* who I'm really dealing with, you can forget about Marley Diana Cole!"

"You're taking this a bit far, don't you think? We're still getting to know each other, right?"

INEVITABLE

"Are you deaf or motherfucking dumb, Trey? Take me home!"

"What's with the insults, woman? I will not take you home until you listen to what I have to say." Marley was hysterical. She wanted to go upside his head with the stainless-steel frying pan on the stove.

Trey grabbed her hand and led her back to the sofa. "Yes, you are correct. I was married, but I'm not anymore."

"What the fuck is this then?" She grabbed his ring finger. "And why do you have those photos in your office?"

"The photos are of my wife Robyn and our unborn child Rianne. We had already named her after Robyn's mother Annie and my father Richard." Trey was becoming emotional at the thought and looked down to hide his watering eyes. "Robyn was on her way home from work one night but never made it. I remember calling her asking what she wanted me to pick up for dinner. She always answered my calls, but she didn't that night. I didn't know that she was already dead. It was a result of a hit and run. I lost her over two years ago."

Marley was in complete shock and felt her heart sank into her stomach. She slumped onto the couch. "I am so sorry," she said as she put her head in her hands. "I feel so awful."

Trey shook his head. "It's fine. I should have mentioned it before I brought you here. I suppose I am still dealing with their deaths. I keep our photos on display to remind me of the wonderful times we shared. I miss her." He looked at his wedding band. "I haven't dated since her death, which is why I still wear the ring."

Marley nodded her head. "I understand...I really do. I know what it feels like to lose someone."

"I guess I just haven't met anyone that could come close to taking her place...ya know? I told myself that I would not remove the ring until I found the right one. I hope this doesn't creep you out or anything. It's just out of respect."

It was then that Marley's perception of Trey changed. *Was he ready to start dating? Or was he using the next woman as a means of getting over his deceased wife? Either way, she felt some type of way about him.*

INEVITABLE

Marley looked perplexed. "So, do you think you're really ready to start dating? I've never been in this type of situation before and I just want to make sure we are clear about what is going on."

Trey sat next to her and looked her in her eyes. "All I know is that since she passed, I have not even been remotely attracted to any woman that I have encountered. Not while working. Not at the grocery store. Not even at the networking functions I attend. But when I saw you at Apache, you struck a nerve…a good nerve. You had me feeling electric on the inside, and I acted on it. What's so wrong with that?"

Marley blushed. "Nothing," she said as she smiled. "*Electric?* Wow. Let's just agree to take things one day at a time."

"Agreed."

INEVITABLE

6

Elicia blow-dried her hair and stood on the scale. In the past eight weeks she had lost a combined seven pounds, which would be fine if she didn't already weigh 135 pounds. *I look like I'm on drugs*, she thought. Her separation from Nasir had her going crazy. Even though he worked her nerves, she missed her husband. Instead of pouting and waiting on him to come home she found herself working out, taking various cooking classes, and throwing herself into her upcoming makeup line, FaceIt.

As Elicia walked to her car she noticed a woman making obvious eye contact. *What the hell is she looking at?* thought Elicia as she tossed her gym bag on the back seat. She turned around to find the strange woman standing only a few feet away from her lighting a cigarette.

"Look, you don't know me, but I know you. My name is Teri and I wanted to speak with you about Nasir.

"Excuse me?" asked Elicia as she removed her jacket. "Surely, you are mistaken."

The woman blew the smoke out of her nose. "No, I'm not. Look, can we have lunch? There are some things I think you need to know about your husband."

Is she serious? thought Elicia. "Look, I don't know you and like I said before you **must** be mistaken."

The woman shut Elicia's car door. "Look, I'm trying to provide you with vital information. What do I have to do to prove to you that we are talking about the same man?" The woman then began rambling random facts about him.

"Nasir Harrison. 39 years old. Birthday is May 2, 1976. Born in Syracuse, New York. He has two siblings, but speaks to neither of them. His social security number is 562-"

"Alright!" yelled Elicia. "We can go across the street to McDonald's. You have five minutes."

INEVITABLE

They both took a seat in the back of the restaurant. Elicia bounced her knee uncontrollably as she couldn't believe she was sitting across from the woman who was fucking her husband.

"Who are you and how long has the affair been going on?" inquired Elicia as she looked at her watch.

The woman sighed. "What?" she giggled. "You got it all wrong, sweetheart. I'm Nasir's first cousin. I don't know an easy way to tell you this, but he is mildly schizophrenic and bi-polar."

"What?" asked Elicia as she closed her eyes. "What the hell are you talking about?"

"I'm only telling you this because even though I have never met you, I know that he loves you."

Elicia was speechless. "I'm a psychologist. What? Why? How could this happen and I not know?"

"We don't know exactly when the actual disorder emerged, but he was diagnosed when he was 17 around the time his parents were shot during a home invasion. I do believe that it was triggered when he witnessed his best friend – my ex-husband Eric being murdered during a car-jacking in 2011. This is one of the reasons why he moved away from the hood. He wanted better for himself, but the thug life always seemed to find him."

Elicia was heartbroken to know that her husband was going through something this severe but didn't bother to confide in her. She knew about his parent's deaths but didn't know that he had also lost his best friend to senseless violence. She continued to listen.

"Shortly after Eric's death, Nasir stayed with me at one of my parent's rental properties in Nashville. We both needed to get away to sort out what had happened. I could hardly grieve myself for having to keep an eye on Nasir. He would wake up in the middle of the night in cold sweats. He would tell me that people were following him. I would catch him talking to himself. Eric's death really took a toll on him. He was like the brother he never had."

INEVITABLE

"I feel like I'm going to be sick," said Elicia. "Excuse me while I get something to drink."

When Elicia returned, Teri finished explaining. "In the beginning he was diagnosed with post-traumatic stress disorder but I knew it was much worse."

"So, how did you help him through it?"

"Well, I eventually started attending counseling sessions with him, but that didn't last long. He would start disappearing in the middle of the night...not returning home for days and selling shit out of my house."

"So, he was on drugs as well?" asked Elicia as she blinked in disbelief.

"I couldn't prove it, but he was. He started hanging out with people that weren't good for him."

"Like Darnell?" asked Elicia.

"Like Darnell," she responded with weariness in her voice.

"He was finally properly diagnosed when I had to check him into the psychiatric ward for attempting to kill himself. The doctors put him on a less potent medication that made him feel more in touch with reality."

Elicia wiped the tears from her eyes and sank down in her seat. "So, you're telling me that my husband is crazy?"

"No, I'm telling you that you are married to a man who is sick. A man, who at this point and time, doesn't need you to turn your back on him."

"Wh-...How did you find me?"

"Nasir showed up on my doorstep about two weeks ago asking for money. I know when he is not taking his medication. I've seen the symptoms many times before."

"Medication??? He hadn't told me any of this. We've been married for two whole years and I actually thought it was me." Teri slid into the booth next to Elicia and hugged her tightly.

INEVITABLE

"I know that he never mentions his family – not even his sisters Nivia and Nyla…but we do know about you. I talk to him enough to know that he loves you."

Elicia was flabbergasted. "So, where is he? What am I supposed to do?"

"I don't know. Like I said, I saw him two weeks ago. All we can do is stay prayerful and ask God to bring him home."

Elicia nodded her head in agreement.

"Here is my number. Call me if he comes home or if you need anything." She pulled out another cigarette as she left. Elicia still had so many unanswered questions. She was shaking so much she could hardly drive home. She pulled into her driveway and mustered up enough strength to gather her belongings. As the car door slammed she realized her keys were still in the ignition.

"No! No! No!" she cried. She dropped her bags and sank to the ground in tears.

Get it together Elicia, she told her inner-self. She grabbed her iPhone and began to search for a locksmith's number.

"Are you okay?"

She looked up at a man standing in front of her and burst back into tears. The stranger grabbed her things and helped her up.

"I'm sorry," she sniffed. "I locked my keys in the car."

"Wait one minute," he said.
He left and returned with a Slim Jim. He opened her door and Elicia was relieved.

"Hello, I'm Gabe. I just moved in across the street about a week ago."

She smiled. "I'm Elicia and thanks."

"Nice to meet you. Are you okay?"

"Yes, I've just had a long day."

INEVITABLE

"Well if you need anything, just let me know. We all have those days."

Elicia watched him walk away in his plaid Polo shirt, khaki pants, and loafers. She noticed how confidently he walked and wondered if he was living with someone. Once she finally made it into her house she kicked off her sneakers and collapsed in the bed.

***

"I'm glad that you finally made time for your little brother," said Gerrod as he bit into his cheeseburger later that evening. "I would much rather be sitting in front of a home-cooked meal made by my big sis, but I keep forgetting you're big shit now!"

Giselle laughed and threw a fry at him.

"The shit is stressful, but this is what I wanted, so I'm handling my business," she said.

"Have you spoken to Mom and Dad?"

"For what?"

Gerrod laughed. "Because they're your parents…why the hell wouldn't you?"

Giselle sucked her teeth. "I'm not going there with you. As long as I know that they are fine, I'm good. I still do my part. I send money home."

"G, when are you gonna let that shit go?"

"I don't like liars. Daddy is a liar and Mom is stupid for staying with him."

Gerrod shook his head. "You are out of line. They are your parents. And sometimes life just happens to the best of us, including you. If mom can accept it, you definitely shouldn't have a problem with it."

Giselle loved her brother but hated how he felt the need to throw in her face that she didn't have a relationship with their parents. When she was younger, Giselle walked in on her father cheating with a close neighbor. It hurt her to the core. *Who in the hell is bold enough to do something so low down and then get a slap on the wrist for it?* She didn't think she would ever understand the concept of infidelity in relationships. Giselle believed that when someone hurt you, cutting them off was the best thing you could do to prevent it from ever happening again.

She unwrapped her hamburger and ate in silence. Gerrod stared at her and shook his head.

"Look, I just want our family to be tight again like the old days. If you don't want to talk about it anymore, then change subjects."
"Thank you," said Giselle with an attitude. "How are you and Eva?"

"*We* are just fine, still trying to make a baby…but getting nowhere. According to my sperm count, she should have been pregnant by now. Six months of straight fucking and nothing."

"Well," said Giselle, "when God is ready for you to bear child little brother, you will."

"So, what's up with you, "Ms. All-work-no-play?" he teased.

"For your information, I **have** been seeing someone. His name is Hill and he's likable enough. I'm not going to offer too much information on him because I don't want to get my hopes up, but if he keeps on doing what he's doing…he just might be my GPS and your future brother-in-law."

"What in the hell is a GPS?" he smirked.

"Giselle's Potential Shawty."

They both laughed. "You, big sis, are *so* lame."

***

After lunch with Giselle, Gerrod made his way home and was surprised to find that Eva wasn't there. He called her cell phone and received no answer. When the phone rang Gerrod expected it to be Eva.

"Hello Eva?" he asked.

"Yes, I'm trying to reach a Mrs. Eva Mosely. This is her physician's assistant calling from A Preferred Women's Health Center. I need to inform her that she left her insurance card at my office. She left about ten minutes ago. I tried to reach her on her cell but it went straight to voicemail."

"Well, this is her husband. She hasn't made it home yet, but when she arrives I'll be sure to let her know."

"Thanks," she said. When Gerrod hung up he formed a smile as big as the Cheshire cat himself. He grabbed his keys and quickly hit the nearest floral shop. He bought three dozen roses, balloons that read *I Love You*, and picked up two bottles of sparkling wine.

I'm going to be a father, he anxiously thought as he sped home.

Gerrod took the rose petals off the stems and made a trail from the front door to their bedroom on the second level. In their master en suite, he ran a warm bubble bath, lit mango scented candles, and allowed Raheem Devaughn's CD to set the mood. He heard the door monitor beep and ran downstairs to greet his wife. Eva placed her keys and purse on the entryway table while taking in the surprise.

"What is all this for?" she asked.

Gerrod kissed her on the cheek. "This is for you being the most beautiful woman in the world."

"Aww baby, thanks."

Gerrod was too excited to notice that Eva didn't seem like herself. He grabbed her hand and led her along the rose petaled hardwood floors up the stairs and into the bedroom. Gerrod backed her into a corner and kissed her feverishly. As his tongue slow danced around her mouth Eva massaged the back of his head. He removed her silk cami and licked her succulent nipples. Eva threw her head back and closed her eyes. Gerrod grazed her torso with his lips and spread Eva's legs apart. She grabbed onto their nightstand.

"Gerrod, I need to sit down. I don't feel well."

Gerrod smiled. He grabbed her hand and led her to the bed. "Is there anything that you want to tell big daddy?" he asked, "because I think I already know."

INEVITABLE

Eva frowned. "You do?"

"Yes, the clinic called this afternoon and said you'd left your insurance card there." He rubbed her shoulders and kissed her neck.

Eva clasped her hands together. "And you're not angry?" she nervously asked.

"No, why would I be angry that you are having MY baby?" A tear rolled down Eva's cheek.

"Excuse me," she said and ran out the room.

Gerrod was confused. He found her sitting on the chocolate leather ottoman in their living room. She was stiff as a board. "Baby, what's wrong? I thought you would be happy for us. We've been trying to do this thing for forever. Are you scared? Because I am, too." He grabbed her cheek. "We have everything we need to raise a child. I love you." Eva stared at the floor and slowly stood up. "I had a consultation today," she sniffled.

"To find out your due date, right?" His voice cracked.

"No, for tubal ligation."

"Wait. What? I don't understand."

Gerrod stared at Eva in disbelief.

"What in the hell are you talking about Eva?"

"I'm sorry!" she scoffed as tears streamed down her face. "I was going to tell you. I just didn't know when. I never intended to hurt you Gerrod."

Gerrod's eyes were beginning to sting. "We have been trying to have a baby for six months straight...and out of the blue you go talk to these people about getting your tubes tied?"

Eva grabbed his hand and he snatched it away.

"You don't want me to be the father of your child? What, you don't trust that I would do a great job? Is that it?"

INEVITABLE

"I've never been 100% sold on having kids, Gerrod. You have always wanted that more than me."

"So, why were you making me believe that this was something you wanted?"

"Because I wanted to make you happy."

"I don't get it. We're financially stable, we have a nice home, we're respectable people. What is it? Why don't you want a child with me?"

"It's not just your decision to make."

"How can you say that when you just came from an appointment discussing a very important topic that involves *me* yet you didn't consult with *me* first. I'm your fucking husband!"

"Do you really want to know why I went Gerrod?" she huffed as her chest heaved up and down.

She stared him in his eyes. "I'll show you why."

What the fuck is she doing? thought Gerrod as she stormed off. Eva returned with a wooden box and handed him a small key.

"Open it."

"Why?"

"Open the damn box, Gerrod! If you want to know why I went, please open it."

Gerrod opened the box filled with internet postings and newspaper articles. Gerrod frowned as he read the headlines aloud.

"Young Black Teen Gunned Down in Front of Family...Police Kill Unarmed Black Teen...Officer Found Not Guilty in the Shooting Death of an Unarmed Black Father of Three"...

He stared at her in disbelief. "What the fuck is this, Eva?" "Are you telling me you don't want to have my child because I'm black and you're white?"

INEVITABLE

She took a seat at the dining table and balled her fists.

"No." she sighed.

"I'm telling you that I am scared for my son. No matter what he does he's not going to be labeled as bi-racial. He's going to be labeled as Black."

Gerrod shook his head. "He *is* going to be Black."

"I don't want our son to end up another statistic. I thought that everything would be okay by now. But look at the world we live in Gerrod. We are living in 2015, not 1915! Look at how many articles I was able to scrounge over the last year or so. There are over sixty articles in that box." She gave him a cold stare. "60!"

He pushed back from the kitchen table. "Eva, I don't know what to tell you except that I am a Black man and this is my reality every day."

"I just want to protect our child. But what if I can't? What if I fail him as a white mother?"

"What in the hell do you think I'm here for?!" he shouted as he beat his chest while jumping up from the table. "This is about you and your selfishness, Eva! Not about our unborn child. I'm out of here."

He grabbed his keys and left. Eva let him go because she knew that there was no stopping him.

***

Hill promptly arrived at 6:55 pm to find Giselle waiting at the office. "You look amazing," he said as he kissed her cheek and handed her an envelope with an ink pen attached.

They drove to a cozy Italian restaurant in an unfamiliar area on the outskirts of Atlanta. When they finally arrived to the secret location, Giselle found herself getting nervous. The restaurant looked closed and Giselle was sure he had the wrong address.

"There's nobody here," she said as she stepped out the car.

INEVITABLE

"We don't need anybody but ourselves, right?" he asked with a mischievous smile.

He was interrupted by her phone ringing. "Hello?" she answered. Hill watched Giselle's eyes widen as she listened to the voice on the other line. She hung up. "I'm sorry, but I need you to take me to my car," she said firmly.

Hill looked hurt and started to ask why, but didn't. "Look, I apologize," she said, "but I have an issue that I need to deal with." She wanted to explain to Hill what was going on but decided to do it later. She could tell by the way he sped off, after taking her to her car, that he was pissed.

Giselle arrived to find Gerrod sitting on the steps with his head in his lap rocking from side to side as if he were a little boy. Giselle ushered him into the house, dropped her bag and made flavored tea.

"Tell me what happened, Gerrod." she asked with deep concern.

"I cheated on Eva." He wiped a tear from his eye. Alcohol seeped from his pores.

"You what?!" yelled Giselle. "Are you fucking crazy?"

"Eva doesn't want to have my baby…so I cheated."

Giselle shook her head. "That doesn't make the shit right, Gerrod. Are you trying to be like dad now? You, she said while pointing at him, are a trifling ass man." She paced back and forth across the floor pausing whenever she had something to say.

"I mean, do you not know what "for better or for worse" means? Point blank, period, you're wrong. You could have gotten back at her another way besides cheating. I don't even know why you would even think *I* would approve of this. You're acting like our father."

Gerrod stood up and stumbled. "I can't believe you're taking her side."

"Believe it," she sputtered.

"Why you always clowning pops?"

INEVITABLE

Giselle paused and rolled her eyes. "Look, we discussed this earlier. You know why. We all know what he did. He embarrassed us. In front of everyone."

"You're right," he stammered. "I know what he did," he grimaced. "But you've done some shit too, right?"

He stared at his sister with the coldest eyes she had ever seen. She decided that it was the alcohol that had him bent.
Giselle leaned over the table. "Look, right now we are talking about you fucking another woman while married. Leave me the fuck out of this," she firmly said.

"I knew you wouldn't understand my position." Gerrod grabbed his coat and proceeded to leave.

"Sit down, Negro!" she demanded. "I gave up a date for **your** damn drama, so you are going to listen to what I have to say. Look, I'm not trying to make you feel worse than you already do, so what do you want from me besides the truth?"

"I don't want anything from you. I just want you to listen." Gerrod said wearily.

Giselle sucked her teeth. "Who in the hell did you cheat with?"

"Tyra."

"Tyra? How could you?!" Giselle was infuriated.

Tyra was a so-called *friend* of Gerrod's who would do just about anything to be with him. He hadn't spoken to her in years and knew that he could still get her to do anything he wanted her to.

"I can't believe that you wanted your ego boosted so bad that you would go back to the same woman that you had to get a restraining order against. Are you fucking crazy?"

Tyra was short, petite, and what some would call passionate. Gerrod met her on his 27th birthday at Trapeze Swingers Club. She was a regular there and as soon as she spotted Gerrod she made it her business to find out who he was. She decided against intercourse that night but did pleasure him orally. Gerrod was so impressed with her skills that he exchanged numbers. He loved his wife, but Eva wasn't freaky enough. At first his relationship with Tyra was cool, but once they did decide to have intercourse, things got crazy. She constantly called his phone, came by his job every other day, and would pop up at his house in the middle of the night. She even came to Giselle's firm looking for him. Giselle checked her quick and Gerrod cut it off. But Tyra was not having it. As a result, he had to get a restraining order.

"Yes, actually I am. I'm crazy for thinking that this marriage shit works. I thought she was different."

"You have to at least consider her point of view, G," said Giselle. "Eva knows how much you want a child. I think you need to calm down. It was only a consultation."

"I need a drink," said Gerrod. "Where's the liquor?" He headed towards the chiller and grabbed a bottle of Vodka.

"What in the hell do you think you're doing with that?" asked Giselle.

"I'm going to drink my problems away. I need to stay here tonight." He headed to her guest bedroom and closed the door.

Gerrod swigged the bottle of Vodka as he undressed. He stood in the full-length mirror and admired his physique before grabbing a towel and washcloth from the linen closet.

As he fumbled through the drawer for toothpaste, he picked up a bottle of pills prescribed to Giselle and noticed the expiration date.

Giselle suddenly knocked on the door startling him. "You good in there?" she yelled.

"Um…yea. I'm good. Looks like you stopped taking your meds."

Giselle cleared her throat. "I think it's causing me to break out in hives. Anyways, good night."

"Yea, good night."

***

INEVITABLE

"Welcome back, beautiful people! You're now tuned in to *Dynamic Discourse*, the show that examines cultural relevance regarding numerous topics in the world today. Thanks for joining us. I'm your host Dr. Marley Cole ....and joining me is my co-host Sophia Lebanon."

Marley smiled at Sophia as she motioned for her to get ready to receive calls.

"Before the commercial break we were discussing the shooting in Oregon that left many for dead. Again, I'd like to offer condolences to all the families and students who were affected by this tragedy. To our selfless educators, you are in our thoughts and prayers."

Marley was in a trance as she sat and thought about her own life one day possibly being in danger. *Why should this even be a topic of discussion,* she thought as she fervently shook her head. Her outspoken co-host, Sophia, interjected as the phone lines lit up.

"Yes, it's important that we understand how serious of an issue this is. I, too, am a professor here at Clark University and the last thing I want to think about or would want to think about as a parent is my child not returning home. This is incomprehensible...as this is the 9th U.S. school shooting in 2015 alone."

She took the next call as she sipped her tea. Marley watched the phone in keen anticipation.

"Caller, you're on Dynamic Discourse."

"Yes, my name is Cynthia Riviera and I wanted to make a comment regarding the recent school shooting in Oregon."

"Hi Cynthia, we're all ears."

"One way that I think these types of things can be prevented is if educators are allowed to carry guns in the classroom. By doing this, they would be able to protect themselves and the students in case an idiot decides to go postal."

Marley watched Sophia's eyes almost bulge out of her sockets.

"I'm not so sure that I agree with that, Cynthia," retorted Sophia. "If the gun falls into the wrong hands someone could get seriously hurt."

INEVITABLE

"The guns are always in the wrong hands and it's time they are put in the right hands. I'm not saying it should be mandatory but for educators that want to protect themselves and their students, it should at least be an option." Cynthia was passionate in her statement.

Marley tried to digest the caller's comments. "So, let me give you a scenario, Sophia and I want you to hear me out before you respond. When the police enter that classroom and the first person in line of sight is a teacher...with a *gun* in their hand, what do you think is going to happen next? Do you think they're going to stop and ask, *are you the active shooter*? Absolutely not! They're going to do what they are trained to do and that's kill!"

Sophia smirked. Silence flooded the line and Cynthia spoke up again.

"That's a good point, doc. But that doesn't mean that they shouldn't be able to protect themselves."

"So, if you were an educator and you were allowed to protect yourself in that way, what would you do if your class was held at gun point by an AR-15 and you only have a .32 caliber? What is the likelihood of you surviving?" Marley loved how Sophia provoked intellectual arguments, but sometimes she felt as if she took it too far.

"At least I would have gone down with a vengeance!" spawned Cynthia. Marley decided to redirect the conversation to prepare for a commercial break.

"It doesn't matter how big your gun is. The truth of the matter is that all weapons pose a safety threat and we have to do what's in the best interest of the students."

Cynthia denounced her claim and went on to discuss her personal plight with intruders in the classroom. By the end of the show, Marley was exhausted. As she walked to her car she thought about maybe one day possibly losing a student, or even her child to gun violence in the classroom. The idea of it all made her shudder.

INEVITABLE

7

"So, are you saying that you're celibate, too?" asked Marley as she whittled the chicken in her salad.

"For the most part I am," Trey said as he sampled the buttered rolls the server had just placed on the table. This was their fourth date since they'd reconnected at the Biltmore and Marley was enjoying every minute with him. The two had been to the movies, a jazz café, and an art gallery showing. The chemistry was definitely there but Marley was still unsure of what they were actually doing. She did not want to find herself all wrapped up in a man knowing that she could possibly end up just being the "rebound chick".

"What does that mean?" she quizzically asked.

"It means that I have refrained from physical sexual activity, but when I feel the urge, I do what I need to do." He winked at her from across the table.

"Gross," she whined as she dabbed at the corner of her mouth with the cloth napkin.

"Tell me this. Why is it considered sexy when a woman pleases herself, but frowned upon when men do it? We have needs as well. Wouldn't you want to know that your man is sexually pleasing himself versus going all over town to get one off?"

"All I'm saying is that's too much information." She pushed the tomatoes to the side of her plate while avoiding eye contact with him.

"I know that you do it," he assumed. "You look like the type. Most successful women who have good character find ways to please themselves instead of jumping from man to man."

Marley didn't want to admit it, but Trey was right. She made sure she was satisfied at least twice a week. It was, after all, a stress reliever.

"Look, I know that we haven't been seeing each other for very long, but I really dig you, Ms. Cole." Marley smiled. "The pleasure has been mine as well," she said. He then rubbed her hand as though she was the most precious thing to him. His touch sent tingles up Marley's spine. She shivered and stared at him.

INEVITABLE

He suddenly pulled a brochure from his back pocket and laid it on the table. It was a detailed itinerary for a 7-day cruise to the Cayman Islands.

"I would like for you to go with me…if you don't mind."

Marley was floored. "What? We just met. I don't know…I'll have to think about it."

"If it makes you feel better, you can invite your friends. It would give everyone some time to recharge. Just consider it. Nothing has to be finalized as of yet."

Marley had always wanted to take a trip out of the country, but she envisioned herself doing it with her husband, not someone she barely knew. She decided to give it some thought. *It would be a nice break from cold weather…*

The two left the restaurant and headed to Marley's home. She wanted to change clothes before they went for a two-mile hike. Trey grabbed his bag and ear muffs and headed in behind her.

"Nice," he said as he surveyed her spacious loft while taking off his jacket. "Thanks," she responded. "The guest bathroom is around the corner if you would like to change."

Trey returned with a pair of black Nike shorts and matching cut-off. Marley's mouth salivated at the sight of him. They both decided to stretch in her living room before leaving. Marley sat on the floor with her legs spread apart and her back against the wall. Trey sat in front of her and spread his legs so that their feet would touch. He grabbed her hands and slowly pulled her towards him. He caught a whiff of her Donna Karan perfume.

"1-2-3-4-5," he said and then let her go. She did the same. After doing a couple more basic stretching exercises Marley felt like lifting weights in the two-car garage where she had converted half the space into her personal gym. She grabbed a towel and led the way. Trey checked out her frame as she sashayed in her hot pink workout pants. Marley grabbed the 10-pound weights and went to work. "You can grab the heavier weights behind the barbecue pit." Trey stared at her then shook his head attempting to repress his obvious desire for her.

INEVITABLE

"You're not holding those properly," he said as he stood behind her and grabbed her arms. She felt his penis erecting. He kissed the back of her neck and inhaled the scent of her hair. He grabbed her waist and slowly traced his tongue around her ear. Marley felt herself becoming weak and moaned. She turned around and backed away. He moved in closer and grabbed her hands. Marley watched him in amazement as her vagina began to throb. Trey pushed her against her garage door and hungrily kissed her. Marley jumped when Trey's penis grazed her lower stomach. She squirmed away from him and backed several feet away.

"I apologize Marley…I, I don't know what came over me," he stammered.

She cleared her throat. "No, it's my fault. We just might be moving too fast. Maybe you should go."

Trey stared at his fully-erect manhood and sighed. "I'm so sorry, Marley…really." He grabbed his bag and left.

After his abrupt departure, Marley grabbed a bottle of Fiji water and gulped it down. *That was intense*, she thought. *I'm going to have to watch myself around him.*

***

The news about Nasir had sent Elicia into a state of depression. She didn't know what to do. She wasn't sure if he was ever going to return. She rolled out of bed around noon and brewed coffee-which was something that Nasir couldn't do to save his life. Elicia was feeling nostalgic and remembered the times he would attempt to bring her breakfast in bed. She would always pour the coffee down the bathroom sink before he would return. A knock at the door shook her out of her trance. To her surprise, it was Gabe. Elicia looked terrible and considered not answering the door, but did anyway.

"Good afternoon, Gabe," she said nervously as she tied the sash of her powder blue robe.

"I'm sorry to bother you, but you have been on my mind for the past few days and I just wanted to check on you to make sure you were doing better."

INEVITABLE

Elicia blushed. "I'm good," she said. "I was just about to make some coffee…would you like some?"

Gabe smiled and entered her kitchen. "Thanks," he said, "I make the worst coffee ever."

Upon their first encounter Elicia was too distraught to really pay any attention to him, but today she observed his physique from head to toe. Gabe was about 6'4" and pure caramel. He sported plaid Ralph Lauren lounge pants, a black pullover hoodie, and tan Timberland loafers. He smelled of Issey Miyake cologne and was not wearing a wedding band. Elicia tightened her robe some more.

"So…what do you do?" she asked as she poured him a cup.

"Well, actually I work for the Atlanta Fire Department. I'm a Fire Marshall." Elicia studied him and took a deep breath.

"That's a very noble job. I've never met a firefighter…heard stories, but have never met one before."

Gabe's right eyebrow rose. "Stories? What types of stories?"

"That's a topic for a different time." They both laughed.

"So, you're married?" he asked as he blew on his hot beverage.

Elicia rubbed the back of her neck. She sighed. "That's something I'd rather not get into."

Gabe looked uncomfortable. "I apologize. I'm not here to cause any trouble."

"No, you're fine," she said. "Right now, my husband and I are beginning the process of divorce and it's been a difficult adjustment."

"Wow, he must be crazy to leave a fine woman like you."

Elicia's face flushed. "Yeah, something like that," she said.

"I've been looking for a church home since I moved to the area. Do you know of any?"

INEVITABLE

Elicia's heartbeat raced. "Yes, actually I attend a church that's not too far from here in Brookhaven. I'm going tonight for Bible Study if you'd like to attend."

"I would enjoy that." said Gabe as he finished off his coffee. "I'd better get going. I have a few errands to run and I'm still in the process of unpacking my things." He stood up and grabbed his keys. "So...I'll see you tonight?"

Elicia smiled. "Yes, be here around 6:30. I'll drive."

Once he'd left, Elicia stood with her back against the door. She placed her hand over her heaving chest. *What in the hell am I doing?* she thought as she peeked out the sidelight and watched Gabe walk away.

Gerrod found himself once again at Tyra's house trying to figure out what was going on with his life. He glanced at her as she lay naked on the sleigh bed.

"I'm so glad you've come to your senses, baby!" she exclaimed as she threw her arms around him. "I knew that it would only be a matter of time before you realized that I'm all the woman you need."

He moved to the other end of the bed to watch television. "Go fix me something to eat," he ordered as he grabbed his boxers. Tyra pranced around the room in her orange thong while looking for a shirt. She slid on her gold Michael Kors flip flops and did as she was ordered. Gerrod checked his voicemail and was not surprised to have four messages. After listening to Giselle complain about leaving her guest bedroom a mess and two telemarketers begging him to switch to their premier services, Gerrod was ready to turn his phone off. He was somewhat relieved to find that the last message was Eva pleading for him to come back home.

He listened to the message again before finally hanging up. He wanted to call Eva but his pride wouldn't let him. He popped a Viagra pill and called Tyra back into the room.

Even though she was small in stature, Tyra Bradshaw was definitely a beautiful woman. Her soft, chocolate skin and long jet-black hair made

INEVITABLE

her appear exotic and mysterious. She wore green contacts and had just enough ass and breasts to keep any man warm on a cold winter's night. Her smile lit up a room and she had a likable personality, but nevertheless, Gerrod could not take her seriously. Maybe it was her whiny, high-pitched voice.

"Yes, big daddy?" she answered ready and willing to do anything his heart desired.

***

"Come give daddy that pussy!" he commanded as he threw her on the bed.

To get her ready he massaged her womanly pearl with his tongue. "Mmmhmm," she moaned as she raised her legs and placed them onto his shoulders. Gerrod's head moved in a circular motion as Tyra's compact frame shivered all over the bed. He roughly flipped her over on her stomach, like a rag doll, as he planned on serving it up.

"On all fours, NOW!" he shouted as he stroked his manhood. Tyra followed his instructions and screamed to the top of her lungs once he finally entered her. "Yeeeesssss!" she squealed as he thrusted himself repeatedly inside of her. "I want you daddy…I want you!" she moaned as she began to throw her ass back. Gerrod took his hand and pushed the small of her back down while purposely going deeper with every stroke. "Stick it out like I taught you!" Even though she was in pain Tyra enjoyed every minute of it. She quickly spun around and threw him on the bed so she could show him what she was made of. She mounted herself on top of him and bounced up and down. She knew exactly what she needed to do to make him explode as she sped up her pace, brought it back down then gyrated counter clockwise as though she was trying to screw the top off of a jar. He smacked her ass and her juices gushed all over his muscular thighs. "You got some good pussy!" he moaned as he picked her up and walked her around the room. Tyra was in lustful heaven as he watched her eyes roll to the back of her head. He put her down and instructed her to go out onto the apartment balcony. She bent over the railing while he hit her from the back. Tyra was immersed in his desire for her and didn't care who heard her profane screams.

"I love the way this shit looks!" roared Gerrod as he continuously smacked her ass. He took his right leg and lifted it over the balcony. Tyra yelped as if it was too much. "Shut the fuck up and take daddy's dick!"

he said as he pulled her hair. Things began to feel too good to Gerrod and he let out a growling sound.

"I'm cumming…shit…I'm cumming!" Tyra turned around and allowed his milky juices to shower her breasts and stomach. As she passionately kissed him, Gerrod felt a weight lift off his shoulders.

INEVITABLE

8

Things around the firm hadn't been the same since Samantha quit. Giselle was put in charge of selecting her replacement but wasn't having any luck. The majority of the applicants were under-qualified with little to no experience. Giselle wanted Simon, Franklin, and Mosely to continue to reign supreme in the entertainment field and would not settle for anyone but the best. After the last interviewee left, Giselle sighed in frustration and threw her pen across the desk. "Damn," she murmured as she reclined in her chair. She was starting to feel the true responsibility that came with being partner and needed to get away to decompress. She hadn't spoken to Hill since their previously interrupted date. She didn't feel like explaining her brother's situation and at this point didn't really care if he called or not. She briefly recalled how Hill looked that night and began to get aroused. Dwayne stood at the door and waited for Giselle to motion him in.

"Morning, beautiful," he sang as he placed a Starbucks Caramel Frappuccino on her desk. Giselle grinned. "You sure do know how to make a woman smile," said Giselle as she licked the whipped cream topping.

"I thought you could use a break of some sort. You've been looking very stressed. I guess your man ain't doing what he's supposed to."

Giselle smirked. "Please, I told you that I don't have a man. Hill and I are just friends and we haven't spoken in days now."

"I thought you liked him."

"I do."

"So, why haven't you spoken with him?"

"I don't know. I suppose I've been busy trying to find Samantha's replacement and just going through a lot of personal issues."

"It doesn't make sense for you to work all the time and not enjoy life. If that man was making your stubborn ass even semi-happy then you need to call him." Dwayne turned around and walked out.

Giselle knew that he was right but didn't know how she would explain herself to Hill…not that she was obligated, but she felt as if something needed to be said to clear the air. She fingered her rolodex and pulled out his card. She decided to invite him on a date.

"Hello Giselle," he answered.

"Hi Mr. Stokes," she responded with her fingers crossed. "Look, I know these past two weeks have been crazy and I haven't been in contact with you, but I'm dealing with family issues and it's been a madhouse around the office. Anyways, I apologize for what happened before. Would you care to join me for dinner? My treat."

Silence flooded the line. "After our last encounter, I'm not sure if you're ready to accommodate someone as demanding as myself. Like you said, you have a lot going on and I don't want to interfere." His tone was cool.

"So, are you telling me no?" retorted Giselle. She crossed her fingers tighter and squeezed her eyes shut while praying to herself. There was another brief silence.

"I'm telling you *no* if you feel like this is something you **have** to do."

"Look, I would never extend an invitation to anyone if it's not something I want to do…trust me. I really would like to get to know you."

Hill sighed. "Fine, Ms. Mosely, you can have me. I'll pick you up around 8 tonight and we can go from there."

"No, you will not," said Giselle. "I am making it up to you, so I am requesting that you meet me at my house around seven. Cool?"

"That's fine," said Hill. "See you then."

INEVITABLE

***

"Wow," said Elicia as she met Gabe at her car. "You look very handsome."

"Thanks," he said, "It is my responsibility to come dressed in the presence of the Lord."

Elicia couldn't decide whether this was a date or not and couldn't shake the guilt. When they arrived at the church, Gabe grabbed Elicia's hand and led her to a pew in the front of the congregation. She recognized some of the members giving her strange looks. She wasn't doing anything wrong…was she? Two friends attending Bible study was harmless…right?

Today, church, we are going to talk about God's plan. Some of you are sitting in the midst of confusion and are constantly wondering why God is putting you through trials and tribulations in life, but I'm here to tell you today that those who trust in the Lord for ALL things will survive. Say this with me, All things". "All things," the church responded in unison. *Sometimes we don't have the answers to what God is trying to do in our lives. This is where faith comes in. Open the good book to Hebrews 11:1.*

As Elicia intently listened to the sermon, she felt the spirit of the Lord move over her and instantly felt at peace. She knew that things would work out in the end. Gabe admired Elicia as they walked back to the car once service was over.

"That was a great message," he said. "Yeah, the pastor is awesome. Not only is he a leader, but he's an excellent teacher. He makes things clear…you know?" Elicia nodded her head in agreement as Gabe put his seat belt on.

"So, are you hungry?" he asked. Elicia was famished but didn't know how she was supposed to feel about being out in public with another man. "Sure," she said reluctantly.

INEVITABLE

"Why don't we go get my car and I can take you to a nice spot in downtown...so you can stuff your face."

Elicia laughed. "That would be great."

Gabe's customized black Escalade with a license plate that read FFLOWE was lavish and roomy on the inside. They arrived at the Sun Dial restaurant and Gabe escorted her through the door. Elicia wondered to herself why, of all the places in downtown, he'd taken her to a restaurant on top of a *hotel*. Once they were seated he ordered them both a glass of wine. He noticed that Elicia seemed uncomfortable.

"Elicia look," he said, "I know I don't know your situation or what's going on in your personal life, but I am not here to interfere or confuse you. I just want to be here for you in your time of need."

Elicia took a sip of her drink. "I appreciate that, Gabe," she said. "I just have so much going on. I often wonder what God is trying to show me in all of this."

"Just be patient, Elicia. Sometimes love takes a while to work itself out. If your husband is a smart man he will come to his senses."

"I wish it were that simple Gabe, but it's not." Elicia suddenly found herself explaining her situation about Nasir to him. Gabe stared at her in disbelief once she finished.

"That's amazing," he said as he savored his bacon and horseradish salmon.

"What's amazing?"

"That a woman so beautiful is being caused so much pain but is handling it with grace. I wish that there was something I could do to assist you."

Elicia smiled. "You've done enough. Excuse me while I go to the ladies' room."

Elicia stared at herself in the mirror and tried not to break down but couldn't help herself. She watched her mascara run down her face. Her nose was bright-red and she knew Gabe would become more concerned if he saw her like this. *Why am I always breaking down in front of this man?* she thought. When she returned, he grabbed her hand.

Gabe noticed her puffy face and that her mood had suddenly changed. "Why don't we just go?" he asked. "You probably have a lot to do and I don't want to keep you out too late." He helped Elicia put on her coat. He grabbed her face and stared into her watering eyes. "Everything is going to be alright…you've got to believe me."

"So, this is how you treat him?" yelled a voice from across the room. Elicia turned around to discover Teri sitting at the bar with a female companion. "I tell you the truth about my cousin and you go and hook up with the next man you come into contact with? What kind of woman are you?" She marched over to her as though they were the only two in the restaurant. Elicia could see some of the guests turning to observe what was happening and rolled her eyes in disgust.

"So, are you following me, now? And not that I owe you any kind of explanation, but who I go out with, in public, is *none of your damn business*. And for the record, he is a friend." Elicia tried to speak in a hushed tone but was becoming more infuriated by the second.

"Yeah, right," said Teri as she flung her blonde streaked bangs out of her eyes. "You are a low-down bitch for cheating on Nasir. You know that he is **sick**."

Gabe stepped in between them. "Look," he said. "I don't know you, but I will not allow you speak to her like this. She hasn't done anything wrong."

He looked at Elicia. "She is a wonderful woman, from what I'm learning, and certainly does not want to discuss her business in public. Elicia, let's go." Elicia grabbed her handbag and rushed to the elevator ahead of Gabe. She couldn't wait to get to the bottom floor and when they finally did Elicia let out a sigh of relief.

INEVITABLE

"Unbelievable!" she said as she sat in the car. She was pissed. "Just who in the hell does that bitch think she is? I have supported her cousin for *years*. I was there when he didn't have shit, and I'm still here."

"Calm down, Elicia," said Gabe. "Everything will be fine."

Elicia didn't mean to but began lashing out at Gabe. "It's your fault that this bullshit happened. Why did I even agree to go out with you? And why in the hell would you take me to a restaurant on top of a hotel? Did you think we were gonna get a room and I was going to give you sex because you went to church with me? Well, you're out of your fucking mind if you were thinking that because I am NOT *that chick*!"

Gabe's feelings were hurt. "Elicia…those were not-"

"Just shut the fuck up, Gabe, and take me home." They rode in silence for the remainder of the drive back to their neighborhood. When they finally pulled up in front of Elicia's house Gabe started to get out of the car to walk her to the door. "Don't bother," said Elicia as she hopped out and slammed his truck door as hard as she could. She let herself inside her house and realized her head was spinning. She felt faint and slumped to the floor. Her stomach started to churn. "Why did I do that to him?" she sobbed aloud as she shook her head. She did not mean to hurt Gabe and felt herself on the brink of a nervous breakdown. She opened the door and found Gabe still standing there looking helpless. He grabbed her and embraced her as tight as he could. Elicia cried like a baby.

***

Giselle frantically moved around the house as she prepared for her date with Hill. She wanted to look sexy, yet simple, but couldn't seem to pull anything together. "It always happens this way!" she whined. "I have the outfit in my head for weeks, then when I put it on it looks a hot mess!" She poured a glass of Viognier to calm herself. She needed to loosen up. Giselle had an arrangement of sushi on the dining table and *Mystic Voyage* by Ronny Jordan serenading the entire house. As the wine moved through her body, Giselle allowed the music to take control and felt sexier than ever. She quickly decided on a light gray jumpsuit, diamond studs and stacked silver bangles. She admired her selection as she twirled in front of her floor mirror. She was relieved to find that Hill equally matched her sexy when she opened the door.

"Come in," she said feeling calm and ready for the evening ahead. He handed her a bouquet of purple calla lilies as she hugged him. She inhaled his scent and breathed slowly. She grabbed his hand and led him to the table. He beamed and said, "Someone has been doing research I see?"

"Always two steps ahead of ya," she said giddily. "And I see that you remembered my favorite color. The flowers are beautiful!" She quickly filled a crystal vase with water and placed the flowers on the dining table.

They both sat down and gazed into each other's eyes. Giselle found herself more attracted to Hill than any of the other men she had met in Atlanta. His features were unique, but familiar at the same time. A certain kind of understanding came with him and she hadn't even begun to know who he really was. But tonight, Giselle didn't want to read more into what seemed to be the perfect opportunity to let her hair down and be herself. The only rule she had for the evening was no sex. Not for him. Not for anyone.

Hill helped himself to the spread. "I love sushi, Giselle. It's a peaceful food. It's delicious."

Giselle frowned. "Can I be honest?" she said.

"Let me guess, you don't like sushi," he retorted.

"I'm not saying that I don't like it. I welcome learning about different cultures. I've travelled outside the country many times."

"But you're still saying you don't like it."

Giselle moved her seat next to his.

"All I'm saying is teach me about it. I'd like to know why you love it." Hill explained to Giselle the various types of sushi, and after learning the ingredients, she settled on the Nigiri Sushi made of vinegar rice topped with cooked fish and vegetables. Hill decided on the homestyle Nigiri formally called Okonomi Sushi. Giselle enjoyed the light taste that her selection provided. She didn't feel stuffed yet was satisfied.

"You care to have this dance?" asked Hill as he extended his hand. Giselle noticed how comfortable she felt. He pulled her close as they grooved to the Isley Brothers' *Living for the Love of You*. She became engulfed in the moment and realized that she hadn't felt this way in a while. No work. No friends. No drama. Just her and Hill suspended in a moment of sheer bliss. This was the kind of good that only came once - or maybe twice in a lifetime. Hill's hands melodically played all over her body. His fingers on her hips keyed in all of her senses. She felt as though this was "goodness" that only someone special could provide. Giselle didn't want to fall for Hill, but right now she was hypnotized.

"So, let me ask you this," he quizzed while they continued to dance. "Why did you get sushi if you don't like it? You don't have to pretend with me, Giselle." He kissed her forehead.

"It's not that serious, Hill. Nobody's pretending," snapped Giselle.

"I don't mean to come incorrect or anything. I just want you to know that you can be yourself around me at all times. Because that's what I plan on doing with you." He caressed the back of her head and kissed her neck. She blushed.

"It's finally dark out." said Giselle changing the subject. "I wanted us to go to Centennial Park and enjoy the rest of the evening."

"Well, let's go then," he said as he playfully pinched her side. She threw on a shawl and set the alarm on her security system as they headed out the door.

They arrived at the park to find it a bit crowded. They sat on one of the old, green benches closest to the street. Hill lightly suckled Giselle's neck as she watched a young, Asian couple playing with their baby nearby. For a second, she thought about what it would feel like to be a mother. Distracting her thoughts, Hill's warm tongue aroused her, but she managed to maintain her composure. The scenery was beautiful. Old couples, young couples, new couples. All races. Everyone was together.

INEVITABLE

As Michael Jackson's *Thriller* echoed throughout the park, Giselle and Hill, along with most of the crowd, nodded their heads in appreciation while watching the light show. "I'm not saying that it's better than what I would have done, but I'm certainly loving this date so far," he joked.

"Of course, you do!" cracked Giselle. "Women are considerate of a man's feelings. Men are just…men." Hill playfully yanked her closer to him and bit her cheek. Giselle laughed loudly, but no one cared that they were enjoying each other.

"So, how'd you know I liked sushi?" he asked.

"I saw your article in Rolling Out. Needless to say, I was quite impressed."

Hill laughed. "Wow, a compliment from the most critical Black woman in the world." Giselle nudged him. "Take that back," she laughed. "Just because I have standards doesn't make me critical. From my perspective, Black men complain more than Black women."

"I'm not like every man." said Hill as he sat forward with his hands in his lap. Giselle watched his facial expression become serious. She wondered where his mind had gone for that moment.

"Would you like to ride?" Hill asked as he stood up. Giselle gave him the look of death. "Excuse me?" she retorted. He pointed to the horse and carriage moving up the street.

"Oh," she said, slightly embarrassed. Giselle was under his spell and felt that she might agree to anything he asked her to do tonight. Once they mounted the carriage Giselle relaxed. She felt like royalty. She didn't want to go back on her "no sex" rule but suddenly felt an itch that needed to be scratched. They rode around the park three times before calling it a night.

"Before you take me back to my car, I'd like to share a piece of my private life with you." Hill's tone was matter-of-fact. Giselle looked puzzled. Hill grabbed her car keys out of her hand. "I'll drive."

INEVITABLE

"Negro, are you crazy? You want me to let you drive my *car*? You do realize you have no respect for speed limits, don't you?"

"Nah, I'm always safe – especially when I'm carrying precious cargo," he retorted arrogantly as he showed his beautiful smile. His masculine, yet understanding smile made Giselle warm. They rode for over an hour before he turned onto *Canary Drive* and pulled up to a white, one-story cottage with a charming wrap-around porch. The house was surrounded by pine trees with a bird bath cemented by the front window overlooking the driveway. She glanced at the mailbox number.

"Get out," he said as he walked around to open her door. Once inside, Giselle peeped her surroundings. "So, is this where your secret rendezvous are held?" she was half joking, half serious.

The inside was mostly vacant. No furniture, television, or anything that could possibly provide entertainment. Giselle suddenly felt her anxiety kick in. *What if he tries to rape me?* she thought. *We are in the middle of nowhere.* She quickly texted Marley and Elicia the address just in case anything popped off.

Hill cleared his throat. "No. It's where I come to get away from it all. It was my grandmother's house. She willed it to my mother, her only child, after her death four years ago. When I decided to relocate to Atlanta, I felt it was best to rehab it instead of selling it. I've been considering leasing it out in the summers, but for now I'm just enjoying its tranquility."

He took Giselle's hand and guided her to a small music room in the back of the house. White, built-in shelves that aligned the walls were filled with timeless music. "This is righteous," Giselle whispered as she looked around. She casually perused his collection and was completely in awe. "I love music, too," she grinned. "You have ALL the classics," she said in amazement. "I thought I was the only music junkie I knew."

Headphones, vinyl records, and a record player were sprawled on the floor. It was a cozy, yet peaceful setting for two. They sat in the room for what seemed like hours listening to music and drinking wine that Hill had brought up from the cellar. "His death was tragic," blurted Hill as they listened to *Butterflies* by Michael Jackson.

"God yes, but everything happens for a reason. He was ready for him to come home, ya know," said Giselle as she stared into space remembering the late entertainment icon. She thought about some of her clients and how their artistry paled in comparison.

Hill cleared his throat. "Wow, a woman who speaks of the Lord. Is there something religious about you?" he asked. *This man was deep*, she thought.

"Yes, it is," said Giselle. "I love the Lord and I have a very intimate and sweet relationship with him."

"I do, as well," Hill said as they toasted. "I mean, I'm working on some things, but aren't we all?" He stared Giselle in her eyes. She wondered what he meant.

"It's after midnight."

"So, what are you saying?" he asked.

"I'm saying that it's late and I need to get home, especially considering the fact that you hijacked the entire date with your little music room." She smiled. "But I loved it. I can even feel your grandmother's presence. I know she's proud of you."

Hill sat against the bookcase and extended his legs. He motioned for her to come to him. The Zinfandel had her mind, body and soul fully relaxed and she couldn't resist. She kissed and held Hill thinking about a possible future with one of the most powerful attorneys in his field. In her opinion, this was the perfect ending to a perfect date.

***

Later that morning, Giselle jumped up as she was suddenly awakened from her sleep. Her heart was palpitating and there was extreme pain coming from both of her hands. She frowned as she fumbled with her lamp. She sat up, as best as she could, and held her trembling hands in front of her. Her knuckles were swollen.

What the hell? she thought. She chalked it up to the boxing lessons she had been taking although she'd missed the past couple of sessions. She grabbed several ice cubes from the freezer and dropped them into a bowl. She took a seat on the bar stool and stared at her knuckles. Very cautiously she submerged them into the ice.

"Oh…my…God," she whispered with her head down. She made a mental note to call her doctor.

***

"And what if I am interested in Trump's proposed policies, is that a problem? You're right, he has never held a government position before but I'm only trying to understand his viewpoints."

Elicia noticed a change in Gabe's tone. Their lighthearted political debate had taken a left turn.

"Follow me," he said. He led Elicia up a winding staircase. At the top of the landing was an open loft area that overlooked the bottom floor of his condo. In the right corner was a sliding red door that she cautiously peered through. She was immediately taken aback when she saw Gabe's book collection. He had converted a small walk-in closet into a mini library.

"Wow," she said with astonishment. "You are definitely well-read *and* creative."

Gabe beamed proudly at his modest but impressive collection. "Yeah, I'm big on knowledge. I am the master of memoirs, manuals, and manuscripts. Even though I might seem a bit rough around the edges, I've always valued education."

Elicia began reading titles of books that she had never heard of. "*Hard Choices, Living History, A Time for Truth: Reigniting The Promise of America…One Nation: What We Could All Do to Save America's Future, Take the Risk: Learning to Identify, Choose and Live With Acceptable Risk…*"

INEVITABLE

As she fingered the spine of several books, one intrigued her the most. "*Our Revolution,*" she faintly whispered. "What is a Republican doing reading up on Bernie Sanders?" Gabe grabbed the book out of her hand. "Like I said, I educate myself. I just wanted you to see that I'm not a dumb dude." He tucked the book away and started back down the stairs to the kitchen.

"You know, I like everything about you," he admitted.

"You can't possibly like *everything* about me." She gushed. "I'm not perfect you know."

"I know that. I'm just saying that you come close to perfect in my book."

She sprayed whipped cream in her brew. "Be honest. Name one thing that you would change about me if you could."

"Besides the fact that you're still married?"

Elicia squinted at him. "Yes, besides that," she mumbled.

"To be honest, I wish you wouldn't wear makeup."

Elicia jerked her neck. "What do you mean? It's what I do. I have my own makeup line."

"And I think that's great. But you don't need it. You have flawless skin."

She didn't know if she should be offended by his honesty.

"So, are you asking me to **not** wear makeup?"

Gabe shook his head. "No."

Elicia let out a sigh of relief. "Good. Because I'm not one for opinions."

"What do you mean?"

"In my past, I've had a few guys tell me that because I don't need makeup I shouldn't wear it."

INEVITABLE

"I agree."

Elicia shrugged her shoulders. "I love makeup. It enhances a woman's natural beauty. It gives us confidence."

"False confidence for that moment. Once the babydoll lashes and foundation come off, then what?"

She rolled her eyes. "In the words of makeup extraordinaire Bobbi Brown, *I believe all women are pretty without makeup- but with the right makeup can be pretty powerful.*"

He leaned in and kissed her on her forehead. "Don't let me stress you out."

"I'm not stressing," she said with a slight attitude.

"Look, I really didn't mean to upset you. Go ahead and be *pretty powerful* with yo' bad self," he said jokingly.

"Thank you." Elicia thought about how Nasir never supported her dream of starting a makeup line and a sadness came over her.

***

"I just don't understand why God would send him my way," said Marley. "A widower."

"Maybe he's taking a chance on you," said Elicia.

"I just don't know," said Marley as she almost dropped her cell phone. "What happened between us was so intense. It's almost unexplainable."

"You better stop playing with fire," teased Elicia. "I can't believe you gave the man blue balls!"

Marley sucked her teeth. "Don't remind me. I don't know why I was so drawn to him. I just can't get over the fact that this man used to have this beautiful wife who was obviously his best friend and then she suddenly gets killed! No matter how much I try to shake the shit, it won't go away."

INEVITABLE

"It sounds to me like you are sabotaging a perfectly "potential" relationship all because the man is obviously still in love with his dead wife," said Elicia.

"I'm not!" shrieked Marley. "I just don't have any time to be wasting my time. Maybe that sounds a bit insensitive, but we both know that I am not getting any younger. I just hope he's truly able to move forward and accept that I am not her. Speaking of relationships, what's going on with yours?"

"Which one?" asked Elicia. "If I had any clue I would inform you. I still haven't heard from Nasir. Gabe has been doing a great job at keeping me sane. That's for sure."

Marley giggled. "***You*** are the one playing with fire. You know Gabe is trying to get next to you while you're trying to act all naïve about the situation."

"No, he's not," retorted Elicia. "Gabe knows and understands that Nasir has my heart. He respects what I've got going on."

Marley rolled her eyes. "The man is practically over your house every night, Elicia. Please tell me you are not this gullible!"

"Call it what you want. Gabe knows what's really going on. You just worry about you and Trey and I'll worry about me and whoever. Deal?"

"Sure, Elicia, sure." said Marley. She knew her friend better than she knew herself.

9

Gerrod sat up and rubbed his head. He looked over and saw Tyra sleeping peacefully. It had been weeks since he'd spoken to his wife. He still couldn't get over the fact that she'd hurt him…bad. Going back to his old ways was the only option in his book. He missed her but couldn't bear to see her face. He turned his phone on and noticed that his father had called seven times. He didn't care to talk but called him back anyway.

"Gerrod, what's goin' on with you, son?"

"What do you mean?" Gerrod asked nonchalantly.

"I dunno what kinda mess you done got yo'self into but you need to talk with yo' wife. Why you not at home?"

"Because she's a liar and I don't deal with liars. We've been together for this long and she never really brought up an issue about us raising a mixed child in a racist world. I mean, we have talked about it but I never really knew she had this much anxiety around it. As a Black man, I deal with shit every day that doesn't make any sense but I'm still here doing my part. I'm determined not to be somebody's fucking statistic…I just don't understand." His father sighed. "Ya need to wash away this nonsense and go back to ya wife. She needs ya shoulder right now. How can ya make it betta there?"

"Why should I listen to you? What could you possibly tell *me* about marriage?" Gerrod regretted speaking to his father this way but was angry and needed him to understand that what Eva did was unforgiveable.

"Boy, forgiveness is da key."

"Well, I can't forgive Eva. Cheating is one thing, but lying about wanting to have my seed is…is…" Gerrod's mouth went dry. "Look pops, I'll talk to you later." He hung up.

INEVITABLE

Tyra jumped up and threw her arms around his neck. "So, does this mean that you don't plan on going back to her, ever?" she asked. He removed her arms.

"Stay out of my damn business. I'm going for a drive." He grabbed his jacket and left. What his Dad said to him really hit home. Although he was angry with Eva he didn't necessarily want to be without her. When he let himself in he found Eva sitting in the kitchen in the mint green silk robe he'd brought her last Valentine's Day. The house was a mess and Gerrod wondered what in the hell she had been doing for the past few weeks.

Eva immediately shot Gerrod the look of death. "For better or for worse," she said as tears began to run down her face. She took her ring off and threw it at him. Gerrod didn't understand what was going on. **He** was mad at her, not the other way around. She pointed to the door and screamed, "Get OUT, before I call the police!"

"Call the police?" retorted Gerrod. "What the fuck is going on?"

"You are a liar and a cheater. You promised me that no matter what happened to us that you would never go back to that bitch! I guess it was only a matter of time."

Gerrod shook his head.

"It's just like you to play the blame game. **You** fucked up, not **me**." Eva disappeared and quickly returned with two suitcases already filled with his personal belongings. She threw them at his feet along with their framed wedding photo.

"You're right, I fucked up and married a lying ass no good son-of-a-bitch who is just like his low-down father. NOW GET OUT!" Gerrod's knees weakened as he made his way to his car. He didn't understand what had just happened. Where did she get off snapping on him when she was the one who was keeping secrets? Gerrod felt justified in his cheating. *I'm ready to live my life for me. Fuck a marriage.* he thought to himself.

INEVITABLE

***

Marley loved her job but sometimes felt overwhelmed with all the red tape that was involved. She'd finished lecturing for the night and stayed behind to grade papers. She removed her purple Mary Jane stiletto pumps and leaned back in her chair with her eyes closed. She let out the most masculine yawn as she massaged her neck.

"Maybe I can help you with that." Marley nearly jumped out of her skin. It was Trey. He had obviously come straight from the gym, because he looked like he needed a shower. Never-the-less, Marley found it attractive.

"Wh-What are you doing here?" stuttered Marley as she fumbled with her red pen.

"Why haven't you returned my calls?" Trey stood there looking pitiful yet seductive.

"Look, you're a great guy but-"

"But what?" he interrupted. "I don't understand. I thought we hit it off well. I thought we had mad chemistry."

"We did, I mean we do, I mean..."

"Exactly," he responded. "You don't even know why we are no longer speaking. Listen, I apologize for what happened the last time we were together, but I still would like the opportunity to get to know you. I think you are an amazing woman. You know that. And furthermore, we are consenting adults. Why are you acting so childish?"

Marley rolled her eyes. She quickly slipped on her heels and began to gather her paperwork. "I like you Trey…I really do, but I honestly don't believe you are ready to start dating again."

"And who are you to say that? Look, I'm sorry I got an erection, you're attractive…what do you expect?"

Marley felt herself becoming aroused.

INEVITABLE

"I won't allow myself to move on knowing that I could have hit it off with one of the sexiest and smartest women in the "A". So ***please***, give me one more chance. It was an accident."

He grabbed her hands. "I made a mistake. And plus, I miss yo' crazy ass." Marley smirked and sighed. His begging made her heart skip a beat but she refused to show it.

"I guess we can give it another try. And I kinda miss you, too..."

Trey grinned and tried to hug her. Marley pushed him away. "A hand shake will do," she stated firmly. "You don't look too clean right now."

Trey took three steps back. "Don't tell me you're afraid to get a little dirty." He playfully pushed Marley down in her recliner. "It's time," he said, with a serious look in his eyes.

"Time for what?" she asked. She felt sweat starting to form under her arms.

"For me to please you." Trey removed her shoes and pantyhose while staring deep into her eyes. He took the gym towel from around his neck and placed it under her. Marley didn't want to move too fast but, once again, felt locked under his spell. Trey's tongue was just right. Not too wet or sloppy, but perfect for her pulsating love box. He spread her vagina lips apart and blew on her clitoris. Marley began to squirm around in the chair and gripped the arm rest for support. He gently licked her sweet spot and gradually increased his speed as she moaned. Marley took deep breaths and wrapped her legs around his head. "Mmmm baby, yes!" she whimpered. She grabbed the back of his head and pushed his tongue deeper inside of her. Marley forced herself to come back down to Earth. She was afraid of what would happen next. "Trey I don't think-" He immediately told her to hush and that he only wanted to taste her essence for now...that he'd dreamed about tasting her. This turned Marley on even more. She allowed him to resume their love session without further interruption. She floated all the way to Heaven and back.

He wiped his mouth and goatee with the towel. "Baby, you taste better than I imagined." Marley's face flushed red. She excused herself and went to the ladies' room. While she respected Trey for only wanting to go so far, deep down, she wished he would have given her what her body needed. It had been a long time since Marley was pleasured by a man and she was horny as ever. Self-pleasure could never compare to a man's touch. When she returned, she found Trey sitting at one of her student's desks.

"Teach me everything you know," he said with a big grin on his face.

"Oh, I will…in due time," she giggled. For a second, she wondered if his deceased wife was able to fulfill his sexual appetite.

***

"So, what do you want me to do about her?" asked Giselle. She was greeted by several complaints upon arriving to the office.

"I don't know what you are going to do, but *something* has to be done. This woman is making everyone's life around here a living hell." said Dwayne. Giselle took a deep breath and stared at him. "Send her in."

Although Giselle was partly responsible for hiring the new paralegal, she hadn't had much interaction with her thus far. Dwayne left and returned with Neena. To Giselle's surprise she looked much different from the day she interviewed her. Neena sashayed in her office wearing a tan BCBG Maxzaria suit and chocolate-colored Gucci pumps. Giselle didn't want to admit it but her body was in perfect shape much like her eye brows and burgundy lip liner. She smelled of Chanel No. 19 perfume and gently patted her coiled afro as though she was standing in front of an invisible mirror.

"Good morning, Giselle," she confidently stated as she looked around her office.

"Good morning," she replied. "Please have a seat, and you can refer to me as Ms. Mosely." Neena shot her an odd look and sat down. Giselle closed her door.

INEVITABLE

"It has been brought to my attention that a few members of the staff have been complaining about your professionalism." She handed her a pamphlet on the firm's policies and procedures.

Neena rolled her eyes. "I have this already," she responded. Giselle stood. "Well now you have another one."

"I have invited you here to inform you that you are still on your probationary period. After 90 days, you will be evaluated and from there we will make the decision whether or not you are highly-qualified for the position."

"But you hired me."

"True, but you are also expected to endure a probationary period to prove your value just like everyone one else who's come before you. I would advise you to adhere to the guidelines and do the job that you were hired to do."

"Look, the others are just jealous. They recognize something in me and immediately want to throw me under the bus. It happens everywhere I go…believe me. People are just intimidated by excellence." She quickly checked her nails.

"I understand that, Ms. Champion, but regardless, you still have a job to do and you must adhere to all guidelines. The distinct orders that are given should be taken care of in a timely manner. Please do not go out of your way to complete someone else's assigned tasks."

"Why not? Especially if I am more proficient. It's not my fault that Dwayne is slow answering the phones and delivering messages because he chooses to socialize instead. Since I am on top of my game and complete my duties ahead of deadlines, I take on the leadership role of assisting him. What's wrong with that? What I am doing is for the greater good of the firm. It's called being a team-player."

Giselle had to admit that she was sharp. Neena graduated from Columbia University at the top of her class and seemed to have similar ambitions as Giselle. Giselle was actually glad to have someone of her caliber working at the firm.

"I understand where you are coming from. But, I also want you to understand that performing someone else's job, especially without their consent, makes them look incompetent."

Neena shrugged. "Fine Ms. Mosely, I'll stay in my place…but just know that I won't be in this position for long. I have high aspirations just as you did, and I do not plan on sleeping my way to the C-suite."

Giselle gave her the look of death.

Neena held her hands up in defense. "Now, before you get all ghetto on me, Ms. Mosely, please know that I am not talking about you. I heard the story about the woman who I replaced. Black women really need to get it together."

Giselle calmed down. "I know what you mean and understand what you are facing, Neena. If you need anything, at all, please do not hesitate to come and speak with me."

Neena stood and shook Giselle's hand. Giselle pursed her lips as she watched her leave. She then called Dwayne back into her office.

"She's sharp," said Giselle. "I knew there was a reason I hired her." Dwayne rolled his eyes. "She aight…I just want her to leave me the hell alone."

"I don't think that she is bothering you. I do, however, think that you are concerned that she might do your job better than you."

Dwayne sighed. "No, that's not it. If you would have wanted her to do my job, you would have hired her for my position. I just can't have her making me look bad."

Giselle laughed. "Well, I would suggest that you stay on top of your work and do not allow her to interfere."

"Will do," he said as he shut her door. Giselle felt that she'd probably ruffled Dwayne's feathers but wasn't bothered by it. He knew that everything she ever told him was out of love.

INEVITABLE

***

Elicia simmered the king crab legs and took the apple pie out of the oven. She ran upstairs to change clothes before Gabe joined her for dinner. The two had become very close, and Elicia was slowly beginning to forget about Nasir. Gabe's company allowed her to keep her mind off all the divorce drama. Gabe made her happy.

He embraced her and kissed her cheek. "Hey queen," he said as he took a seat in the living room area. Elicia brought him a glass of wine and joined him. "Dinner is almost ready."

"It smells nice," he said. "Look, I've been meaning to talk to you."

He sat down his wine glass and grabbed Elicia's hand. She blushed. "I really don't know how to say this, or if it's even right for me to say this, but I will no longer repress my feelings. I think I am falling in love with you. I mean, I know you got a situation, but I love what we have. I love you."

An awkward silence erupted. "I…I don't know what to say," Elicia was stunned. "I'm married."

Gabe stood up. "But you're getting a divorce." His sudden change in tone startled her. Elicia froze. She had never witnessed this side of him.

"Look, I'm not trying to confuse you or make your current situation more difficult than it has to be, but I can't be around you and not acknowledge the connection that exists or the feelings I have for you. You are the most beautiful, intelligent, and sexiest woman I have ever met. I want to learn everything about you. I think about you all day, every day. I want you all to myself and I don't believe in sharing."

Elicia just sat there. While flattered, she didn't know what to do. Yes, she was attracted to Gabe, but her heart belonged to Nasir. The thought of not being with him saddened her. She knew Nasir was unfaithful but now believed that complications in their marriage arose from his illness. At that moment, she remembered her vows, *"For better or for worse, through sickness and in health, 'til death do us part."*

INEVITABLE

"I'm not sure if I love you," she said.

Gabe moved towards the door. "Honestly, I don't want to put you in an uncomfortable situation, so maybe its best if I just leave."

She grabbed his hand. "You know I want you to stay."

Gabe smiled. "I do want to stay, but **will you stay** when your husband returns?" Elicia sighed as Gabe walked out the door. She needed her girls.

***

"I had a surprise date with Hill tonight so this better be important." Elicia, Giselle, and Marley gathered at Pano & Paul's for light appetizers and drinks. Marley rolled her eyes. "I also had plans with Trey and you both know what that man does to me!"

"Gabe told me he has fallen in love with me!" she blurted out.

"Well, everyone knew that except you," retorted Marley. "You knew that man was going to fall hard for you sooner or later…which is why I don't understand how you continuously hang around him."

"To be perfectly honest, I don't see anything wrong with it," said Giselle. "It's better than her sitting in the house moping about Nasir, when he's out doing God knows what."

"She just can't forget about her husband because a new man comes into her life. She knows nothing about this Gabe guy." Marley was annoyed.

"She probably knows just as much as I know about Hill," retorted Giselle.

Elicia sighed. "I love my husband, but right now he is not here and I don't want to be alone. Gabe and I have never messed around…we haven't even kissed, but I love being around him."

INEVITABLE

"Sounds like you want him around if you ask me," said Giselle. "And you're a grown ass woman so if that's what you want to do then do it." Marley reluctantly nodded her head in agreement as she felt somewhat torn about her friend's predicament. "It sounds like this Gabe character is everything that Nasir isn't."

Elicia thought about it and realized they were right. She wished she would have met him years ago. What would her life be like at this very moment? She began to get emotional.

"Pull it together, Elicia," Giselle said bluntly. "You will get through this."

"I think we should go somewhere fun," interjected Marley. "Trey keeps mentioning this trip to the Cayman Islands and I feel like we should all go. Just to get away…to relax."

"Trey asked you to leave the country with him already?" Giselle sounded reluctant. "I guess he wants another case of blue balls." They all broke into laughter as Marley threw a piece of bread at her. She couldn't bring herself to tell them about their freaky rendezvous at the college.

Giselle excused herself to answer her phone. "Hey you," Hill said. "What's going on? Can I have you to myself or what?" Giselle's face flushed. "Um, of course. She glanced at her Movado watch. About what time were you thinking?"

"I need you now," he responded in a sexy baritone. "I'm sitting outside of the restaurant." Butterflies formed in Giselle's stomach as she began to imagine Hill's strong embrace.

She grimaced into the phone. "I asked you not to arrive until 9. We *just* got our appetizers because the place is packed tonight."

"I can wait if that's what you want me to do."

"Gimme a minute." She couldn't resist his chivalry.

Giselle returned to the table. "I can't believe that my brother is calling me with his bullshit again." She grabbed her coat. "Ladies, I have to go."

INEVITABLE

"But you didn't drive," reminded Elicia.

"Um...he's downstairs waiting on me." Giselle almost twisted her ankle hurrying out of the restaurant. Marley and Elicia looked at each other and rolled their eyes. "Liar!" they both said in unison as they burst into laughter.

"I'm just glad she's finally happy," said Marley.

Giselle found Hill standing against his car and immediately threw her arms around his neck. As they kissed Giselle felt Hill's hand grab her backside and she stiffened and pulled away.

"What?" Hill asked. "I can't do that?" Giselle felt like a teenager in high school.

He saw how stiff she became and let her go.

"I have a surprise for you," he bragged while opening her car door.

They drove west for about 45 minutes and finally arrived to a dark, wooded area. Hill popped the trunk of his car.

"What in the hell is going on, Hill? It looks scary out here. Why aren't there any lights?"

He grabbed a blanket and basket out the car and headed up the wooded path. Giselle didn't move. He motioned for her to come but she wouldn't budge.

"Giselle, come on! We'll be fine. Trust me."

She reluctantly got out the car and tried to keep her balance as she moved towards Hill. She was grateful to have worn her Tory Burch flats. They walked for what seemed like forever and finally reached a well-lit area off the lake.

Hill spread the blanket on the ground and pulled out chicken salad sandwiches, pretzels, fruit, and wine from the basket. He retrieved a small analog radio and turned to his favorite jazz station. He fed her one of the ripe strawberries.

INEVITABLE

"This is nice. A little chilly out but nice," said Giselle between bites. "It's so peaceful here." Hill nodded his head. "I agree. I come here all the time to journal and clear my head."

She wiped the juices from the corner of her mouth. "A man that journals? You obviously ain't from around here," she teased.

"I'm an original." he smiled.

"Look, I have something to tell you and if after I say this you decide that you don't want to continue whatever this is we're doing…then I understand," Giselle said while methodically re-wrapping her neck scarf. She paused to await Hill's reaction.

Hill slipped off Giselle's shoes and started to rub her feet. "I'm listening."

"I made a promise to myself, after my last breakup, that the next man that I became involved with would have to wait at least a year to become…you know…freaky."

Hill burst into laughter. "Why would I lose you over sex?"

Giselle shrugged her shoulders. "I just want you to be clear on where I stand. I don't want to have any regrets…ya know?"

Hill shook his head. "Trust me, I would rather make love to you mentally first, then physically."

Giselle started giggling uncontrollably.

"You sound like a pimp. Men don't think like that anymore!" She threw a strawberry at him.

"I told you I'm not like other men." He pulled Giselle closer and kissed her. She found herself wrapped up in their lip locking session as they both reclined on the blanket. Hill caressed Giselle's backside and this time she allowed him. She didn't mind a little touching…just as long as he respected her wishes. Giselle felt herself getting hot and bothered and cut the foreplay session short.

"So, tell me about your last relationship," Hill said. Giselle bit into another strawberry and rolled her eyes. "Well, it's been a while since I've been in anything worthy of being called a relationship…but the last guy I dated for longer than a month ended up being an asshole. The end."

Hill laughed. "Well…could you be a little bit more specific? Can you tell me what actually happened without the sarcasm, please?"

"His name was Immanuel and I met him at a coffee shop. He was cool. Out of all the men I had met in Atlanta I can honestly say that I liked him the most. He was a stockbroker and worked long hours. The time we spent together during the first few months was great. He wined and dined me and it seemed as if he was genuinely interested in me. You know, music, politics, education, fashion…everything. He was also very romantic…which was what I loved the most."

"So, what was the most romantic thing he did for you?"

"He took care of me when I had strep throat, and while that might not seem romantic…it really was to me because I was quite the bitch."

Hill gave Giselle two thumbs down. "That's not romantic. That's mandatory."

"Well, you did ask me…am I correct?" Giselle retorted with a slight attitude. Hill threw a napkin at her. "Finish," he said.

"We had fun together. I felt like I could really be myself around him."

"So, who were you in your other relationships?" Hill joked.

"I was me, but only to a certain extent. I was going through some things at the time."

Hill raised his left eyebrow.

"Look, I just don't feel like I'm able to trust any man. Like I told you before, when something feels too good to be true, it usually is. So, as a result, I just don't give my all."

"What did the brother do?" This very moment would have been perfect to disclose to Hill the reason they broke up. She chose to lie instead.

"What does every man do when a good woman comes into their life?"

Hill looked perplexed.

"They find some way to fuck it up. He cheated on me and when I found out, he defended his actions by saying, "*Marriage is the only relationship that truly matters.*""

Hill fed Giselle another strawberry. She resisted licking the chocolate from his fingers.

"Well, that is somewhat true, Giselle."

"So, you're saying that it's okay to cheat in a committed relationship? You can cheat on me during our entire relationship but expect me to believe it will cease on our wedding day? That's unrealistic!"

"I personally don't believe that applies to me. All I'm saying is, I see his logic."

"There is no logic there, Hill. If you love someone, you should commit yourself to them. Period. And to think, he had me meet his mom and everything."

"So, what does that mean? Answer this, why does a woman think that just because a guy introduces them to his mom that they are automatically 'the one'?"

"Why would you even waste your time introducing your mother to a chick who isn't?"

"You do have a point. But most of the time you think the person *is* 'the one' and for whatever reason it doesn't work out. It happens to the best of us. So, you found out this dude was dating someone else and then what?"

"Then I dismissed his ass and have been single ever since."

INEVITABLE

"You sound like an ABW again."

Giselle nudged him. "Whatever Hill, after a while you have a right to be angry. No one wants their heart to be dragged around the ring. You get tired of that shit. I am getting tired of dealing with pigeons and peacocks. I need an eagle."

"Giselle, what are you talking about?"

She became serious and sat up ready to defend her statement. "Pigeons defecate on you all the time. They are only for self and don't have good intentions. Peacocks act like females. Anytime you need anything from them they complain…you know, huffing and puffing with their feathers out. But an eagle, an eagle takes care of everything. He makes sure that his woman has every need met and boldly rises to the occasion."

Hill looked at her like she was crazy. "I never thought I'd see the day that women would start making men synonymous to birds. Very interesting analogy." He shook his head. "Well, do you still talk to the guy?"

"No, for what? In my book, exes cannot be friends."

"Now, I do agree with that. An ex is an ex for a reason."

Giselle laid back down and looked Hill directly in his eyes.

"So, tell me about the last chick you dated. Is that the reason why you mysteriously appeared in Atlanta?"

He playfully changed subjects. "Did you hear that, G? I think my cell phone is ringing."

Giselle laughed and playfully hit him on his chest. "I'm serious, Hill."

"Well…we were friends, first, then dated over a year and were planning to get married, but our trust issues got the best of our relationship. I can honestly say that she was the only woman I truly loved. It was through her that I learned that relationships are hard work. The beginning of our courtship was an adjustment for me because I was in the process of finding myself, but when I finally came face-to-face with who I was and what I wanted, it was too late."

"Wow," said Giselle. "Sounds like she had your nose wide open."

"I don't know about all that, but I did love her deeply at one point. We were alike in a lot of ways."

"She sounds perfect, which means you messed up. What happened?"

Hill became uncomfortable and lied. He wanted to tell Giselle what had caused the split but couldn't bring himself to do so.

"I was getting nervous about the commitment that was supposed to be forever. So, I mistakenly cheated on her."

Giselle shook her head. "So, you're one of **them**. Just for the record, I don't trust you. How do you mistakenly cheat on someone?"

"Damn, how are we supposed to progress if you carry this negative attitude about relationships everywhere you go? And for the record, I know that you don't trust me…you've made that quite evident."

Hill stood up and walked towards the lake. He pitched a few rocks and watched them skid across the water.

Giselle walked over to Hill and hugged him from behind. "I didn't mean to upset you. I just wanted to let you know where I'm coming from."

He turned around and kissed her forehead. "It's cool…but I get it. I'm just going to have to make you love me for who I really am."

"*Make* me love you? What does that mean?"

"It means that I am going to make you love me for who I really am," he repeated.

"But will you ultimately love me for who I really am?" She nervously played with his hand.

INEVITABLE

Hill kissed her. "Of course, I will love you for who you really are. I'm ready and willing to take on that challenge."

She kissed him on his cheek. "Well, Mr. Stokes, I just have to might take you up on your offer."

INEVITABLE

10

Four months after their first encounter at Apache Café, Marley finally decided that Trey was ready to be in a relationship. They spent as much time as they could together and she enjoyed every moment. They were on their way to the movies that Saturday afternoon and Trey wanted to make a quick stop. The weather was great outside considering it was early February. The car thermostat read fifty-one degrees at 12:34 in the afternoon. Marley wore a black sweater dress and mustard yellow blazer with a gingham print scarf and Trey sported a maroon button down with dark jeans. When Marley realized that they were entering a cemetery her heart skipped a beat. Trey got out of the car and opened her door. He grabbed her hand and led her to his wife's grave. Marley didn't know why but she felt uneasy. Trey laid down flowers and silently prayed. Marley stood back and gave him his space. When they reached the car, Trey let out a deep breath.

"I apologize if that made you uncomfortable. I went to put flowers on Robyn's grave last week and it was too much for me…so I left. Her birthday was February 1st. I always made it a point to keep her birthday and Valentine's Day separate. I decided that I needed you to come with me to visit her. I wanted her to meet you…for her to feel how beautiful you are. Forgive me if I've offended you in any way."

Marley rubbed his hand as she tried to hold back tears. "It's fine, I'm here for you."

"So, what do you think about having a family one day?" he asked.

His question hit Marley like a freight train. "It's a possibility. I mean I want to get married, but I'm not too sure about kids."

"I used to feel the same way. I was selfish once…always focused on growing my company and thought that having a child would be more of a hassle than a benefit. I heard Robyn crying late one night, while we were in bed, and asked her what was wrong. She told me that she didn't feel complete…that she needed to have a child and that she always wanted to be a mother. She actually wanted two kids…a boy and a girl. Shortly after that, I realized that I wasn't in my marriage solely for me and decided that I was ready for the challenge. The day I found out that she was pregnant, it gave me purpose."

Marley continued to stare at him with admiration.

"It's funny, I now wonder why anyone wouldn't want to have kids. I often think about my nieces and nephews and see how they bring so much joy into the lives of-."

"Okay Trey, enough about kids. I fucking get it." Marley cut him off mid-sentence while trying to stop her boiling tears from falling. "I'm sorry, Trey. I didn't mean to snap at you."

He turned the car off and turned to her. "What is it?"

She hesitated then closed her eyes trying to garner the strength to tell him. "I have a 9-year-old daughter somewhere out there who I know nothing about."

"Are you serious?" Trey was shocked. "You can find her you know."

"No, I can't," she sniffed. "How do I explain to her that she was a mistake? I was raped Trey, by my own boyfriend. How do I explain that to a 9-year-old? Tell me!"

Trey looked hurt. "Wow, you're a strong woman, Marley. You did what you felt was best for you and her at the time. Please don't beat yourself up about it."

Marley sucked her teeth as she looked out the window. "Yeah, whatever."

Trey attempted to comfort her. "You would make a great mom. It's not too late to reach out to her."

"That's easier said than done," Marley whispered with defeat in her heart.

"You know, I think we should just skip the movie. I have something better in mind."

INEVITABLE

They pulled in front of a high-end spa. She noticed that it was 2:03pm on the dashboard and felt a tinge of hunger. Trey hopped out the car and came back ten minutes later and opened her door. He took her by the hand. "I just want you to relax a bit. I've booked a facial, manicure, pedicure, and massage just for you. But first, would you mind joining me for a gourmet lunch?"

Marley embraced him tightly. In less than two hours she had *officially* fallen for Trey Roberts.

***

Elicia grabbed her briefcase out of her truck and looked forward to an evening of quiet. At times, she wished that she could just switch professions or focus on her makeup line. Being a psychologist was not an easy gig. Not only did she have to put her personal life aside, but also take on the problems of others. She checked her mailbox and noticed Gabe pulling into his driveway. She hadn't spoken to him in weeks and hated to admit that she was going crazy without him. She yearned for his companionship and wished that they could go back to the way they were. He waved at Elicia as he unlocked his front door. She waved back. Once inside, Elicia made herself comfortable and began to sort through her mail. The paperwork for her separate maintenance had arrived. After Nasir left, Elicia thought more about it and couldn't bring herself to outright divorce him. She decided that a separation was best just in case they worked it out. She made herself a cup of tea and read through the legal jargon. Elicia still didn't know if she wanted to sign it. She called both Marley and Giselle but didn't get a response. She didn't know how or why but she found herself knocking at Gabe's door once again.

Upon opening the door, Elicia abruptly pushed past him and twirled around on her heels to hand him the documents. "Hello to you, too," he said as he shut the door behind him.

Gabe sifted through the legal paperwork as he walked to the living room to sit down.

"Separation documents? I thought you were getting a divorce. So, you lied?"

"No," said Elicia defensively. "I didn't lie. I thought that I could go through with the divorce, but I couldn't. I was only trying to do the right thing." She followed him in and sat next to him.

"And what is that exactly?"

Elicia found herself becoming infuriated. "I didn't know if I was thinking hastily or not. I did the next best thing, which was to file a separate maintenance."

"Well, why are you bringing me the documents?"

"Why are you being such an asshole?"

"I'm not being an asshole. I'm trying to figure out how these papers are supposed to make me feel. Why did you bring them to me anyway?"

Elicia was confused. She did not understand why he seemed so annoyed.

"I brought them because I thought it would make you happy."

"Are you going to sign it? And even if you do, what does that mean for us? I'm sorry, but I can't get happy about a possibility."

Elicia snatched the papers out of his hand and headed to the door.

"Just forget it, Gabe. I thought you would understand, but you obviously don't."

He stopped her before she could leave.

"I apologize. My intentions are not to upset you, but I have been in this position before. I get excited about a woman…she leaves her man…but doesn't leave with me. My heart can no longer take the bullshit."

Gabe caressed Elicia's face.

INEVITABLE

"Look me in my eyes and tell me what your intentions were behind these papers."

Elicia snatched a pen off his coffee table and signed the last page. She then gave Gabe one of the most passionate kisses that she could muster up. Gabe lifted her into his arms and laid her on the couch. He ran his thumb across her lips and stared at her.

"So, does this mean that you're all mine now?" His tone was cold.

Elicia forced a smile. She noticed how tightly he gripped her waist. "I'm not saying that just yet. I just want to continue to get to know you."

Gabe tried to look happy and hugged Elicia as she stared at the documents on the table.

Elicia silently prayed that she had made the right decision. Gabe, on the other hand, braced himself for the worse.

***

Giselle drove around downtown trying to find a parking spot. She was meeting Samantha for lunch and she hadn't spoken to her since she'd exposed Justin at the firm. They hugged as they both entered Café Intermezzo. Once they took a seat by the window, Giselle finally got a good look at Samantha and noticed how amazing she looked. She had lost at least 15 pounds and was dressed like she was ready for New York Fashion Week.

"Girl, you are definitely looking good! What's been up?"

Samantha playfully brushed her shoulders off. "Well G, I am officially in love and finally getting married!" She flashed the emerald-cut diamond ring and Giselle showed her approval.

"So, tell me about your fiancé."

"Well he's a brother and is a prosecutor at a local firm. To top it all off, he's 47 but looks 35 and doesn't have any kids!"

Giselle's eyes got big. "47? Isn't that a tad too old for you?"

Samantha shook her head. "That's the thing. I think that the age difference was what I needed. I was tired of dealing with dead beat little *men boys.*" **He** is very mature and plus men our age are not ready for commitment. All they want to do is hit it and quit it. He has changed my life."

"Little *men boys*?" Giselle chuckled. "Well if you're happy, go for it. Life is too short to be anything less."

The two toasted their water goblets.

"So...." said Samantha, "What's really going on with you and Mr. Stokes?"

Giselle slowly took a sip of her water and sat it back down. "What are you talking about, Sam?"

Samantha rolled her eyes. "I can't believe you are insistent on lying about you and this man being in a relationship. You better claim him because a lot of women want what you have."

"Do you love him?" she asked.

Giselle didn't know. She knew that she cared for him deeply, but love had never really crossed her mind. They had only been dating for a couple of months.

"I would rather not discuss my personal relationship, if you don't mind. We should be celebrating you."

"Well, if you love someone, I feel like you need to make it known. Because when you don't, it leaves room for others to interfere."

"So, what are you trying to say, Sam?" Giselle asked. She was becoming irritated.

"I'm saying that you are NOT the only woman in the world after Hill Stokes. Women are constantly flaunting themselves around the office. They don't care about you and are willing to do whatever to get at that man. **Your** man."

INEVITABLE

Giselle leaned back in her seat. "What exactly is he doing?"

"I don't know, but you need to check his intentions."

Giselle felt her heart sank. While she wasn't sure what to make of her conversation with Samantha, she became uneasy.

"Anyways," said Samantha as she fumbled through her Gucci handbag, "I came to bring you this." She handed Giselle two wedding invitations. "These are for Elicia and Marley. Tell them they can both bring dates. The more, the merrier." Giselle stared at the invitation. The date was less than a month away.

"Wow," said Giselle. "What's the big rush?"

"The big rush is that we are in love honey! They say that you will know when you find the one."

"So, you really trust him like that? Seriously, Sam. What do you know about this man? You do realize what Chrisette Michelle meant by 'a couple of forevers', right?"

"G, when will you ever fully know everything there is to know about a man? Hell, I don't even know everything about my daddy or even my four brothers. You can be with and around a man for years and still not know certain things about him. I might be rushing into this, but I can't help what I feel. Whatever God wants me to know, he will bring to the light."

Giselle let what Samantha said sink in and was actually proud of her for taking control of her happiness. She wasn't the same person anymore. Maybe her fiancé was what she needed to blossom. Her confidence illuminated the entire restaurant.

"So, I don't get an invitation? What's up with that?"

"Well, you didn't receive an invitation because I would actually like for you to be my maid of honor." A tear popped out of her right eye as she smiled. Since my move to Atlanta you befriended me and were there for me when others weren't."

Giselle handed her some tissue from her purse and thanked her for the kind words and for selecting her to take on a very important role in her wedding. The two hugged and finished their meal. Giselle didn't want to focus on what Samantha had told her about Hill but couldn't think about anything else. She drove home in silence.

***

Marley tried to wait patiently for Trey to return from the store, but let her curiosity get the best of her. She decided to snoop around his condo and went to the bathroom, first, to check his medicine cabinet. She didn't find anything unusual and proceeded to check his bedroom drawers.

"What the fuck?!" she gasped. To her dismay, she found a drawer full of sex toys, lubricants, condoms, and all types of freaky paraphernalia. She also noticed the XXX DVD on the television stand. Marley felt her stomach turn sour. She didn't know what to think. He swore to her that he hadn't had sex in over two years. Marley should have known that something was up with him.

She returned to the couch and unsuccessfully tried to keep her knee from bouncing. A few minutes later he came through the door.

"Babe, we are all set." Trey beamed as he placed the bag on the kitchen counter. "I have the ginger ale and Hennessey. Let's do this!"

Marley cracked a smile but was sure that her attitude would eventually surface. He turned on some music and commenced to make their drinks. He noticed the change in her demeanor.

"What's going on, Marley? You good?"

He pulled off his shirt and exposed his muscles that Marley would have normally lost her mind over.

"You told me that I could come to you if I had any concerns, right?" she asked while ignoring his bare top half.

"Definitely, anything you want to know."

Marley jumped up and grabbed Trey's hand. She led him to the bedroom and exposed what she had discovered less than ten minutes ago.

INEVITABLE

"It's definitely not what you think." Trey was very nonchalant in his response and it pissed Marley off.

"Well what is it, Trey? Help me to understand why a celibate man is storing all of this freaky ass shit at his house. You've got to be fucking kidding me? First, I find out about your deceased wife and now this!" She plopped down on his waterbed then quickly jumped up when she realized the sexual acts he might have committed when he wasn't with her.

He sighed. "The videos that I shoot from time to time are pornographic."

"What?!" yelled Marley. "You are truly a piece of work, Trey. And you actually think that I am one of those desperate women who overlooks the obvious just to say that she has a man! Do you really think that I am supposed to believe that you shoot adult films in your spare time?"

"Look, I haven't given you any reason not to trust me before, so why would I start now?"

"You are lying. I know you are." She stared him down while silently wishing she hadn't stumbled upon his extracurricular activity.

Trey walked out of the room to avoid further confrontation. Marley followed him.

"I cannot believe you, Trey. You are a sex-addicted liar. You put on this façade as if sex doesn't mean shit to you and now I'm seeing why. You probably have different hoes in here on a regular."

"Maybe you should leave, Marley."

"Why? So, you can bring the next string of bitches up in here?" She grabbed her drink off the counter and threw it in his direction.

Trey calmly grabbed a dish towel to wipe his face and pointed towards the door.

"Get out of my house, Marley," he demanded.

"Or what? Are you going to call one of your lil' freak bitches over to get rid of me?"

INEVITABLE

Trey slammed his fists on the counter.

"You are so mentally fucked up and don't even know it. Just because you live a lie doesn't mean we all do!" He said it to hurt her.

Marley lost it and started beating him all over his face and chest. "Don't you ever talk to me like that again!" she screamed as she continued flinging her arms in an uncontrollable rage.

He grabbed her by the arms and shook her until she calmed down. "I didn't sign up for this psychotic bullshit, Marley! Now, get out of my house and please don't contact me ever again."

Marley snatched away from him and grabbed her purse. Trey gratefully watched her make her exit.

INEVITABLE

11

Giselle had previously scheduled to meet Hill later on that night but couldn't shake what Samantha had revealed to her. While she didn't have much to go on, she didn't want to even think about allowing Hill to play her. She decided to go home and dismiss their date. Around 6:20pm Hill began to blow Giselle's phone up. She reluctantly answered.

"Hey baby, your eagle is awaiting you. Are you alright? You're never late."

'Look, maybe we should cancel for tonight. I'm not feeling well." She hung up the phone.

Giselle walked around her opulent abode with a glass of wine in one hand and the remote to the sound system in the other. As Algebra Blessett bellowed throughout the room, Giselle began to feel lovely on the inside. She was in self-contemplation mode…trying to sort things out in her mind. She'd drifted off into a light sleep and was startled by Hill ringing the doorbell like a maniac. Giselle lazily opened the door and sashayed back to her chaise lounge. She didn't bother to acknowledge his presence although she did note that he was looking extra dapper and had on a new cologne. He immediately demanded to know what was going on.

"What did I do now, G? We had a date and you deliberately stood me up. What's going on? Turn your music down…you couldn't even hear me ringing the doorbell." Giselle sucked her teeth and lowered the volume.

"I fell asleep," she retorted without looking in his direction.

Hill moved towards her and she shooed him away. He backed up.

"So, you aren't even going to communicate to me what I've done wrong?"

Giselle rolled her eyes. She didn't feel like talking. He was blowing her high. "Tell me about the women you work with."

He took a seat across from her. "What do you want to know?"

"Bottom line, are any of them trying to fuck you?"

INEVITABLE

"Giselle, where is all this coming from?"

"Answer the damn question, please." She'd put on her prosecutor hat and wasn't backing down.

Hill was stunned by the accusation. "I haven't given you a reason to not trust me. Why are you tripping all of a sudden?"

Giselle had heard this defense, too many times to count, and wondered what made him different from any other guy? She put her guard all the way back up.

"I hear there's a lot of pathetic broads all up in your face five days a week and I wanna know what you do about it?" She studied his body language to see if he had anything to hide.

"I can't believe you are even asking me this bullshit. I'm a professional and I always behave as such. Don't even sit here and try to make me believe that men don't try to get at you." Giselle didn't respond and continued to stare a hole through him.

"We are both attractive people...what's wrong with that? We make calculated decisions that allow us to maintain our respected positions. If this means that I must be overly-courteous to my staff, even when I know they're just using what they possess to move rank, then that's what I'll do. I'm no fool, baby. We live in a world of opportunists and I am well-aware that women put in overtime for my attention in hopes of becoming Mrs. Stokes."

What Hill explained made Giselle's heart sink like a ship. She thought deeply for a few moments about how she had just been approached at the post office and gas station earlier that day - probably because she appeared to have her shit together and who wouldn't want to associate themselves with success? She realized that she was allowing her insecurities to get the best of her.

"You're right, I apologize. I'm just used to protecting my heart."

Hill rubbed Giselle's face with the back of his hand. "You are not the insecure type, so please don't act this way. It's not attractive."

Giselle was aroused by his cologne. "What are you wearing?" she asked.

INEVITABLE

"Jean Paul Gaultier's Le Male." he smiled.

*Oh, you are **definitely** all male*, thought Giselle.

"Why did you have to go ruin the evening with this mess, G? We could have been having a night on the town. I had a surprise for you." Hill was irritated.

Giselle let her robe casually drape off her shoulders. She smiled. "Well, why don't you give me my surprise now?" she playfully demanded as she held her hand out. He sat behind Giselle on the chaise and started to massage her shoulders. "Mmmm," she moaned. "This feels nice, but where's my surprise?" Hill reached into his pocket.

"This…is for you. I hope I am making the right decision."

Giselle opened the box and inside she found a key. "What is this for, Hill?"

"The key to my castle, of course! No, I'm kidding," he laughed. "If you ever need a place to unwind, feel free to crash at my cottage. I trust you."

Giselle was speechless. She was growing fond of Hill by the day but found his proposition premature.

"Are you sure you want to do this? Because I honestly can't see myself giving any man a key to anything of mine, unless we're married."

Hill looked hurt. "What do you mean? We've been doing this for a little over three months."

"And, what exactly is that supposed to mean to me, Hill? I still barely know you."

"You know me enough to let me come into your home and take you out on lavish dates, but not enough to give me a key to your apartment?"

"I didn't ask you to do this!" she snapped. "And I don't have to give you anything. You don't pay shit in here."

"Why are you so selfish, G!? Obviously, we are not on the same page. I'm sorry I came by." He took the box from her and headed out the door.

INEVITABLE

After Giselle had simmered down, she realized that Hill was only testing her trust in him. *Why do men always have to play this fucking game?* she thought to herself. Her high was officially blown.

***

"Look, I'm on my way over so we can talk." As Gerrod hung up the phone, his stomach began to tighten. What was he going to say to her? What was she going to say to him? He'd still been having his occasional flings with Tyra. Just last week, he'd brought her over to Giselle's house, when she was out of town on business and banged her in the laundry room. He didn't know if he was ready to face his wife yet.

When Gerrod stepped inside the foyer, he was enthralled with what he saw. Eva looked totally different from the last time they'd spoken. She'd cut her hair and gotten a spray tan. She seemed to be glowing from the inside out. He suddenly realized how much he missed his best friend.

He followed her to the kitchen and cleared his throat. Eva, trying to seem uninterested, took a seat at the breakfast table and resumed reading her magazine. Gerrod stood there waiting for her to make the first move.

She finally turned her attention to him. "Look, I apologize for what I did, but I never meant to hurt you. I didn't know how to tell you my fears about raising a Black child and I'm sorry you had to learn the way you did, but I'd never intentionally sabotage our marriage...never. Although I don't desire to have kids at this very moment, I do realize that what I did was selfish. I just want to do right by you...my husband."

Gerrod tried to remain calm but his emotions overcame him. Eva ran to him and wiped the streaming tears from his eyes. They embraced for a long time. Gerrod inhaled the scent of her hair and perfume. He carried his wife upstairs and made passionate love to her for the rest of the evening.

***

"So please tell me how we ended up here?" Elicia listened to Giselle and Marley inform her on the latest happenings as they met briefly for brunch at Ray's on the River.

INEVITABLE

Elicia smiled. It felt good being drama-free although deep down she was still hurting. "Well, I guess I can give you my advice free of charge." She faked a smile.

Marley rolled her eyes. "Let's hear it dammit!"

"First you, Giselle. I think you are so used to what men have done to you in the past, including your dad, that you assume all men are the same and because of this you will never progress. It's good that you have your independence and survived unfortunate relationships, but you have to remember that all men are NOT the same. Love is about taking chances but most of all, you have to be willing to trust and forgive when a mistake is made."

Giselle dipped her tomato in ranch salad dressing.

"And you, Marley…where do you get off snooping around that man's house? Have you no shame? I'm sure just as easy as it was for you to invade his space you could have opened your mouth to ask for a tour. I'm just saying!"

Marley frowned and pushed Elicia in the shoulder.

The trio sat in silence to get through their meal. "Well, I just don't understand why I have to give up a damn key just because *he* wants me to have his key," pouted Giselle. "I don't **need** it, nor do I **want** it. Me having a key to his place is not going to stop him from seeing other people if it's what he wants to do. That key silently speaks commitment and I don't think I'm ready for that."

"Why does everything have to be so deep for you?" Elicia couldn't understand her friend's logic.

"Because I'm deep."

"Whatever, Giselle. You are crazy. I don't see what the big deal is. Once again you are looking for something to complain about." Marley took a long sip of her Bellini.

Elicia listened to her friends go back and forth as she took several bites of her French toast.

"I just feel like I don't know him well enough." sighed Giselle.

INEVITABLE

"Well tell him 'no' again and explain why." said Marley. "Again, I don't understand why you are making such a big deal out of it. Put the key in the lock. If not, move on."

Giselle frowned.

"You don't have to be so blunt, Marley."

"She's the same way you are when you're in a crazy predicament. You get the business straightforward…no chaser." Elicia sucked on the lemon from her water.

***

The next day Marley texted Trey to apologize for snooping around his home. He wanted to discuss the issue further. Marley didn't care to. He finally convinced her to meet him for lunch at Paschal's.

"It's just me, taking pictures and filming people having sex," he whispered.

"I'm sorry, but that's disgusting," she whispered back.

"Well, I'm sorry, but it is a lucrative side hustle that I couldn't refuse. Look, I only do it once a month and it's an all-day thing. I put in my 8 hours and walk away with 4 g's…just for filming people while they get their freak on. You should go with me one day. You might enjoy it." He winked at her.

Marley shook her head. "Like I said…disgusting." She was starting to wonder if her Prince Charming had a problem. Most men she'd dated loved sex, but Trey seemed to be obsessed with it. She decided not to press the issue.

Trey looked at his watch. "We have an important appointment that we can't miss," he blurted. Twenty minutes later they pulled up in front of an office building. Before she could object, Trey told Marley to relax.

The two went inside and took a seat in the lobby. Marley didn't understand what was going on but remained quiet. A stout, Caucasian man in a tan suit approached them and shook Trey's hand.

"Nice to meet you, Mr. Roberts. You both can follow me to my office."

INEVITABLE

They sat down in the leather maroon chairs. "Good afternoon. I'm glad that you have decided to locate your daughter after all this time."

Marley glared at Trey. "What is this? What's going on?"

The unfamiliar man picked up a green file folder. "Well according to this record, Mr. Roberts is trying to locate his daughter after almost ten years. Marley looked confused.

"Well, actually, Mr. Thompson, it's for my friend here."

"What's going on, Trey? What is he talking about?" Marley's palms started to sweat.

"Baby, I know I might have overstepped my boundaries, but I contacted Mr. Thompson so that we could begin to take the necessary steps to find Adah. His firm specializes in adoption law." he nervously explained.

"How dare you, Trey?" Marley abruptly stood up almost knocking over her chair.

"She's *my* daughter and you have more than overstepped your boundaries."

"I am only trying to help," Trey pleaded.

"I didn't ask for this, Trey. We didn't discuss this. I can't believe you took matters into your own hands. Who said I was even ready for this?" Marley grabbed her purse and stormed out of the office.

Trey apologized to the attorney and explained how he was only seeking to help Marley locate her biological daughter. He signed some paperwork and stopped by the restroom before leaving the office. By the time he'd made it outside, Marley was nowhere to be found.

12

"I thought I'd lost you," said Gerrod as he stared at Eva in the dresser mirror. "I was a wreck."

"So, are you ready to talk about the real issue?" asked Eva as she tousled with her hair.

"Real issue? I thought we already talked about it. You apologized and I accepted."

Eva turned around and glared at him. "Are you serious, Gerrod? Let's not forget the role you played in all of this as well. You cheated on me…your wife."

Gerrod smacked his lips. "I cheated because you lied to me."

"So, every time I do something that you don't like you're going to go out and cheat on me? What kind of marriage is that?"

"Let's just drop the shit, E…we made up…let's leave it at that." Eva was not ready to let it go.

"No, we will not drop the fact that you fucked around on your wife…and probably multiple times. Am I right?" Gerrod left the bedroom and went into the bathroom to relieve himself.

"So, what if I did?!" he yelled to her as he shook himself off. "We both hurt each other. Let's just get over it!" He was beginning to infuriate Eva and she went downstairs to cool off.

***

Trey called Marley's phone four times before she decided to answer.

"What is it, Trey?" she asked. The fact that she was annoyed was obvious to him.

"Please let me know where you are. We need to talk."

INEVITABLE

"I am just fine...I took an Uber home. And, no, we don't need to talk. Look, I'll catch up with you some other time. I need to clear my head." She was ready to hang up.

"We really need to talk about what happened, Marley."

"If it's not too much, I would appreciate it if you would stay out of my private affairs."

"You know I was only trying to help."

"Help?! You deliberately went out of your way to make me feel like a bad person. You wanted to remind me that I have failed as a parent."

Trey didn't understand her logic and became exasperated. "The Trey-hurt-Marley bullshit is really starting to get on my nerves. I'm trying to show you that I care and everything I do comes across as some conspiracy to hurt you."

Silence flooded the line. "I want to fill a void that I know you have in your heart but yet I'm wrong?"

"You just don't get it, Trey."

"*I, Trey Roberts,* don't get how the loss of a loved one could damn near destroy you?! Of course, I don't." He hung up on Marley.

Although Trey had overstepped his boundaries, Marley also knew that he had good intentions. She could not stop thinking about Adah. She often wondered how she looked and what her personality was like. She pulled out her computer. Upon logging into Facebook, she entered the name *Michelle Stevens*. Her palms began to sweat. Michelle was Adah's adoptive parent. She'd thought about finding her daughter on social media for a long time but had pushed it to the back of her mind. She wasn't sure if she was ready to meet the little girl who she'd once carried inside of her. After searching for over an hour, Marley came across a profile page for *Michelle Stevens-Jackson*. She was a plain Jane but still beautiful. "Married last year to Lance Jackson. Nice figure. Hmmm...similar complexion as Adah's. She could pass for her mother any day," mumbled Marley as she trolled their pictures. After a few minutes, Marley came across a photo album entitled *My Gift*. She took a deep breath and tried to control her trembling hands.

INEVITABLE

***

"So, can I say what really needs to be said before we go any further?" Gabe gave Elicia an uneasy stare. They celebrated the finalization of her and Nasir's separation by taking a weekend getaway to Hilton Head Marriott Resort & Spa in Charleston, South Carolina. Elicia wanted to unwind and focus only on Gabe while getting in a little time for herself. She'd packed a couple of books to indulge between their scheduled outings. Both needed pampering and opted for the Spa Soleil as soon as they checked in. As the therapist strategically massaged aloe scrub onto Elicia's lower back, she tried to prepare herself for Gabe's daily interrogation. The room smelled of jasmine and sweet honey. The cream walls were a complement to every piece of furniture in the room. The massage table was heated which put Elicia in total bliss. She closed her eyes tighter praying that Gabe would drop the issue.

"What if he comes back?" he asked.

Elicia sighed. "He's not coming back. He's moved on…I've moved on." She sucked her teeth and rolled her eyes. "Gabe, sweetheart, please…we are supposed to be enjoying ourselves." He persisted anyway while their masseuse pretended to ignore the conversation.

"Are you telling me that you can just get over someone you've laughed with, cried with and had sex with just like that? Have you ever really thought about what you would do if he suddenly popped up?" Elicia grabbed Gabe's hand and looked him in his eyes.

"Would you please try to relax for once, Gabe? You are going to ruin our weekend with this nonsense. You have absolutely nothing to worry about." Elicia turned on her side, away from him, and tried to enjoy the rest of her indulgence.

***

Marley clicked on the photo album and was shocked to see a little girl who resembled her in many ways. She knew that it was her daughter. She could feel it. Tears fell from her eyes as she continued to scroll through the albums Michelle had created over the years. Adah was gorgeous and even shared the same mole over her right brow. Marley stumbled upon a picture of Michelle holding an infant and an adoption certificate. Her stomach began to churn as she slammed the laptop shut.

***

Giselle didn't want to fight with Hill any longer over something so insignificant and invited him over to talk.

"It's only a key. I could see if I was asking you to move in with me. I just thought you might like to have it. You're so busy and sometimes I feel that everyone needs to be more selfish and steal moments to unplug from this digital world we're living in and reconnect with their inner spirit."

Giselle hadn't thought about it like this. "Well, are you giving me a key to both of your places?" she asked as she batted her eyelids. This caught Hill off guard. "Why do you need a key to both places?"

"If I am going to give you my only key, you are going to give me *all* of your keys. Hill, I have never seen the inside of your home. We quickly drop in and drop out and I always get left in the driveway when you go in to *grab* something. Wouldn't you find that a little suspicious if you were in my shoes?"

He sighed with growing impatience. "Baby, I didn't know you felt that way."

Giselle was confused. "Are you trying to hide something, Mr. Stokes?" she asked.

"Of course not. I've just always had adventures planned for us outside of the home so I never really thought much about it."

"It's because you *are* hiding something. Too good to be true." She rolled her eyes.

"What are you talking about now, G?"

INEVITABLE

"Take me to your other place!"

"That's forty-five minutes away and it's already after 10pm. You know I have an early appointment tomorrow. Why are you doing this?"

"Because we're not supposed to have any secrets…that's why." She grabbed her bag and headed to his car. Silence flooded the air until they arrived. The house had a three-car garage and was beautifully furnished with high-end pieces. The neutral wall paint was offset with bold, abstract artwork. Giselle admired the portraits of Hill and his family. She immediately decided that he favored his mother and noted that his father was strikingly handsome. Hill also had pictures of his younger sister.

"Your family is gorgeous, Hill. You and your sister look so much alike. When will I have the pleasure?" He didn't say anything. Instead he went to the kitchen and poured himself a drink.

"I don't communicate with my family unless I have to and that's pretty much never," he said between sips. I love them to death, but my success has caused a wedge between us. While I am obligated to assist whenever they are in need, I have to take care of myself first. If you want something, then I am a firm believer that one should at least try and go after it themselves. You miss 100% of the shots you don't take. My family sat on their asses for years while I carried most of the weight. Once I realized what was going on, I cut them off." Giselle didn't realize she had hit such a sore spot.

"Look, I love my family, but they are not in my life like that."

"Mine either, so it's cool," said Giselle as she rubbed his hand. "Why do you have such a large home and no one to share it with?"

He peeled a banana while partially ignoring her question. "My sister crashes here from time to time…which is why I am hesitant to give you the key." Giselle understood. She would hate to intrude on someone else's space. They both turned to the door to find a woman entering the room. Giselle recognized her from the picture. As she extended her hand, she caught a glimpse of Hill's obvious apprehension of their unexpected guest.

INEVITABLE

"Giselle, this is my sister, Hayden."

"Hello, nice to meet you. Your brother is a wonderful man." Giselle forced a smile.

Hayden giggled. "Oh, I'm sure he is. Excuse me." Giselle watched her disappear to the back room. She had had her share of sisters to deal with and learned that ignoring ignorance, in some situations, was the best thing one could do.

"Let's get out of here," said Hill as he rushed to toss the banana peel in the kitchen trash.

When they arrived at Giselle's home she handed him her spare key before they entered. Hill beamed. "That's my baby." He squeezed Giselle tightly and let himself in.

INEVITABLE

13

Giselle stood in the middle of the dressing room wiping away Samantha's tears. "Maybe you're right. What if he's too old? What if it doesn't work?" Samantha paced the Atrium in her tailored off-white Priscilla bridal grown.

"You have got to calm down," said Giselle. "Your hysteria is making you sweat." She picked up her train and sat her down. "You are the prettiest, classiest, and sexiest bride I have ever seen." Samantha forced a weak smile. "Now, act like it. If this man makes you happy, and wants to give you the world, then take a chance on him. I'm learning, myself, that love is about taking chances. Absolutely nothing is certain. But what you can be certain about is your affection for him."

As Giselle made her way up the aisle, she was taken aback by the beautiful view. Asiatic lilies, green button spray chrysanthemums, and white roses provided a breathtaking sight. She tried not to blush when she saw Hill wink at her. Marley, Trey, Elicia, and Gabe were sitting nearby. She imagined what it would be like on her own "big day" and most importantly, who would be standing in Trevor's spot. Giselle stared at Samantha's soon-to-be husband. She had to admit that he was handsome. Dressed in an off-white tuxedo accented with a lavender vest, Trevor was definitely an attractive man. She remembered his best man, Jason, from rehearsal. He looked equally edible. The weather was perfect as Samantha made her grand entrance to Tony Terry's *"When I'm With You"* instrumental. As they went through the traditional ceremony, Giselle couldn't help but notice the chemistry between Gabe and Elicia. She, for once, looked truly happy and Marley and Trey appeared to have made up given she was leaning on his shoulder crying during most of the ceremony. *Love is definitely in the air*, Giselle thought to herself as she bowed her head for a brief prayer delivered by the officiant. After the lovely couple declared I do, the wedding party moved to the pavilion for the reception. The newly *Mr. and Mrs. Trevor Drake* arrived and everyone stood and applauded. Samantha had finally found her happiness.

The buffet was impeccable and satisfied everyone's appetite. There were so many selections to choose from that the guests didn't know where to begin. Lemon and lime chargrilled chicken salad and Irish smoked salmon were the main courses featured on the menu. The side items were highly-complementary. The redolence of spiced parsnip and apple soup, red cabbage with crispy bacon, french beans with dates and potato soufflé lingered in the air. For dessert, the guests chose between pear and ginger cake served with vanilla ice cream and lime sorbet. At the end of the reception, Samantha and Trevor were whisked away in a pearl-colored 1939 Packard limousine to the airport for their honeymoon in Montego Bay. The night was still young and Hill invited everyone back to his condo for a night cap.

While Elicia was looking forward to getting to know Trey and Hill better, she didn't necessarily want to do it that night. Ever since she and Gabe returned from their weekend getaway, he had been getting on her nerves bringing up Nasir's return every other day. Elicia really hadn't given much thought to him coming back but certainly didn't want to spend her every waking moment talking about it. Their relationship was changing, and she just wanted the old Gabe back.

Each of the couples made it to Hill's place just after midnight and delighted themselves in vintage wine and jazz. "So, how did you two meet?" asked Hill as he poured Gabe a glass of Montaudon Brut.

Gabe started to speak. "We-." "Well, actually, he moved in across the street from me," blurted Elicia. She smiled and wrapped her arm around his. "He's my personal firefighter." He sat up a little straighter on the barstool and sipped his drink.

Gabe awkwardly turned to face the other ladies sitting on the couch in the living area. "So, Giselle…do you think Nasir will ever come back?" Elicia almost choked on her cheese bite. Giselle felt uneasy but decided to answer the question anyway. "At this point I don't feel like that should be the focus. I don't know anything about what's going on with Nasir. But what I do know is that Elicia seems happy. All I ask is that you continue to provide that service for her." Elicia let out a sigh of relief.

Trey immediately picked up on how uncomfortable the atmosphere had become and changed the subject. "So…did Marley mention the Cayman Islands to you all yet?"

"I've always wanted to travel there," said Hill. "I heard the women are spectacular!" Giselle playfully nudged him in his side. Trey stood up and turned the music down. "I've asked Marley to invite you all on a 7-day excursion. I think that it would be an awesome experience."

"How soon are you talking about doing this?" Hill asked.

"In about six weeks. That should give everyone plenty of time to prepare. All you need is your birthday suit and your black card!" They all chuckled at Trey's humor. Giselle needed a vacation. She hadn't taken off longer than a weekend since her promotion to partner, so she was down.

"Sounds like a plan to me," said Gabe. "Well it's settled…we are going to the Caymans!"

***

Marley didn't have much to say as Trey drove her home that night. He went to open her door and she jumped out and started to walk away. He grabbed her waist from behind.

"What did I do now, Marley?"

"Nothing, I just wish you would have waited and got a confirmation from me about the trip before you presented it to my friends." She pulled away from his firm grasp.

"Well, you never said anything about not **wanting** to go so I just assumed-" She cut him off.

"What did I tell you about assuming things?"

"I can never win with you, Marley. Why are you so afraid to venture outside of your comfort zone?"

"I don't mind doing new things. I just don't want you taking control of my life. First Adah and now this…I feel like you're doing way too much."

INEVITABLE

Trey looked at her in disbelief. "Doing too much?"

"I am open to new things, Trey. I just for like things, that involve me, to be run by me before decisions are made without my consent. That's what any normal person would want - including you, right?"

An icy breeze shot across the night and Marley realized that they were bickering on her doorstep. "Look, I'm tired and I'm going in. I will call you tomorrow." She kissed him on the cheek and let herself in.

On the other side of the city Elicia and Gabe were sharing a similar situation as they sat in his car in front of her place. "You HAVE to stop this, Gabe. I feel like you are ruining our relationship by worrying about something that at this point and time really doesn't matter." She looked out the window trying to hold back tears.

"It only doesn't matter because he hasn't returned…yet. You have to understand where I am coming from. This whole situation makes me uneasy. You signed the paper, not him."

Elicia sighed. "And you make me uneasy, Gabe. Please stop with the insecurity." She got out of the car and headed inside.

***

Giselle didn't want to spend the night at Hill's but didn't feel like making the drive back to her house. As they cleaned up the mess the guests left behind, Hill chuckled to himself.

Giselle read his mind. "I can't believe Gabe put all that out there like that tonight."

"You? At least you weren't in the hot seat." Hill shook his head.

"Now that I think about it, I guess I can see where my man was coming from. I don't know what I would do if your ex-husband, boyfriend, or whoever just popped back into the picture…especially one that you were once in love with." Giselle rinsed the wine glasses before carefully placing them in the dishwasher. "I also don't think anyone is going to be able to take you away from me, either." He kissed Giselle and grabbed her backside.

Giselle could taste the wine on his tongue. "And how can you be so sure, Mr. Stokes?"

"Because you're mine and I'm not going to let them." Giselle admired his confidence.

***

Trey did what he thought was best and continued to give Marley her space. He was fed up with her shooting down everything he attempted to do for her. Marley, on the other hand, was quite confused and gave him a call after not hearing from him in over a week. He didn't answer.

Trey, it's me Marley. Give me a call when you get a chance. Maybe we can do breakfast around 10. After she hung up the phone, she stared at it. He *always* answered her calls. Three hours later she called again. Still no answer. He didn't have to work and she wondered what he could possibly be doing, on a Saturday afternoon, that had him so occupied. Marley tried everything she could to keep her mind off of him: grading papers, catching up on her favorite HGTV shows, doing laundry, getting her bi-weekly pedicure and manicure…but nothing worked. By 7:00pm she couldn't reach Giselle nor Elicia and this made the situation worse. She called again. *Trey, I don't know what type of games you are playing, but if you are seeing someone else you need to let me know so I can move on with my life.* She slammed down the phone and realized what she had just said. Her phone rang and she immediately went in.

"Trey, where in the fuck do you get off not calling or answering my phone calls! Who in the hell do you think you are? I haven't done shit to you and if you got another bitch waiting then be with her but keep your shit real with me."

Silence flooded the line. "Is that how you always talk to him?" asked Giselle. Marley was embarrassed.

"Giselle! I thought you were Trey." She grinded her teeth with impatience.

"Why are you so angry with him?"

"Because he hasn't called."

"Why hasn't he called?"

"Because we had a disagreement."

"A disagreement about what?"

"About him trying to control my life."

"And how, exactly, is he trying to do that?"

"Look, I don't care to talk right now. I'll call you later." She hung up the phone. She quickly showered and rushed over to Trey's house. She got there in record speed and was pissed to find his car in the driveway. She made sure to look extra sexy so she could make an Oscar-worthy scene. She wore a green silk romper accented with gold jewelry and her gold Sam Edelman stilettos. She didn't care if she was overdressed. She was fierce and wanted Trey to see what he would ultimately be missing out on. She grabbed her gold clutch off the passenger seat and strutted to the door. She knocked and didn't get an answer. She rang the doorbell multiple times and still didn't get an answer. Her heart sank but she wouldn't dare show it. She turned around and slowly made her way back to her car.

"Marley, what are you doing here?" Trey barely shouted to her.

She turned around and found him 12 feet away in nothing but his boxers. Her nipples hardened, and she almost forgot why she'd come over. He yawned.

"Why the fuck haven't you answered your phone, Trey? I know you saw me calling!" She was steaming as she stomped up to him.

Trey rubbed his eyes. "I've been sleep, Marley." He turned around and walked back through the door. She stormed in right behind him.

INEVITABLE

"Motherfucker you haven't been sleep for seven whole fucking days! So why haven't you called?"

"You act as if I'm a problem. I thought it would be best to give you some space. Plus, I had a long week dealing with meetings and conference calls and needed to catch up on some rest."

"So, you're dumping me and weren't going to tell me?"

"I'm confused," he said. "When did we become official?" That statement hit Marley like a ton of bricks and she turned around to leave.

"Where are you going?"

"Home. I don't have to deal with this shit!"

"What are you talking about? You come over here waking me up from some damn good sleep, cursing me out and now you're leaving with an attitude? You are really crazier than I thought."

"Crazy? I'll show you crazy." Marley picked up a mug on his coffee table and threw it across the living room. It smashed the picture of Trey and his family that sat on the mantle. Trey hurried over to the picture and tried to salvage the pieces. "Get out of my house, woman!" His eyes were burning red and she ran out crying hysterically. Trey slammed the door and grabbed a broom. He swept up the glass that covered the floor.

Marley was in such a frenzy that she could hardly drive. She fled to Elicia's house and was relieved to find her there. As she explained to her what had just happened Elicia looked at her in disbelief. When Marley finished, Elicia was silent.

"Well, aren't you going to say anything?"

"What are you so afraid of, Marley? You act as if this man has given you a reason to behave this way…unless there is something you aren't telling me. He sounds like a good man. *You* sound like an idiot. To be honest with you, I think *you* need therapy."

"Do you still have the weed?"

INEVITABLE

"What?" responded Elicia as she rolled her eyes. Marley totally ignored the "therapy" suggestion.

"The *mar-i-jua-na*. Do you still have it? I need to take the edge off."

"You are a professional woman. An educator. Don't ruin yourself."

"Look, I'm grown as hell and if I want to smoke I should be able to do so!"

"I flushed it down the toilet," Elicia lied as she looked away.

Marley knew when her friend was being dishonest. "I know you have it, now go and get me a joint!"

"But you don't smoke!"

"Well, I do today." Elicia reluctantly obeyed her friend's orders and went to retrieve Nasir's old sack.

Marley quickly lit the joint and coughed ceaselessly. "I don't get it," she said as she tried to catch her breath.

"That's because you don't know what you're doing." She grabbed the joint and showed her how to inhale. Elicia had smoked with Nasir, on a few occasions, early in their marriage. Marley followed directions and began to make funny faces. They moved their session to the couch. Within minutes they both were spaced out and Elicia found herself in just her underwear. "I am floating!" said Elicia as she blared Erykah Badu. Marley laughed so hard that she tumbled to the floor. "This is fucking awesome!" she said. She was instantly reminded of their college days.

"You know what your problem is?" asked Elicia.

Marley hit the joint again. "What?"

"You are too fucking uptight. You're boring. You, my friend, are used to living a boring life. Trey is just trying to bring some excitement and you," she said while blowing smoke out her nose, "are going to miss out on a good thing."

"Really?" asked Marley as she tried to sit up. "I'm not boring. I'm sensible."

Marley lit some strawberry incense, that was sitting on the nearby end table, and this stimulated her high even more. "I haven't felt this at ease in a while."

"You know what, Elicia?"

"Yea?"

"I love you, man!" They both laughed until they cried.

Marley suddenly realized it was one in the morning and that she had a tutoring session at 8. She jumped up. "I've got to go!" she shouted.

"What the hell is wrong with you? You can't drive in your condition."

"I have a student early in the morning. Can you take me home then?"

Elicia rolled her eyes. "Fool, I'm high, too!" All they could do was laugh.

Marley took a shower to wake herself up. She knew she had no business driving home but did so anyway. What was normally a 40-minute drive took over an hour. She was shocked to find Trey in her driveway. He immediately jumped out the car.

"What in the hell happened to you? Are you alright? You look…different." He grabbed her hand and began to check for bruises. Marley, still slightly under the influence, smiled. "I'm fine Trey. I'm fine." He followed her inside of the house. Marley noticed how good Trey looked. She immediately felt her sexual appetite arise. The weed intensified her erotica. She moved in to kiss him and he stopped her. He sniffed her hair.

"Have you been smoking?" She giggled. "Yes," she said as her eyes barely stayed open.

"What in the hell is going on, Marley? Are you kidding me?"

INEVITABLE

She didn't remember much after that. Marley was awakened by her cell phone ringing off the hook. Her student was calling to cancel, due to some sort of emergency, and she couldn't have been more ecstatic. She rolled over and found Trey lightly snoring while sleeping fully-clothed on his back.

***

"How long am I going to have to put up with your shitty attitude? I should have stayed gone if that's the case."

"How dare you!" said Eva as she put her finger in Gerrod's face. "YOU better be lucky that I let your cheating ass come back! Nobody else would put up with this stupid shit but me!"

"Well, what do you want me to do? I apologized. I can't do much more than that."

Eva paced the floor. "I didn't say you had to do more but be sensitive to the fact that you CHEATED on your wife. I simply withheld information from you. What's worse?"

"Two wrongs don't make it right, Eva."

"Why did you have to run to her? You had to get a restraining order against her, remember? Why don't you ever think?"

He smacked his lips. "That was years ago."

"It doesn't matter. The mere fact that you had to get one should speak volumes about why *she* should be left where she belongs. In the past!"

"I'm done talking about this, Eva, and I mean it." He grabbed her hand. "Let's just work on making us better…please?" Eva knew that it wasn't going to be that easy. She snatched away her hand and told him she was heading to the gym. Gerrod poured himself a bowl of cereal. "Whatever," he said aloud as he watched her go.

INEVITABLE

After binge-watching The House of Cards on Netflix, Gerrod noticed that it was getting late. Eva had been gone for four hours and left her phone on the kitchen table. He figured she was still mad at him and prolonged coming home. By midnight he became worried. He called her mom and sister and they hadn't seen her. He jumped in his car and headed towards the gym. He was relieved to find that Eva's car was one of the few in the parking deck. The gym doors were locked and the lights were off.

INEVITABLE

14

Hill leaned against the corner of the bathroom doorway with a towel wrapped around his lower half. Even with a face full of shaving cream he looked quite striking. Giselle glanced at her bracelet watch. "We are going to be late, Hill! Get in the shower already!" He winked and closed the door behind him.

It was a breezy but sunny day in Atlanta and the two decided to take a tour of the Martin Luther King Center. Hill's phone vibrated on the dresser as Giselle applied finishing touches to her makeup. She glanced at the phone and thought about the conversation she'd had with Neena earlier in the week. She stopped applying the powder and replayed it in her mind. Neena had stopped by Giselle's office in the middle of her working a case.

"How's everything going?" she said as she let herself in. "If you need any help with the Lorner vs. Jackson case, please know that I am at your service."

"Thanks," Giselle said as she offered her a seat noting how Neena was always willing to do whatever was needed to get the job done.

"I haven't seen you around the office in a while," she said as she tugged at her hair.

"Yeah, I've been pretty busy with this arduous case and swamped with meetings. So, what brings you by?"

"Well, I kinda wanted to talk with you…off the record."

"Off the record?" repeated Giselle.

"Well, I have this situation and I just don't know how I should handle it."

"I'm listening."

"I've been talking to this guy, for the past few months, and things have been getting really heavy between us. We're not exactly what I would

INEVITABLE

call 'official' but we've been spending a lot of time together and I am starting to develop strong feelings for him. But, I've run into a speed bump and I'm not quite sure how to handle it."

"Spill it, Neena."

"Okay, here goes. I went through his phone and found out that he is still sending text messages to females he used to deal with."

"Why would you go through his phone? Do you not trust him?"

Neena rolled her eyes. "Ms. Mosely, I go through all phones, all the time. I'm not trying to get played!"

"Well, what did the messages say?"

"There was one in particular - it read: Last night was unforgettable. I am going to be dreaming about you all week."

"So, who was the message from?"

"Some bit-…excuse me, woman named Rylee. What kind of name is that anyway?"

Giselle glanced at her desk clock. "So, did you confront him?"

"No, and that's where you come in. What would you do?"

Giselle had never found herself in this type of predicament before. She never checked Hill's phone because she was somewhat afraid of what she might find.

"Well, if you both haven't agreed to be exclusive then technically you are not his woman…so you really don't have the right to say anything."

"I do if we're sexing! So, are you telling me that you don't go through your man's phone, ever?"

"No…because I trust him," she lied. Giselle was ready to get back to her work.

INEVITABLE

"Well, I thought this guy was trustworthy until now. I honestly don't know what came over me. The opportunity presented itself, and so I decided to investigate."

"That's what you get for playing detective, Neena." Giselle laughed.

"So, I shouldn't say anything? Because this is NOT a laughing matter."

"I think that you should just be cool. Make sure that you are using condoms and stop jumping to conclusions."

Neena sucked her teeth. "I guess nothing matters except marriage anyway."

"And what is that supposed to mean?" asked Giselle.

"It means that men feel that they can do whatever they want until they marry you and even then, most stray." She stood up and smoothed out her skirt. "Thanks, Ms. Mosely."

As Giselle snapped out of her thoughts, Hill's phone vibrated again. She picked it up and quickly placed the phone back on the dresser. After all, she did trust him, but for some reason her heart started to race. She removed herself from the bedroom before temptation set in again. She cut up slices of apples in the kitchen and poured herself a glass of sparkling water. Before she knew it, she had returned to the bedroom. She peeked in on Hill and saw that he was still handling his business. After quietly closing the door, Giselle immediately ransacked the phone. His incoming and outgoing call list contained numerous men and women, but Giselle assumed they were all either clients or business associates. The text messages, however, were another thing. She began to whisper them aloud. The most recent one was from his sister, Hayden. *Why did you try to shun me from your GIRLFRIEND? You are dead wrong but it's all good. What is done in the dark will be brought to the light!*

What is she talking about? thought Giselle as she continued to scroll. *How do you want it today? Because the last time you complained. I just want you to be pleased.* Giselle's heart beat faster yet she continued to scroll through the messages and stumbled across another one dated

INEVITABLE

February 23, 2016 at 8:52pm. *Please be on time. It's already getting late.* She was so entangled in the messages that she didn't realize Hill was standing behind her. She almost dropped the phone when she heard him clear his throat. He frowned as she stared at him. "So, is that what you do? You go through my phone when I'm not around? Is that really necessary?"

"Why actually I think it's *quite* necessary considering you have questionable texts from - she looked at the phone - Tamara! Who the fuck is she?"

"Are you serious, G? You're acting out of character again." Giselle threw the phone at him.

"Yes, I'm serious."

Hill became infuriated. "Why are you so insistent on me fucking you over? I am a good man! Probably the best man you'll ever be lucky enough to encounter, and yet you continue to mistreat me. You should know me by now. I would die before I hurt you."

Giselle rolled her eyes. "Hill miss me with the Joe lyrics! I knew you were too good to be true." She tried to exit the door but he blocked her path. "Move Hill…I'm not playing with you."

"And I am not playing with you, either. Call her," he said.

"I'm not calling that bitch because if I do I might curse her out."

"Go ahead. Be my guest. Place it on speaker so I can hear." Giselle picked up the phone and reluctantly dialed the number. While she didn't know what she was going to say she still wanted to confront Hill's possible lover. On the first ring a woman picked up. "Mr. Stokes, the documents you requested for the Timmons case are ready. I tried the new proofing system, that you suggested, and it works phenomenally. Did you want me to fax the documents over to your home office or send them through mail? There's 47 pages total."

INEVITABLE

Giselle handed Hill the phone. "Actually, you can hold them until Monday. I have a few more critical changes to make. I'll talk to you soon." He hung up.

Giselle plopped down on the bed. "Hill, I apologize. I was wrong for going through your phone. I don't know why I did it. I do trust you. It's just that-"

"Let me guess, I don't know what you've been through." Hill's tone was cool. Giselle stared at the floor.

"Look, this will never work unless you trust me. I haven't given you a reason not to trust me so why are we going through this?"

She shrugged her shoulders. He grabbed her chin and kissed her. "You have to stop listening to people on the outside and replace your past hurts with new experiences with me. You are a beautiful woman, but honestly babe, your outer appearance doesn't match your inner core. Shake the façade if you are not going to embody it from head to toe. Your insecurities will eventually harm what we've worked so hard to build."

Giselle had heard this several times before, in previous relationships, but found it difficult to overcome. She was so used to putting up a wall that bailing at the first sign of unloyalty was easy. How could a woman like Giselle have it going on but not have it going on at the same time?

"Well, how do I do that, Hill? I try but it is a constant struggle. I can do it sometimes but other times I let my self-doubt get the best of me."

"Have you ever considered counseling?"

"Counseling? I'm not crazy, Hill."

"Counseling isn't just for mentally unstable people, G. It might help you tremendously. I definitely feel it's something you should consider." Giselle sucked her teeth. Hill buttoned his shirt. "Trust me…I've tried it and it actually works."

INEVITABLE

***

Trey awakened to Marley making breakfast. He stared at her without uttering a word. "Look, I don't have anything to say, Trey. I was wrong for what I did. I apologize."

Trey grabbed a piece of toast. "Is that supposed to make me feel better? I'm convinced that you don't want me around, Marley. My only goal was to make you happy."

"Who said anything about not wanting you around?"

"Your actions."

Marley was silent.

"I would hate to see how you would act if we **were** to become exclusive…and while that is something that I eventually want, I don't need nor want it if I'm not trusted." He grabbed his keys and left.

***

"So, you mean to tell me you gon' give me $500 to set this building on fire?" The man stumbled around as he looked Gabe in the eye.

"Yeah, just make sure you follow through with the plan. This has to be fool-proof."

"So, I go in, throw this on buddy in the green shirt and drop the match - that's it?"

"That's exactly what I want you to do."

"But what if I get caught?"

"Look!" he bellowed. "You're not going to get caught. I'm going to make sure of it."

He handed the homeless man the money and a plastic bottle filled with gasoline. "Don't fuck this up or I'm coming for you next." Gabe glared at the disheveled drunk and then rushed back to the station. He gave Elicia a call.

"Don't you wanna come get in my big red truck?" Elicia giggled as Gabe begged her to come to the station. "You know I've been on call for two days straight and I miss my sunshine."

As of late, the two had been on good terms. Gabe had finally dropped the Nasir issue and tried to focus his energy on making memories with Elicia. She had spent the night with Gabe at the station before but didn't get much sleep. The twin beds were too small for them to cuddle, let alone anything more, and she felt like she was back in college again. She did, however, like seeing him in action. It was something about a man, risking his own life for others' safety, that turned her on. Elicia grabbed her overnight bag and pressed the gas to get to her man.

***

"You got here pretty quick." Elicia kissed him slowly then wiped her clear gloss from his lips. She buried her head in Gabe's neck and embraced his aura. Immediately turned on she straddled him on the bed. He palmed her breasts and slid her shirt off. This was new for the both of them but Elicia decided to flow with it. He unloosened her bra and like a tiger took one of her breasts in his mouth. His tongue wrestled with her nipple and Elicia threw her head back. Her breathing grew heavy as he removed her skirt. He pushed her panties to the side as he rubbed his fingers against her moist clitoris. Elicia squirmed to help him take them off. Gabe flipped her on her stomach and ran his fingers across her back. Elicia licked her lips. "Mmmmm…"

Their moment of intimacy was interrupted by the fire alarm. There was an instant knock on the door. Gabe jumped up. Elicia grabbed her shirt and bra.

"Are you gonna wait on me?" he asked while quickly lacing up his boots.

"Yes," she said between breaths. "I'll probably take a quick nap. We might have a long night ahead of us." He grinned and kissed her cheek. "Keep your phone close to you."

INEVITABLE

***

"Can you please let me know where you are taking me, Trey? This is not exciting anymore." The two headed out on a crisp evening. Trey had promised her the most exciting night of her life. They pulled up to the historic Tabernacle. He had instructed Marley to dress sexy, but comfortable. He sported an all-white Armani fleece with Armani jeans. He perfectly accented the ensemble with a gray ivy cap and loafers. Marley wore a zebra-printed Betsey Johnson strapless dress and black and white stilettos. Her red lip and matching manicured nails provided just enough pop to turn heads. She got out of the car and began to scream when she saw the marquee that displayed *Lauryn Hill*. Marley thought her music was dope and was excited to find out what else the night had in store. Every seat in the house was filled and the vibe was laid back and cool. Candles were lit everywhere and each corner of the stage displayed Lauryn in HD. Couples made out, held hands, and rocked to every song she bellowed. Alcohol flowed freely and everybody seemed to enjoy this special moment in time with the incomparable Ms. Hill. She demanded that the audience particularly pay attention to the words and smoothly sang:

Yeah, yeaaah, yeah heh, yeah heh, yeah heh...
See the road to hell, is paved with good intentions
Can't you tell, the way they have to mention
How they helped you out, you're such a hopeless victim
Please don't do me any favors, Mr. Intentional
All their talk, is seasoned to perfection
The road they walk, commanding your affection
They need to be needed, deceived by motivation
An opportunity, to further situation
Why they so important, is without explanation
Please don't patronize me, Mr. Intentional
Oh, ohhh, ohh ohhh....

The music icon stopped strumming the guitar and let the beat of the drums take over. Marley bobbed her head and swayed back and forth with Trey. She was having the best time of her life and did not want the night to end. Both had been drinking and were in their own worlds. As they exited the Tabernacle Trey grabbed her hand. They stopped and waited to safely cross the street. She pulled herself closer to him and asked him to forgive her one more time. He smiled and kissed her passionately.

"I have one more surprise for you tonight. All I'm asking is that you keep an open mind."

"Anything you want to do, handsome, I'm down." Marley was tipsy. They drove approximately two hours to what appeared to be an open field.

"What in the hell is this, Trey?" He didn't respond. They traveled along a dirt and gravel pathway for ten more minutes and came upon a gated area. Still slightly intoxicated Marley tried to make out her surroundings.

All of a sudden, they were blinded by a flashlight. A White male, who stood around 6 feet, and sported a tailored suit walked up to the car and asked Trey for the password. "Mansion Sex," he whispered as if someone was listening. The man pressed a button on a small remote and the gate doors slid open. Further up the private driveway stood a three-story mansion with a neon-pink sign that read *Sexxus*. Marley was speechless.

"Is this what I think it is, Trey? What the hell are we doing here? What if someone recognizes me?" She could almost hear her heart pounding through her chest. Visiting a freak house was not what Marley had in mind but she did tell Trey that she was down for anything. Now she regretted taking so many shots at the concert although the alcohol was now wearing off and she was slowly coming to her senses. When they entered the mansion, they were immediately ushered inside a sex store by a woman dressed in a corset and stilettos. Dildo's, creams, handcuffs, porn, lingerie, etc. was made available to the freakiest of the freaky. Trey and Marley were given robes to change into and were led into the main part of the house. Various types of couples, in all shapes and ethnicities were getting it on in plain sight. Marley was embarrassed and nervously grabbed Trey's hand.

INEVITABLE

Marley didn't feel right. "We're not having sex in here, Trey. Why would you bring me somewhere like this anyway?" whined Marley as she watched Trey strip to his boxers. "I'm not this type of freak." Trey silenced her by slowly unzipping her and watched her dress fall to the floor. He licked his lips.

"Baby you are one beautiful Black woman," he gleamed. Something suddenly came over her. Marley wanted him to continue to undress her. His essence of manhood turned her on. They secured their belongings in a nearby locker and Marley tightly clutched her robe as she allowed Trey to lead her out into the open session. As the tour guide continued to lead them throughout the mansion, Marley was quite surprised of what was happening all at once.

On the first level of the manor was a dance floor full of women. Some were dancing on each other, others were simply nodding their heads to the beat. The strobe lighting created a sensual sensation within Marley and she reminded herself to make a stop there with Trey later on that night. As she passed the X-rated action, a White woman, who appeared to be a size 12, grabbed her hand. Marley allowed her to pull her onto the dance floor. Trey watched in delight as they moved to the music. Marley tried to keep a safe distance but the woman was obviously trying to hit on her. The woman then motioned for her to follow her to the billiards area. She glanced at Trey and he motioned letting her know that he would be nearby. She checked out the woman and admitted that she had flavor. Her demeanor spoke for itself. She was polished and dressed only in red leather underwear.

She finally spoke. "I know you are not a lesbian, sweetheart, but I am."

She walked behind Marley and breathed on her neck. "I'm Lizzy." She took her pool stick and seductively leaned over the table. She didn't know why but she found herself amazed by this woman. Maybe it was her boldness.

"Excuse me," Marley said as she found Trey and moved them along. "Baby, she's pretty and all but I like dick! Point blank." They both laughed.

INEVITABLE

To the left of the game room was a movie room. The door was covered with black velvet draping. Upon entering the room, the couple found an Asian woman performing fellatio on a husky Black man. She stopped when Marley and Trey entered. She glanced at both their ring fingers and saw that neither was married. "Would you both like to join us?" Trey declined and grabbed Marley. He led her to the back of the theater and sat her in a chair. He removed her robe and buried his face in her lovebox. Marley threw her head back in pleasure. She began to moan and smiled devilishly as she watched the Asian woman envy her.

***

Elicia awoke to find that Gabe had called her several times while she slept. She called him back and he answered on the first ring. "Baby, what have you been doing? I've been blowing your phone up like crazy!" Elicia sat up as she noticed the urgency in his voice.

"What's going on? I just saw that you called like a million times. Is everything okay?"

"Baby, I'm afraid not. I think I just rescued Nasir from a burning building. His entire body is covered in third degree burns. The ambulance has already rushed him off to Memorial Hospital. You might want to get down there!"

Elicia began to have an anxiety attack. Her heart sank to her knees. She somehow managed to pull herself together and called Giselle to meet her at the hospital.

Giselle embraced Elicia as she collapsed while walking through the door. Elicia sobbed uncontrollably. Hill walked them to the registration desk.

"I'm here to see my husband, Nasir Jones." The nurse looked tired.

"He's currently in surgery, Mrs. Jones. The doctors are doing all that they can to save him. He's bleeding internally. I'll inform you as soon as I know something."

INEVITABLE

Elicia placed her head on Giselle's shoulder.

"He's going to be fine Elicia, don't worry yourself."

"What have I done, G? I turned my back on my husband when I should have been there. Why did I even get involved with Gabe? This is all my fault!" Elicia sobbed.

Giselle tried to talk some sense into her. "Now you listen to me. As bad as this is, you have to remember that Nas walked away from you. He should've communicated with you…good or bad. Don't blame yourself for what has happened. Gabe is a good man and God sent him into your life for a reason. All of this happened for a reason."

***

Just as Gerrod was about to call the police, Eva appeared. "What are you doing here, E?" asked Gerrod. "I have been looking all over for you."

Eva rolled her eyes. "I've been out here meditating. Why do you care?"

"Meditating? Are you fucking serious? At two in the morning? Do you have any idea what kind of maniacs could be out right now?!" He was furious.

Eva pulled a hot pink C-9 pistol out of her cross-body bag. "I can protect myself." She pushed past him and headed back to her car.

He stormed after her. "I don't understand what it is that you want me to do!" he yelled. "I brought my ass back home to my wife and cut Tyra completely off. Why can't we just move past this?"

Eva stopped in her tracks. She turned around and pointed the gun at him. "You came back home AFTER you fucked around on me!"

Gerrod stepped back. "Okay!" he said. "I fucked up. I cheated. There I said it."

She wiped her tears away. "You are unbelievable!"

INEVITABLE

"Well you hurt me like hell, Eva! You know how bad I want you to have my seed. You went along with the shit like it was something you wanted to do! I trusted you! And for what? For you to tell me I'm not good enough to father our children?" He pointed his finger at her. "You better be glad I came back."

***

Elicia's heart raced as she stared at Nasir wrapped in bandages. His entire body had been burned. What she could see of his face was distorted making him hardly recognizable.

"Are you Mrs. Jones?" Elicia turned around to find two officers standing in front of her. "Yes. We are separated. I haven't talked to him in months."

"I'm afraid to inform you that this case has turned into an attempted homicide by arson. Witnesses say they were with Nasir when going to purchase drugs. Supposedly the transaction involved a large sum of money. On his way from making the buy, he was robbed. The perpetrator led him back to the abandoned building and beat him. And we have evidence that suggests the building was purposely set on fire. We've just gotten word that there was a substance on his clothing that appears to be gasoline."

Elicia felt dizzy and took a seat. "Do you know of anyone who would want to harm him in any way?" Elicia shook her head. She then realized that she didn't know anything about him. Her husband. After the cops left she tried to calm herself but ended up dropping to her knees. "Lord, why me?" she wailed. "Whyyyyyyyyy?!!"

INEVITABLE

15

"All I'm saying is that right now she probably is confused. You just have to be there for her in her time of need." Hill sipped his coffee as Giselle paced the floor. "I hate what has happened to Nasir, but that is no reason to give up on Gabe. Nasir left her!"

"But he's still her husband."

"They are separated! There is a difference!" He grabbed her hand. "Have a seat and calm down. You are stressing yourself out more than you should. Ultimately it's not your decision to make." A tear rolled down Giselle's cheek. "I just want to protect my friend. I don't want her to go back to him…ever."

Elicia clenched her fists as she entered the room. "Whatever decision I make I just need you to support! I am tired of you judging him! You know nothing about him!"

"I didn't mean-"

"Shut up, Giselle! Just shut the hell up! You think you're so fucking perfect with your hot-shot lawyer life. Well, you're not. You're a selfish bitch who only cares about herself. And I don't care what you say or think…I'm going to be with my husband." Gabe walked in as an eerie silence took over the room.

"I knew this shit would happen," he said. Elicia stormed out the room. Giselle jumped up and tried to comfort Gabe. "Gabe, never mind what she's saying. She's delirious and tired."

"Thanks, but I think she's made up her mind. Somehow I knew that he would eventually resurface." He tried to crack a smile and left.

***

"Now if this wasn't spontaneous, I don't know what is!" exclaimed Marley. "I feel…nasty!" she giggled as they walked to the car. "I don't know why but watching complete strangers get busy has me turned all the way on!"

INEVITABLE

"So, what are you saying?" asked Trey. She pushed him up against the car and kissed him.

"Mmmm," she moaned. "Your lips taste succulent, and I want more!"

"Whoa, calm down!" he said. "I think you might have had a little too much to drink."

"I know exactly what I'm doing and I know exactly what I want," she said seductively. As Trey sped to his home, he could hardly control the steering wheel as Marley unzipped his manhood and squeezed some lotion into her hands. While she didn't engage in any of the activities at the freak house, Marley did take notes. She squeezed the shaft of his magic stick and worked him until he started to squirm. "Ooooohhhhhh, baby we gotta pull over! I want you now!" he said hoarsely. Marley didn't respond. She continued the session until they arrived at his condo. Trey snatched Marley out of the car and carried her to the bedroom. He anxiously ripped her clothes off and dropped his pants to his ankles. As he lay back on the bed, she went to his top drawer to grab the condoms she'd put there for when the time was right.

"Where are the condoms, Trey?"

He stood up. "What condoms?"

"I put condoms in your top drawer."

"What are you talking about, Marley?"

"Negro, I'm talking about the condoms that I put in your drawer about two weeks ago. Where are they?"

"I have no idea, Marley. I must have grabbed them for a shoot or something."

Marley laughed. "Do you think I'm fucking stupid? What - was I taking too long to give you some? Is that why you took me to a fucking freak house? To speed up the process?" She watched Trey's dick go limp.

INEVITABLE

He shook his head. "How many fucking hurdles are you going to have me jump through, woman? I have done everything right in this situation and now I am tired. I'm done. Whatever we had is over. You need to go."

"With pleasure bastard," she said as she went into the bathroom and slammed the door.

As Marley dressed she wondered if she had taken things too far again. Why couldn't she trust Trey? He had proven himself time and time again. She felt a lump form in her throat.

***

Elicia had locked herself in her house for two days straight. She took a leave of absence from work and ceased all forms of communication. Gabe had not called. She missed him dearly, but was so confused. Was God trying to show her that it was best to try and make her marriage work? She couldn't cry anymore and went to retrieve the extra blunt she had stashed. She knew both Marley and Giselle would kill her if they found out. She told Marley that she didn't have any more, but knew she would need it, eventually. She only desired to get away from all the drama in her life at this point. Elicia nestled in her cream Bamboo Rayon sheets until she found a comfortable spot. It felt good to clear her mind. The blunt was just what she needed to take the edge off. As she inhaled the weed, she coughed fervently. She allowed the green giant to take her away like Calgon and felt instant relaxation. For that moment, she forgot about all her problems and now understood why Nasir smoked as much as he did. She sighed and smiled to herself. She didn't remember where she laid her smoke down as she drifted off to sleep.

***

Days went by and Eva and Gerrod barely uttered a word to each other. They made sure that they were never in the same room and did not sleep in the same bed. Eva sat in the den trying to work on her next novel when she heard a knock at the door. She jumped up. It was after 10pm. Who could be at their door? Gerrod walked to the door and came back with a large envelope. Inside it was a used pregnancy test tucked in a zip lock bag accompanied by a note. It read: *That bitch didn't want your baby, but I do. You are going to make a great dad. I can't wait. Please come back home daddy. Love, Tyra.* Gerrod stared at the handwriting in disbelief. He knew Eva was waiting to know what was going on, and handed her the note.

Eva's face frowned and tears immediately began to form. Gerrod grabbed her and tried to hug her but she pushed him away with so much force that he almost fell over the couch. "Get away from me, Gerrod! Why does this bitch know my business anyway?!" She slowly turned around and headed into the next room to keep her distance. Gerrod grabbed the envelope and jumped in his car.

He banged on Tyra's door until she let him in. "What in the fuck do you think you're doing, T?"

She smiled. "I see you got my gift to you!"

"Your gift?" he yelled. He threw the test at her barely missing her face. "I thought I told you to stay the fuck away from me and my family! You are ruining my life!"

"Your family?! Don't you mean *our* family?"

"You know that's not my baby. You are a fucking slut. I did what a million other niggas have done to you. Why are you trying to set me up?" Tyra sank to the floor.

"I have loved you for years, Gerrod, and this is how you do me? You think I would set you up? You fucked me raw, remember?! Did you seriously think it couldn't happen to you? Are you that stupid?"

Gerrod paced the floor. "You are a hoe Tyra…point blank, and I don't have time for this shit. I'm not going to tell your crazy ass again. Stay the fuck away from me and my wife!" Tyra stood in wonder as she watched him walk out and slam the door. Gerrod didn't make it to his car before taking several blows to the head.

INEVITABLE

***

Elicia peered through a windowpane as she tried to get her sneak peak of the glass-enclosed wedding chapel at Ashton Gardens. As she took everything in, she breathed deeply sending her thoughts all over the place. She had always wanted an evening wedding. Lilies adorned the end of every pew accented by romantic candlelight. It was simplistic, yet sophisticated. She watched Darnell fix Nasir's tie and smiled. Elicia caught a glance of her best friends and teared up. She never, ever thought she would see the day that she, Elicia Yavonne Harris, would get married to the love of her life. She admired her best friends. They looked absolutely stunning in their cranberry crinkle chiffon one shoulder gowns. Giselle had given Elicia hell about the color but looked flawless never-the-less. She wore her hair in a bun and allowed her golden-tresses to fall towards her face. Marley's jet-black mane was garnished by an Ancient Greek gold plated crown and of course her makeup was fierce. Marley gave everyone a simplistic, yet elegant face beat using FaceIt Cosmetics.

Elicia didn't want Nasir to see her just yet, but was excited to make her debut. She was ready to put their questionable past behind her and move forward. It felt like one of the best decisions she'd made in a while. When the pastor entered the church, she knew that it would be showtime in a matter of minutes. She glanced at Nasir again. He looked worried. As the Wedding March began to play, Elicia watched the flower girl and ring bearer move up the aisle. The guests laughed at how slow the flower girl moved, gently placing down one petal at a time. Elicia smiled at the thought of kids. She was ready to begin her new life.

She grabbed the doorknob of the entrance and abruptly snatched her hand away. The doorknob felt like hot coals. Elicia thought she was hallucinating as she attempted to turn the hot knob again. *What in the hell is going on?* she thought. After her third attempt, she became frustrated. Her eyes locked with Nasir's and he shrugged his shoulders. *Why couldn't his bride get to her groom?* Elicia instantly began beating on the door.

INEVITABLE

"Open up! Open up!" she cried. "I'm getting married!" she bellowed. But it was as if no one in the wedding party could hear her. She tugged on the door once more, this time leaving a noticeable burn on her hand.

"The church is on fire! The church is on fire!" said the Reverend as he toppled onto the stage with his cane. "Everyone must leave now! This wedding is off!"

Immediately the crowds began to panic as a blaze of fire spewed from the empty baptism pool. Everyone scrambled to make it to the doors. Elicia yanked on the entrance door of the chapel. The doors were locked and Elicia could not get out fast enough. She watched the guests as they moved expeditiously across the pews. "Somebody help me! Let me out!"

She threw off her headpiece and began to kick and scream. "Somebody open this door! Please!"

Elicia found herself going crazy in the small space! "Open the door! Please! Open the door!" She beat on the door until she passed out.

"Open the door, Elicia! Please! Open the door!" Gabe banged on the door before rushing in. There he found Elicia's Venetian rug in flames. He quickly grabbed the fire extinguisher.

"What is going on Elicia?!" She jumped up and began to scream once she saw the flames. Gabe's chest heaved up and down as he stared at Elicia in disbelief. After the dry chemicals dissolved in the air he picked up the piece of blunt. Elicia was humiliated. He placed it on the table and helped her into her robe. He carried her to his place and sat her at the kitchen table. As the coffee brewed he massaged her shoulders.

"Are you ok, Elicia? When did you start smoking weed?" She rolled her eyes and laid her head on the table. "I'm just going through a lot right now, Gabe."

"You could have set your entire unit on fire! What would have happened if I hadn't stopped by?"

"What are you doing stopping by anyway?" She looked at him with tired eyes.

INEVITABLE

"Because you left these in your front door." He dangled the keys in front of her face. He rubbed his face in frustration and sat down in front of her.

"Look, we need to talk about what is going on. I just can't believe that you are willing to walk away from me so easily. I thought what we had was solid."

Elicia sighed. "I really don't want to focus on this right now. I have a lot on my mind. Please, you have to understand what I'm going through."

Gabe digressed. "Tell you what, I'll go and pick up those cookies you like, and we can listen to music and just chill for the rest of the evening." Elicia smirked. She knew that her lack of communication was tearing him up but was glad to not have to face it at this point.

"I'll be right back. Get comfortable. I have sweats in a fresh laundry basket in my bathroom." Elicia kissed his cheek before watching him go.

She sat staring at nothing for a few minutes before getting up to use the bathroom. While washing her hands, Elicia noticed makeup remover wipes on the sink. She picked up the container and examined it. As she fumbled around in the laundry basket she froze when she came across a woman's leopard print headscarf and cheap panties. Rage began to fill Elicia's heart. She didn't know if she should confront Gabe or not.

Ten minutes later he walked through the door with her favorite cookies and ice cream. "I was thinking maybe we could make-"

"I'm ready to talk now, Gabe," Elicia interrupted.

He took a seat. "I'm listening."

"First, where exactly do you get off questioning where we stand when you're fucking somebody else?" Elicia threw the scarf and panties at his face. "Exhibit A, liar!" He looked at the underwear and sighed. "Let me explain, Elicia."

"Yes, I will let you explain. I should have known that you weren't this "great guy" from the beginning. A single firefighter…that should have said it all. Know that you are the one who fucked this up. You lost the best thing that ever happened to you. I was actually falling in love with you!"

She stood up and started to leave. Gabe picked her up from behind and she began to scream through her tears.

"Put me down! I hate you! You hurt me! You are a liar!" She kicked and scratched as Gabe tried to keep her under control.

"Listen!" he yelled. He scared Elicia and she calmed down. "I can admit that those are someone else's…that I've had sex with, but you dismissed me. What was I supposed to do? I am a man and I have needs."

Elicia tried to laugh. "Why are you acting as if that makes the bullshit okay, Gabe? Why do you still have her personal belongings here if she doesn't mean anything?" Gabe put his head in his hands.

"It's because she was eventually going to come back, right? I can't believe I trusted you."

"I don't know what you want, Elicia. I felt hurt and betrayed. I understand your situation and I know it's hard, but it's hard for me too. So, now I have to lose the best thing God has ever sent me? She was just a fuck. I don't know why I did it."

"So, who is she?"

"I told you already. She is no one to me. And why are you so pressed about *her* anyway? Didn't you state in front of the entire world who you wanted to be with? I don't even know why we're going through this shit."

It was at that moment that Elicia realized he really did care for her and that she cared deeply for him.

"I'm scared, Gabe," she whispered. "I feel guilty. I cheated on my husband. Even before the accident I knew that I wanted to be with you. I was just trying to make sure that I was doing the right thing."

Gabe stood in front of Elicia. "So, what are you saying?" Elicia sniffed and closed her eyes. "I need you in my life, Gabe. You make me feel safe, protected and special - the way a woman should always feel. I want you to be my man – not anyone else's." He hugged and kissed her neck.

"That's the best news I've heard all week."

***

When Gerrod finally regained consciousness, he realized he was on the floor of Tyra's bathroom. His wrists and ankles were bound with duct tape, and he was propped up against the jacuzzi tub. In front of him was a full-length mirror. It read *Karma's A Bitch* in red lipstick. He stared at the unfamiliar face in the mirror. His left eye was swollen shut and he couldn't move his mouth. He began to breathe heavily and frantically jerked around at a failed attempt to free himself.

Tyra unlocked the door and strolled in the bathroom with black, lace crotch-less underwear and six-inch red stilettos. "I hope you had a good night," she said kissing his forehead.

"Now, what I need for you to do is just sit back and relax. I'm running the show. You are going to do what I say." Tyra put on some soft music and lit candles. Gerrod remembered why he once hated her.

"You really are a crazy bitch," he said while gritting his teeth so hard it hurt.

"You are going to get yours, sweetheart." She laughed and began to dance seductively in front of him. She bent all the way over and touched her toes while placing her clitoris to his mouth. He moved his head away. She turned around and slapped him.

"You will eat my pussy like you used to make me suck your dick. Now eat it bitch," she commanded. He turned away again. Tyra hurried to unlock the door and an unidentified male in a ski mask barged in and hit him in the face with brass knuckles. "Do as she tells you, motherfucker." Gerrod spewed blood out of his mouth. The man disappeared, and Tyra picked back up where she left off.

INEVITABLE

***

"It's not like him," said Eva as she explained all that had been going on to Giselle.

"I still cannot believe that he cheated on you with that stank bitch. My brother really be on some other shit."

"Do you feel like he's with her now?" Eva didn't feel quite right in her spirit.

"I'm…I'm not sure what to think."

"Well, I know where she lives. I'm going to confront that bitch."

"Well you can't confront her without me. Text me the address." Giselle hung up the phone and changed clothes.

Hill shook his head. "You are not going there alone."

"Of course not," Giselle said as she laced up her gym shoes. "I'm calling the police."

"No police…I'll go with you. This could get ugly. If need be I'll talk to my buddy on the force."

INEVITABLE

16

Marley rubbed her eyes as she took a break from her laptop. Every paper she graded was beginning to look the same, so she decided to pack up and go home for the night. She put on her jacket and slipped on her loafers. She promised herself that she would stop working so late at the university, but knew that she wouldn't get much done at home. She missed Trey and realized that it was officially over. He hadn't reached out to her and she had gotten back in the swing of her regular routine. As she hustled to her car she heard footsteps behind her and walked faster. "Good evening, Ms. Cole." Marley cautiously turned around to see a familiar face appear from the shadows.

"Kahmin? Is that you?" He smiled as his face surfaced in the light.

"Yes, it's me. How are you?" Marley quickly scanned the parking deck and noticed that it was empty besides one other car. "What are you doing here?"

He smirked. "Be cool, lil' mama. I just wanted to check on my favorite teacher."

"Excuse me?" asked Marley. As she continued to migrate towards her truck he sped up behind her and grabbed her arm.

"Hold on, baby. What's the rush?" He knocked everything out of her hand and placed his arms tightly around her.

"Let me go, Kahmin. What do you think you're doing?" she whispered.

"All I wanted was one date…so I've come to wine and dine you." Marley could smell liquor on his breath. As she tried to struggle free he squeezed her even tighter.

"Let me go!" she yelled. But he wouldn't. He took his hand and shoved it under her skirt. A tear fell from her face. In an instant, Adah flashed into her mind. She thought about her baby being conceived as a result of a rape. She was not going to endure this pain again. "Help!" she screamed as she tried to get away. Kahmin slammed her against her truck and she kicked him in the groin. He fell to the ground as she fumbled through her bag for her keys. He reached for her and ripped her skirt. "You bitch!" Marley kicked him again and took flight. "Come back here you bitch!" he screamed as he caught his balance on her truck. He took her laptop and busted out one of her windows then started to chase her. Marley was so scared that she didn't even see herself run into Trey. She was hyperventilating.

"What in the hell is going on?!" Trey demanded.

She couldn't talk and pointed in the direction of her car. Trey ran down Kahmin and almost beat him unconscious. By the time the police arrived Marley didn't even recognize her student. His face was covered in blood and his bottom lip was enlarged. By the look of his left arm, it was broken. Trey stared at her in silence. She trembled at the thought of what almost happened to her…again. He took a tissue and removed the sweat from her forehead. He ran his fingers across her cheek.

She sniffed. "What are you doing here, Trey?"

"I'm here every night to make sure you get to your car safely." He squeezed his swollen knuckles.

"What?" she asked as she unpinned her damp hair.

"Even though we don't deal…every night you work late, I make sure you get to your car safely."

She was both shocked and confused by his revelation. "I don't know what to say."

"It's cool. You don't have to say anything. A tow is on the way and will take care of your car. I can take you home or wait for a friend to pick you up." He put his arms around her.

Marley placed her head on his chest as she held back her tears. They rode in silence all the way home. She knew that she was responsible for their situation, but couldn't help but wonder what was going through Trey's mind. They finally arrived at her place and said good night. Worn out by her unfortunate run-in with Kahmin, Marley took two pain pills and crashed.

INEVITABLE

***

Gabe smiled as Elicia finally relaxed and allowed him to give her a massage. "That feels so good, baby!" Gabe slowly kissed the back of Elicia's neck as she moaned in relief. His faded cologne turned her on. He was definitely all the man she could ever need. She rubbed her fingers through his mane and straddled him. She stared deeply into his eyes.

"What did I do to deserve you?" He smiled and unhooked her bra. He tossed her shirt aside and admired her beauty for a minute. His strong masculine hands palmed her left breast as he bit and sucked on her right. Elicia threw her head back. This turned her on immensely and she began to breathe heavily. Gabe slid off her panties underneath her skirt. He took his index finger and rubbed swiftly against her swelling clitoris. Elicia's juices flowed relentlessly as she rode Gabe's fingers. She thought about Nas and suddenly snapped back to reality. She became rigid and grabbed Gabe's face looking him in his eyes.

"Were you getting your needs met by that chick since the beginning of our relationship?" He stared at her in disbelief. "Wh-What does that have to do with what we got going on right now?" Elicia grabbed her bra.

"I just wanna make sure that I'm not rushing things. We're both are attracted to each other but that doesn't mean that sex has to immediately happen once we say we are exclusive, right?"

"Unbelievable, Elicia…you get me all aroused and then want to discuss old shit right in the middle of it? I thought that was the past."

"You told me that you were with this chick because she was just sex, correct?"

"Correct."

"So that means ever since we've been talking *you've* been fucking this chick, correct?"

"Correct."

INEVITABLE

"So, what in the hell do I look like giving all of myself to you and you're giving yourself to her?" Gabe watched his magic stick die.

"How do I know you are done with her, Gabe? How do I know?"

He grabbed her chin. "Because my heart is with you, not her. And don't you ever forget that." He started to lick her nipples again. Elicia finally surrendered.

***

Hill's friend from the force arrived at almost the same time as Giselle, Hill, and Eva. He asked them to stay in the car and knocked on the front door. Tyra answered wearing only a robe and slippers. "Ma'am, I'm here to check out a call I received about a disturbance coming from your home."

Tyra smiled and purposely unloosened the belt on her robe. "I have no clue what you are talking about Mr. Officer."

"Is that blood on your robe?" Tyra tried to wipe it away.

"No officer, that's just a little wine I had earlier."

"Do you mind if I come in? I just want to check around a bit." He called for backup.

Twenty minutes later Tyra and her brothers were in handcuffs. Hill helped Gerrod to the car. Eva couldn't do anything but cry. They rushed him to the hospital. Eva held his hand the entire way. They patiently waited outside of the emergency room when, finally, the doctor arrived. "What's going on doc, is he going to be okay?" Eva said in between sobs.

"Yes, he's going to recover but we're moving him to ICU. His nose, collar bone, and rib cage are broken. He's going to be off his feet for the next two to four months."

INEVITABLE

***

At home, Marley sat and drank her caramel macchiato in a daze. Her experience with Kahmin sent her into a state of fear. She felt vulnerable and scared. She needed to see Trey. She hadn't heard from him since the night before, but she yearned to see him. She continued to stare at the phone as if it was going to magically ring. At that moment, she realized she was ready for love.

***

A couple of weeks later, everyone's life seemed to be back to normal. "Yes, we'd like three Swedish massages please." As the three friends made their way into Jazmin Spa, they all smiled at the fine receptionist that checked them in.

"I cannot wait for this. My life needs a detox." Marley said with a hint of tiredness in her voice. "I think all of us could use a detox at this point." After about an hour of pampering the ladies headed to the back of the spa to get manicures and pedicures. Giselle sipped on a glass of Riesling as the Asian woman went to work on her toes. She sighed.

"I don't think I can hold out much longer, ladies." Elicia shook her head pretending that she and Gabe hadn't taken it to the next level.

"No one told you to go into the situation being Ms. Goody-goody. If you wanna have sex with him then do it." Marley was fed up with how Elicia was treating Gabe.

Elicia started to laugh hysterically and both Giselle and Marley shot her the look of death.

"You did not!! When were you going to tell us?" Marley grabbed her chest in shock.

"Forget that," said Giselle. "I need details." They all laughed.

Elicia threw her head back in delight. "It was incredible!"

INEVITABLE

"Now you know damn well that's not enough, I need more. If I'm not giving it up then I need to at least live out my sexual fantasies through you!" Giselle was being serious.

"We had argumentative sex."

"That's the best kind!" chimed Marley as she munched on seedless grapes.

"What in the hell do you two have to argue about now?"

"That's not important," said Elicia. "We will discuss this later in the privacy of our own homes, ladies. Now, on to Giselle." She shook her head. "What are you going to do about Hill?"

"I don't know. Things have been going exceptionally well with us lately. You both know that sex confuses and changes everything."

Marley sucked her teeth. "Is he not your man?"

"Yes," said Giselle, "but I really wanna stick by my one-year rule."

"I understand where you are coming from, G, but you are a grown ass woman. If it feels right, do it." Marley started to admire her choice of pink polish on her nails.

John Legend's Ordinary People blared from Marley's phone.

"Hello, um yea, sure. I'll be there in about thirty minutes." She quickly grabbed her bag and sandals. "It's Trey. He wants to talk. I'll see y'all later."

"I can't believe you're skipping out on our monthly rendezvous. Wassup with that?" Giselle asked with obvious irritation.

"I'm going to go get my man back," she beamed. Giselle and Elicia shook their heads in disbelief and watched her hurry out the door.

"So back to you," said Giselle as she took another sip of her wine. "What's going on with Nas? Is he better? The past few times I've seen you, you haven't mentioned him."

INEVITABLE

***

Marley could smell Trey's cologne in the air as she entered the restaurant. Her heart beat fast as she approached him and gave him a tight hug. He pulled her chair out for her and rubbed his goatee while looking Marley up and down. He finally spoke.

"So," he bellowed.

"So," she responded.

Trey smirked and grabbed her hands. "What are we doing man? Why can't I get you off my mind, ma?"

"You tell me," she teased. She had to admit that there was something very powerful between them.

Marley sighed. "Look, I can't explain why I am the way that I am. I know I might spaz out from time to time but I'm a good woman."

"Never disputed that."

"Well, why do you act like I get on your nerves all the time?"

"Because you do."

They finished their meal and went for a walk in the nearby park.

About five minutes into their stroll, Trey stopped and turned to Marley. He gave her the most passionate kiss she'd ever experienced. "I just want you to be happy and I know that you'd only be happy with me."

She wiped the lipstick from his lips. "And what makes you think that, Trey?"

"Because no one else is going to put up with you. I want to protect you. I don't ever want to hurt you."

Marley kissed him back making sure to outdo his performance.

INEVITABLE

"Man, I've missed you. So, does this mean you're going to the Caymans with me?"

"Yes!" squealed Marley as she threw her arms around his neck.

INEVITABLE

17

"I'm gwad you still here." Gerrod tried to speak but the stitches in his lip hurt. He handed Eva a piece of paper. It read:

Babe,

This is my fault and I know I fucked up. I want a family with you more than anything. You hurt me and I wanted to hurt you back. I will never hurt you again in any way. I promise to make this up to you. I love you.

Eva smiled as he wiped her tears. "I love you too, baby. I'm sorry for being so selfish. I want you to be the father of my child…of all my children. It doesn't matter what we go through as long as we get through it as a family." He pulled her face close and tried his best to kiss her.

***

When Elicia arrived at the bowling alley she was surprised to find Gabe with three guys hanging out by the bar. She grabbed her compact mirror from her purse to check her makeup. Elicia wondered why Gabe didn't inform her that they would have company. He saw her coming and walked her to the table. "Elicia, I want you to meet two of my homeboys, Shannon and Kenny." Elicia faked a smile and shook their hands. "Nice to meet you both."

"I can't believe that we finally get to meet the infamous Elicia. This man just can't stop talking about you." Elicia blushed and winked at Gabe. "As a matter of fact, I think we need to toast." Shannon ordered four Tequila shots. As they all held their glasses up, Shannon stood. "I just wanna say that it's been a long time since Gabe has found somebody that he is actually crazy about. So, if you hurt my boy I might have to come after you."

Everyone laughed except Kenny, who clearly had been drinking already. He shook his head. "No disrespect, but who are we kidding? This chick is still married, to a crackhead at that, and probably gon' leave yo' ass when dude comes out of his coma."

INEVITABLE

Gabe stood up. "Let's go, you've had too much to drink. I'ma walk you to your car." Kenny rolled his eyes. "Well somebody gotta tell the truth. You pussy whooped and it all might be for nothing."

He snatched Kenny's collar and dragged him out of the place.

"What the fuck do you think you're doing?" Gabe demanded as he slammed him on top of the car. Larry struggled to get up. "Aight, don't come calling me in the middle of the night crying when that bitch break your heart. You fucking up your life for no reason."

"Fuck you, dude," said Gabe as he walked off. He found Elicia sitting alone at a table. Shannon was nowhere in sight.

"I'm sorry, Elicia. I don't know what that shit was all about."

"Why do they know all of that anyway?"

"What…you think I kept all of the shit that we've been dealing with all bottled up inside? All of your friends know."

"Yes, but my friends are mature and act like adults. He disrespected me."

"And I checked him."

"He owes me an apology. I won't be disrespected by your friends."

"I checked him, Elicia. Just let it go."

"No, I won't."

"Are you mad because something he said might be true? I'm not going to be convinced about you or us until you file for a divorce."

"This is becoming ridiculous," hissed Elicia as she stormed out. He followed her.

INEVITABLE

***

Giselle woke up in the middle of the night in a cold sweat. Her chest heaved up and down as she barely made it down the stairs for a glass of water. This was the third occurrence in the last month. The random breakouts and fatigue had heightened as well. Giselle simply chalked it up to aging and being overworked. She was glad that the vacation was still on. In about three hours she planned to meet Hill for breakfast. Giselle couldn't go back to sleep and caught up on her favorite reality show to pass the time away. Her phone rang. It was Hill.

"What are you doing up, beautiful?"

Giselle giggled. "Couldn't sleep. You?"

"Can't stop thinking about you. May I come see you?"

"Nah, I'd rather come and see you." Giselle hung up the phone and jumped in the shower.

As she dried off she noticed a rash on the back of her leg. Giselle finally decided that it was time to make a doctor's appointment.

She arrived at Hill's place in under an hour. "Wow, you look amazing…even in sweats," he said while closing the door behind her.

After hugging her tight, he ran both hands through Giselle's golden tresses while admiring her beauty. To his surprise, several strands came out in his hands. He dropped them before Giselle could notice.

"So, we are less than two weeks away from the Cayman Island excursion, have you been getting your wardrobe together?"

Hill laughed. "Of course. I'm wearing nothing but speedos!"

"Well, I'm wearing thong bikinis only, and maybe a big, straw hat," she joked.

He stood behind her. Giselle inhaled his scent. He smelled of shea butter and soap and Giselle was becoming turned on.

INEVITABLE

Hill kissed the back of her neck. Giselle slipped from his hold and opened his fridge. She poured herself a glass of pineapple juice.

He grabbed her again. "So, what are we doing, Ms. Mosely? We've been going out for a few months now. How long do you usually wait until you become exclusive with someone?"

Giselle wasn't expecting this. It must have been the early morning hours getting the best of Hill. "I mean…I don't know. It depends on the chemistry I guess."

"We have chemistry."

She looked at him. "More than just that. Things like trust."

Hill frowned. "You still don't trust me? Is it because of the Samantha bullshit?"

Giselle didn't know why she couldn't fully trust Hill. Suddenly, the doorbell rang. She followed him to the foyer.

"Not this shit again," said Hill. Hayden stood at the door. She looked rough.

"Well, are you going to let me in?" she said with an attitude.

Hayden smiled at Giselle. "You must really like this one, Hill. She's around all the time."

Giselle cracked a smile, but really wanted to smack her face. "Hi Hayden, it's nice to see you again." She wondered why Hayden didn't let herself in.

Hill was careful not to alarm Giselle and excused himself to speak with his sister privately in the kitchen.

"What are you doing here? You were supposed to be staying at Carmen's for the weekend," Hill demanded staring a hole into Hayden.

"Did you tell her?"

"No. I'll tell her when the time is right."

"Looks to me like you've fallen in love again. Oh, how sweet."

Hill backed Hayden into the kitchen stove. "Why the fuck are you here?"

"I'm fucking here because you're here! Don't act brand new."

Hill grabbed $300 from one of the kitchen drawers and threw it at her. "Get the fuck outta here."

Hayden brushed past him and left out the back door.

***

"When were you going to tell me?" asked Trey.

"I'm telling you now," she said while pulling out her laptop.

She showed Trey the pictures of Adah and her adoptive family.

He smiled. "She looks just like you. Let's contact her."

"And say what?"

"That you're her real mom and you would like to meet her. That simple."

Marley closed the laptop. "What if she says no?"

"Why would she say no?"

"Because she might think I'm trying to steal her or something."

"This is the perfect opportunity. The least you could do is try."

Marley cringed. If she was denied the right to see her daughter she would be crushed.

"I'm right here. We can do this together." Trey opened up the laptop.

INEVITABLE

Dear Mrs. Stevens-Jackson, Hello. I am Adah's biological mother, Marley Cole. I gave her up when she was born because I wasn't in a position to care for her. I love my daughter. I would just like a chance to meet her, if possible.

Respectfully Yours,
Marley Cole
404-677-7771

"I think that's perfect," said Trey.

Trey grabbed her hands and prayed over the email before sending it.

Marley stared at the computer. "If she responds to this message, my whole life is going to change."

"You mean *our* life is going to change," said Trey.

Marley grabbed his neck and kissed him. She couldn't help but feel reassured that they could possibly be one big happy family.

***

Elicia pulled into her driveway and noticed a police car leaving Gabe's house. She also noticed her too-friendly neighbor, Rosalind, looking in Gabe's direction while talking on her cell phone. Elicia got out of the car and waved then waited until it was clear to cross the street. Gabe looked flustered.

"What was that about?" she asked as she slung her leather briefcase over her shoulder.

"That was nothing…just accidentally set off my house alarm and ADT security sent someone out. That's all."

He looked as if he had something on his mind. "Well, are you alright? You are welcome to come over and hang out if you like."

INEVITABLE

Gabe brushed her off. "Look, I have a lot of errands to run. I'll catch up with you later."

Elicia stared at Gabe as he retreated to his house and shut the door. She didn't understand why he was suddenly acting so weird.

***

As Elicia settled in, she went to the kitchen to prepare herself a sandwich and realized she hadn't cleaned up in days. Mail and a few half-eaten takeout containers lined the countertops and dishes peeked over the rim of the sink. She sighed as she put on some music and grabbed her cleaning products. As Elicia rummaged through one of the drawers, for a fresh dishtowel, she came across a picture of her and Nasir when they had first started dating. She remembered angrily snatching it off the refrigerator door after one of their senseless arguments about an unpaid electric bill. She'd contemplated ripping the photo to shreds, when he didn't come home that night, but decided against it. She gazed at the picture for a long time. She grabbed her coat and headed to the hospital. She hadn't seen him in over a couple of weeks because she'd found herself so consumed with Gabe and work.

***

Nasir still looked nothing like himself as he lay there in a coma. Elicia began to sob and grabbed his hand. As she prayed for him she allowed her tears to fall freely. The nurse came in when she heard the wailing and tried to comfort Elicia, but it was to no avail. It wasn't until Gabe walked in the room that Elicia's tears stopped. He looked disappointed.

"What are you doing here, Gabe?"

"I'm paying my respects."

"Why? You don't even know him."

"I've been coming to see him. I'm just paying my respects."

Elicia was confused. "Pay your respects? He's not dead, Gabe."

INEVITABLE

***

Giselle headed to the YMCA beaming from head to toe. She had a good man. A good job. And good friends. She had it all together.

"And you, young ladies have to understand that you were put here for a reason. You have purpose. Go out and make your dreams manifest!"

The ladies in the room cheered for Giselle as she took her curtsy. She felt like royalty.

"Now, I have a few more minutes left to take questions from any of you ladies."

An older woman in a cream-colored pants suit stood up. "Could you tell us a little bit more about the case that made you *famous*?" she said while motioning quotation marks in the air.

Giselle was irritated but maintained her composure.

"Thank you for your question. Well as you all know, my client, rapper Chase K called police after getting into an altercation with producer Yee da Don about six years ago. Chase K shot Yee in the stomach after a heated argument, supposedly over unpaid royalties. The bullet grazed Yee's spine and is still lodged in his back. The doctors were unable to remove it safely but thankfully he lived. Eventually Chase K was released on bail. I argued that it was a self-defense case due to evidence of previous threats and unwarranted harassment. The judge found the evidence sufficient and the case never went before a jury. Chase K was found not guilty. The rest is history." Giselle smirked.

"No. It's history for you. But it's the present for me. Even after all these years my son still can't walk and sometimes will stop breathing in the middle of the night because of what your client did to him."

Giselle was becoming anxious as the woman moved closer.

"Are you a mother?" the woman scowled.

"No, I'm not," Giselle said impatiently.

INEVITABLE

"Well, of course you aren't." She turned and stormed out the building.

Giselle tossed her hair and remained cool.

"Ok ladies, are there any more questions?"

The room was eerily quiet. "Well, it has been great speaking with you today." Giselle took a couple of photos with the group and made a swift exit to the parking lot. She was glad that she had parked away from the entrance so that no one would see her.

She leaned across the passenger seat to fumble through the glove box. "Where are my fucking cigarettes?" she growled. Hill must have taken them out in an attempt to help her kick the habit. She reached under her seat and pulled out her spare pack.

She squeezed her temples as she took a toke. *What in the hell just happened in there?* Was she being stalked?

Once she made it to Hill's house, she told him what had transpired. Her knees began to shake uncontrollably.

"So, what did you do after she left?"

"I tried to pull it together of course."

"What did she look like again?"

"I told you she was older, but looked good for her age. She sported a short gray cut, nicely dressed. But pissed the hell off."

Hill walked to the window. "Well, there are a lot of crazy people out there, so you have to be careful."

"I don't understand why this is my fault…after all these years. If anything, she should be going after Chase K. Should I file a police report?"

"No, I don't think it's that serious. You know this comes with the responsibility. Just be extra careful."

INEVITABLE

"Be careful. Really, Hill?" Giselle retorted.

"The trip to the islands is going to do us all some good."

Still uneasy, Giselle wrapped her arms around Hill and laid her head on his chest. "It can't come fast enough."

***

Days passed and still no word from Adah or Michelle. Marley was becoming discouraged.

"I knew this was a bad idea."

"Give it some time, Marley. Hopefully she'll respond by the time we return from our vacation.

Marley slammed the laptop.

"And for a second I was thinking about what it would actually feel like to be a mom."

"You will be a mom, Marley. I'll make sure of that." Trey rubbed her right temple as she lay on his shoulder.

"Look, I gotta run. I have a shoot in about an hour. You're more than welcome to accompany me."

"Sure. Who knows, maybe it'll cheer me up."

Even though he tried not to show it, Trey was ecstatic.

***

The old brick building was huge and smelled of must and fresh paint. Trey led Marley to a private elevator that they rode to the sixth floor. Marley was officially creeped out. It reminded her of something out of a Jason movie. She stepped off the elevator to find two women butt naked in a shower adjacent to the elevator doors. To the left of the room was a king size bed fitted with the finest linen. At the edge of the bed sat a husky man who looked to be in his mid-twenties stroking his erect penis.

INEVITABLE

"What's going on boss?" he said as he threw his head up at Trey. Trey spoke and introduced Marley to Sampson. He led her to a seat and began to set up his equipment. Marley didn't know if she should be mad at Trey for his chosen side hustle. She couldn't deny her slight interest, though. Marley watched the two women get out of the shower and dry off. Both women were attractive in their own way. They pranced over to Sampson and attacked him. The caramel colored blonde feverishly sucked his tank as the jet-black beauty devoured his missile. Sampson pressed both heads down harder in an attempt to feel the hot wetness that came from their mouths. He pushed both of them off and bent the blonde over. A tattoo on her vagina read "Fuck Me" and he did just that. As he pounded her to cloud nine the black splendor spread his ass cheeks and allowed the second vixen's tongue to linger around his hole. Sampson seemed to be in another world and began to buck the blonde as if she were a racing horse.

"Yyyy…eeee….ssss!" she screamed as he smacked her ass cheeks. Marley was turned on and ready to produce her own show. Trey had brought her a tall glass of Moscato to ease her discomfort. All this seemed to do was turn Marley on even more. She watched Trey keep his distance as he expertly moved in and out of the scene with his camera. He was good at what he did and rarely got in the way.

Sampson grabbed his ass taster and threw her on the bed. He thrust hard into the blonde with his large dick and she went into a trance. He pushed her legs behind her head and ate her pussy like a five-course meal. Marley watched her come multiple times and wished she could trade places. As the woman's lovebox squirted juices, Marley covered her mouth in astonishment. When they finally finished up, everyone sat around and joked as if nothing had happened. Marley waited while the crew showered, packed up and left. She now had Trey all to herself. He gathered his camera equipment and looked sheepishly at her.

"So, what did you think? Was it that bad?" She stood up and handed him his camera cords. "It was…fine I guess. I couldn't do it for a living, but it was cool."

Trey started to unpack his camera. "Maybe we could make a film of our own."

INEVITABLE

"Are you crazy? Me? On camera? No way! I have too much to lose!" She pushed the Canon out of her face.

Trey smiled. "I understand. You're just a little camera shy. For now."

Marley suddenly realized that she might have a sex addict on her hands.

INEVITABLE

18

Giselle woke up feeling refreshed and ready for the Caymans. She stretched, her breasts lifting with her arms as she greeted the morning sun. She showered and threw on a PINK lounge suit. As she tidied up her halo braid, Giselle noticed a new rash on the back of her neck. She smacked her teeth. It had been almost a week sent she'd seen the doctor. Her blood work should have been back by now. Her cell phone rang.

"Yes, Elicia?"

"Can you please make sure that Marley is on time? I'm really not trying to miss this flight."

"Actually, Hill and I are picking up Marley and Trey so we should all be on time." She gave her suitcase a final look-over before shutting it.

"Soooo, are you excited?"

"Of course! I think this is going to be a memorable experience for all of us! Are you planning to let yourself be free with Gabe? I mean, really connect with him spiritually?"

She scoffed. "If you're implying sex, then hell to the no. Once was enough and even that was too soon. We are just getting over a rough patch and I don't want to make any more sudden moves. You?"

"I'm not quite ready for that. You know…I really, really like Hill. But my intuition is telling me that he just might be too good to be true."

"It's okay to let your guard down, Giselle. He's the best you've dated in a while. Don't mess it up with your insecurities. He seems to truly be invested in you."

"I'm not insecure, I'm insightful."

"Well, don't mess it up with your *insightfulness*."

They both laughed. "I'm on my way!"

INEVITABLE

Giselle called Gerrod to see how he was feeling and told him that she loved him. She grabbed her bags and dashed out the door.

***

Once they checked their bags and made it past security, they all relaxed. It would be another hour before their flight departed and they were hungry. After settling on a bar and grill, Hill ordered Vodka shots for everyone.

"I'd like to make a toast to new beginnings and great memories."

"Cheers!" they all yelled in unison.

Before boarding the plane, Hill made his way to the restroom as he was not keen on relieving himself on planes unless he absolutely had to. As he washed his hands he noticed a male flight attendant staring at him.

"Hill Stokes, it's been years."

Hill barely looked up. "I think you must be mistaken." He went to air dry his hands.

"No, I'll never forget that rod."

Hill paused in shock.

"I don't know what you're talking about," he stammered as he pushed past him.

***

Once seated on the plane, Hill took off his jacket and sank back in his plush seat. He all of a sudden felt warm and uneasy. Giselle noticed and grabbed his hand.

"You ok?"

"Yea…yea…just…um ready to get on the ship."

INEVITABLE

When the flight attendant from the restroom appeared from behind the curtain, Hill became nauseous and tried to maintain his composure. They made eye contact and the attendant rolled his eyes.

"How did Trey manage to get us all first-class seats?" Giselle asked.

"I don't know, nor do I care." Hill was obviously agitated. They both reclined and closed their eyes as other passengers boarded the plane.

Before Marley could shut off her phone she received a notification.

Trey playfully shook his index finger at her. "It's time to relax, babe. That means no phones."

She froze. Marley's heart beat fast as she opened the Facebook notification from Adah's adoptive parents.

She gave the phone to Trey. He read the message to her.

Thanks for contacting me. I can admit that I was somewhat hesitant when you reached out. I became overwhelmed with emotion and had to take some time to figure out what was the best thing to do in this situation. After much thought and prayer, I have come to realize that Adah does need to know who her biological mother is. Please give me a call so that we can make the proper arrangements.

Trey's biceps squeezed Marley as they both beamed with joy. Marley thanked Adah's adoptive mother and told her that she would reach back out once she returned from vacation.

"I finally get to be a mom!" she hollered.

Giselle jumped up. "What?"

"Oh, my God, you're pregnant?!" yelled Elicia.

Trey nervously sat forward as Marley bowed her head giggling.

Before Giselle could get another word out her phone rang.

"Yes, I'm trying to reach Ms. Mosely?"

INEVITABLE

"Speaking. Who is this?"

"This is Dr. Langford with Piedmont Hospital. How are you this afternoon?"

Giselle sounded hopeful. "I'm actually on a plane getting ready to take off to the Caymans."

"Wow, that sounds great! Well, when you get back in town, I need for you to come in and discuss your test results."

Giselle's heart nearly stopped.

"Sure, is everything okay?"

"I believe that we may have figured out why you've been experiencing fatigue, the dizzy spells, and the recurring patches on your skin."

She nervously swallowed. "That's great. Can you tell me what it is?"

"I think it would be much better for you to come in and discuss this in person." The doctor became silent on the other end.

"Dr. Langford, I need to know something." She was almost in tears.

"I'm sorry, Giselle. I can't discuss this over the phone. I do not want to be in violation of HIPAA privacy laws."

"Please, Dr. Langford. If I don't know something, I am going to worry when I should be enjoying my vacation. Please! Let me know something!"

The doctor sighed and proceeded to briefly share with Giselle her diagnosis.

"What?!" she exclaimed in disbelief. "How?"

"This is why I wanted to discuss your results in person, Ms. Mosely. I can answer all of your questions and help you through this. Please just enjoy your trip and make sure you contact me as soon as you return."

INEVITABLE

"Yes, thank you doctor."

Giselle silenced her phone, put on her shades and reclined in her seat.

"What's the matter?" Hill inquired. He removed Giselle's shades as tears began to form. The flight attendant noticed that something was wrong and rushed over.

"Hello, I'm Donald and I'll be your attendant. Is everything okay?"

"Yes, thank you," Giselle said as she grabbed a tissue from her purse.

He quickly glanced at Hill.

"You two make a lovely couple. Are you married, engaged?"

Hill sat forward. "This is my woman and we need some time."

"I understand. But may I ask, what do you do for a living?"

"We're both attorneys. Now please excuse us." Giselle put her shades back on.

Donald smiled and winked at her.

"I guess we all get to the top the best way we know how."

Giselle sat up in her seat while abruptly removing her shades again. "Excuse me. What are you suggesting?"

"Child, nothing," he said nonchalantly as he continued up the aisle.

"Why are you crying, Giselle?" Hill was concerned but was mostly consumed with his own unraveling situation.

"I don't want to talk about it. Do you know him? Do I need to know him? He seemed a bit intrusive - almost nosey don't you think?"

Hill distracted Giselle by asking her to select a movie for their two-hour flight. He took a big gulp of wine as he reminisced on how he'd met Donald. He never envisioned in a million years that he would get caught up.

INEVITABLE

Caught Up

"I'm sorry Hill, but your father and I are no longer in a position to help you financially. After the outcome of the lawsuit, we are going to have to file for bankruptcy. We funded your undergraduate education and even part of law school. We love you, son, but you're an adult now and it's time that you start taking care of your own obligations."

"But what else am I going to do, Mom? I was planning to take the bar in February and now I can't because my credit isn't in good standing."

"You should have thought about that before you leased the condo and the sports car. I told you about keeping up appearances. Especially for people who don't matter."

Hill understood where his mom was coming from but he was in too deep and couldn't turn back now. All of his credit cards were maxed out and this façade was now catching up to him. Hill took pride in his appearance and how people perceived him, so he did whatever was necessary to disguise the fact that he was broke.

"Have you tried taking out another loan?"

Hill sighed. "Yes ma'am, I didn't get approved," he huffed.

"Well, then you just might have to borrow some cash from your friends until you can get back on your feet. That seems to be your only option at this point."

Hill hung up the phone and slid from the couch to the floor. He tried to hold back tears of frustration. He realized how close he was to accomplishing his dream of making *Forbes' 30 Under 30* list, yet the bar exam was standing between him and his promising future. He had studied his ass off and was ready for the next level.

Just as he was about to call his Uncle Ray to see if he could loan him the money to get his bills current, his roommate Tristan walked through the door. He dripped in sweat and was drinking from a jug of water.

INEVITABLE

"My man, what's going on? Why you look like you got somebody pregnant?"

Hill sucked his teeth. "Ain't nobody pregnant, man. I'm broke. If anybody got a chick pregnant, it's you. I heard you in there last night. You had shawty screaming at the top of her lungs."

Tristan smirked and pounded Hill's fist. "Yea, I just gave her what she was begging for." He put his hands in his gym shorts and grabbed himself. "These hoes go crazy over the dick!"

"But forreal, I don't understand why you so broke. You got a good job."

"My dude, I have only been a paralegal for two years. You gotta be in that shit for a lifetime just to get top pay. I'm not trying to be the assistant no more. I'm a boss who deserves boss pay. I got major debt and I need major cash…case dismissed."

He grabbed a Heineken and chips while contemplating his next move.

For the past month or so he noticed Tristan had come up. He was dressing fancier and had bought a new sound system for his Impala. He watched him kick off his special edition Jordan's and throw a wad of money on the table.

"Do you sell drugs, man? Because I don't remember you ever having this much dough. Shoe World is not blessing you like that."

Tristan wiped the sweat from his brow with his wife beater and took a deep sigh.

"I'm not so sure you'd be interested in what I do."

Hill sipped his beer. "Look, at this point I'll try anything."

Tristan took a seat on the sofa next to Hill. He hesitated at first but then went on.

"There's this guy named Chance and he works for a male escorting service."

INEVITABLE

Hill stood up.

"Yo man, I'm not down with no shit like that. I'm not gay!"

"I'm not, either. So just listen."

Hill sat on the recliner away from Tristan.

"Chance only fucks with the best. He only hooks me up with high-powered and wealthy doctors, politicians, businessmen and all kinds of rich niggas of the sort. If you ain't wealthy he ain't fucking with you."

Hill look bewildered. He had known Tristan for two years and would have never suspected he would do anything like this. Especially considering that on any given night a different chick would come through their condo.

"So, let me get this straight. You have sex with men for money?"

"Sometimes. It just depends on what they want. But for the most part, yes."

"So, how do you consider yourself to not be gay? You have sex with men. You're fucking gay dude!"

Tristan got defensive. "Look nigga, I'm not gay. I go in, strap up, usually high or drunk, do what I gotta do, get paid and leave. It's just an act. It's a job. A quick way to get money."

Hill shook his head in disbelief.

"A quick way to get money? What if you get caught or, better yet, exposed?"

"Caught or exposed doing what? What do I have to lose? I'm a nobody in the situation."

"I can't believe you have sex with men and don't consider yourself to be gay."

INEVITABLE

Tristan pulled a business card from the kitchen drawer. "Look, I'm done explaining. You said you needed help and this is my solution. Call if you want, I'm hopping in the shower."

Hill picked up the business card and stared at it. He flicked it out of his hand.

"Fuck that! I ain't gay."

***

As the weeks passed, Hill continued to drown in debt. One of the hefty loans he'd taken out during his time in law school had defaulted and he was contacted by a collections agency stating that they would soon begin garnishing his wages. He was working 50 hours a week and wasn't making a dent in his debt. The interest, alone, was killing him.

He stared at the letter on the ottoman and then at the business card Tristan had given him a few months prior. He tried to appear calm and collected around his peers but was secretly on the verge of a mental meltdown. He had hit rock bottom and couldn't see any way out of his situation. He reluctantly made the call.

"How'd you get this number?"

"My roommate, Tristan, gave it to me."

"Yes, Tristan. I know him very well."

"Look I'm in dire financial need."

"Have you ever done this type of work before?"

"No."

"So, how do you know you're qualified for the position?"

"It doesn't matter if I'm qualified or not. I need the money."

"Are you sure this is something you want to get involved with? This can sometimes be a very dangerous world."

INEVITABLE

"What is that supposed to mean?"

"Just what I said. Meet me at the address on the card at 8 tonight."

The line went dead.

As Hill drove to the location, extreme anxiety came over him. He pulled over on the side of the road. He was confused and didn't know exactly what he was doing. He placed his head on the steering wheel. He decided against it and turned around to head home.

Chance rang his phone.

"Are you on the way?"

"I'm having second thoughts. I'm not sure if I can do this."

"I told you to be sure before wasting my time. You said you were sure. Don't bitch up now."

"I can't see myself submitting to a man in that way. I love women. I adore everything about them."

Chance was getting irritated. "What does that have to do with anything? I love women, too. As a matter of fact, my wife and I are celebrating our six-year anniversary in July."

"Wh-what? You do it, too? I thought you were just the connect?"

Chance laughed loudly into the phone. "What can I say? The money ain't bad and as long as wifey is happy, I'm happy. Now get your ass over here. I've hooked you up with a lawyer who's willing to pay up to $2,000 tonight."

"What? $2,000? Are you sure?"

"Yes, I'm sure. So, make a U-turn, jump on the highway, and get the fuck over here. He's waiting on you."

-Click-

INEVITABLE

Hill drove for over an hour before arriving outside a vacant warehouse. When he pulled up Chance came out to greet him.

He got in the passenger seat and extended his hand to Hill. He reluctantly shook it.

"Look, I know you're new to this, but relax. Take this. He gave Hill two white pills. To subdue his anxiety, Hill tossed the pills back with a water he had in the car.

"Tonight, you are meeting with Axel. He owns a couple of casino's in a few different states, so he pisses cash."

"What is he going to want me to do?"

"I don't know but if you want to get paid, you'll do whatever he asks. $2,000 is the minimum he's willing to pay you."

They sat in the car for about fifteen more minutes as Chance shared with him the acts he periodically partook in and how much money he had made over the years. His wife would assume he was on a typical business trip, but it always included his secret pleasure.

A black Rolls Royce pulled up next to Hill's vehicle. Chance got out and motioned for Hill to go with the client.

They drove to an unknown hotel in silence. Hill couldn't stop thinking about what he was about to do.

"Pull over," he blurted.

"What?"

"I said pull over or I'm going to fucking throw up in your car!"

Hill barely made it two feet from the car before puking everywhere. He wiped his mouth and almost fell to his knees. Axel looked irritated and Hill knew he had a decision to make.

Hill slumped down in the seat as Axel pulled back onto the highway.

INEVITABLE

"Look, if you really don't want to do this, then don't. I would much rather give my money to someone who doesn't mind entertaining me for the night."

Hill rolled his eyes.

"How did you think I was going to feel about having sex with a man?"

"Obviously okay with it. But I guess not. Why are you doing this, anyway?"

"I'm trying to pay off some debt. Why are you in my business?"

"Because tonight I'm supposed to be your business. If you don't want to do it, I can drop you off and take my money elsewhere."

"Why do you do this?"

He took a cigar out of his pocket.

"I do it because it relaxes me."

"How can you relax with a penis in your ass?"

"Trust me. It's very relaxing."

Hill shuttered at the thought.

"So, what are you going to do, Mr. Stokes? Please me or leave me?"

He pulled out an envelope.

Hill opened it. "$5,000?"

Axel smiled. "I knew you'd change your mind."

Hill's mind raced as they continued the drive. *I cannot have sex with a man. What will my parents think of me? There's got to be another way.*

They finally arrived at a swanky hotel in the middle of nowhere.

As Hill reluctantly got out the car, he carefully took notice of Axel.

He was in his mid-forties, chiseled and attractive for an older gentleman. Hill could

INEVITABLE

tell that he was very meticulous and took extreme pride in his image.

In the hotel suite were snacks, beer, liquor, pills, and everything to else to make Hill more comfortable.

"Care for a Scotch?" he asked while making his way to the bar.

Hill nervously sat in the hotel recliner. He could see the bedroom across the way and began to feel nauseous again.

"S-sure." Hill threw back the shot and coughed.

"Slow down, champ. We got all night."

"I need another one."

For the first hour or so the two watched ESPN highlights and the news. The conversation was great and Hill was beginning to relax more and more. He felt like he was chilling with one of his homeboys.

After a while, he couldn't feel his face. He began to slowly lose control of what was going on and slumped over on the couch.

"W-what did you give me?" he slurred.

"Just something to make you relax. It's only Oxycodone."

"What? Are you going to rape me?" He tried to sit up but plopped back down.

"Just relax, novice. I got this."

Hill could hardly keep his eyes open.

Axel grabbed Hill and moved him to the bedroom. After Hill was stripped down to his underwear he stared at him in awe.

"Nice package," said Axel as he removed his drawers.

"Wait…what's going on?" Hill slurred.

"Shhh…Ima take good care of you. Trust me."

INEVITABLE

***

Hill awoke the next morning with a pounding headache and a sore derriere. He was naked and wrapped in sheets. He quickly sat up. Out the corner of his eye he could see the money on the nightstand. What had he done? He quickly dressed.

"Yo, Axel? You in there?" he bawled.

"Yea man, I ordered room service."

Hill was embarrassed. How was he supposed to interact with Axel after last night? He decided to play it cool.

Axel rolled up a blunt as he watched *The First 48*.

"About time you woke up. Check-out is in an hour."

"Cool," he mumbled as he made his way to the chair opposite of Axel.

Axel lit the weed and took a puff.

"Do you remember anything?"

"No. I don't think I even want to remember. What did you do to me?"

"Nigga, what do you think I did to you? I fucked you."

Hill's stomach cringed.

"And what did I do?"

"You let me."

Hill shook his head. He didn't believe him.

"I wasn't conscious."

Axel stood up. "Look man, don't go there. You know damn well what it is and what it was last night. You know what you signed up for."

INEVITABLE

"Did we use a condom?"

"What the fuck you think? AIDS been on the rise."

He went and retrieved the money from the nightstand and threw it in Hill's face.

"I bet you conscious now. Let's smoke this weed and go ball."

Hill couldn't deny that the money felt good. He tried to convince himself what he did was normal.

"You right," Hill agreed. "But I'm going to fuck some hoes later!" They cackled on their way to the car.

***

For the next eight months escorting became Hill's normal routine. He continued to see Axel on a regular. They became friends and hung out often. Hill finally felt comfortable enough to have sex with Axel without getting drunk or high. On top of that, Axel still paid top dollar. It was what it was. Hill had other clients but it was strictly professional. He would go in, get intoxicated, do his job, and leave. His biggest payout in one night was at an orgy in Beverly Hills. There he serviced six men for a total of $22,000. Hill decided then that it was time to get out the game.

"Are you seriously going to get out that quick man?"

"I've made plenty of money man. My bills are paid. I'm back on track. I'm good." Hill thought for a moment about his future as a respected attorney.

Tristan shook his head. "But you will miss this money though."

"Like I said, I'm in a good place and I have a nice little stash."

"It's going to run out."

"And I'm going to be an attorney real soon. Watch."

"You're going to break his heart."

INEVITABLE

Hill rolled his eyes. "What are you talking about?"

"I'm talking about Axel. You told him?"

Hill sighed. "No. But he should be good. We're homies."

Tristan chuckled. "Yeah. We'll see."

He decided to tell Axel later that night.

***

Hill strolled into the strip club around 7:30pm. He wanted to break the news to Axel in a comfortable and relaxed setting. He ordered wings and fries for the two of them. He sipped on a beer and got a lap dance until he arrived.

"Dude, the hoes in here are busted. We should've gone to the one up the street. They got better wings too."

"We here now. Get a dance and relax." Hill was ready to get it over with.

As the petite, White woman with fake breasts grinded all over Axel, Hill prepared himself for the worse.

"I'm done with the escorting, Ax. I accomplished my goal and now I'm moving on to better things."

Axel immediately dismissed the dancer and pulled his chair closer to Hill so that they could talk privately.

"What do you mean done?"

"I mean I'm not doing it anymore. I'm not having sex with men for money."

"Even me?"

Hill was taken aback.

INEVITABLE

"Yes, even you. Look, you know I never wanted to make this a lifestyle. I was only trying to make bank."

"I suppose I understand. You can run but you can't hide forever though."

"What does that mean?"

Axel shook his head. "It means that all of this will come back on you in some kind of way…and when you least expect it."

Hill finished his beer and walked out. This was a chapter of his life that he was glad to close.

INEVITABLE

Years Later…

Hill passed the bar and landed a job at Danfield & Associates as a criminal defense attorney. With an eagerness to surpass expectations and an unparalleled work ethic, he finally made partner. After receiving many awards during his nine years of service, Hill branched out and started his own firm. Stokes & Associates quickly became one of the most reputable firms in California. At 43 years of age, life was great. He had even found love. His fiancé, Victoria, was everything he wanted in a woman. She was a flight attendant supervisor and did fitness training on the side. They lived together for over a year, but Victoria was growing tired of the cramped space. While the firm was making great money, Hill wanted to make sure they were financially ready to purchase her dream home and start a family. His past financial woes forced him to become savvy with his income and outside investments.

"It's time to move honey. I mean really. There is no room for my things."

Hill sighed. "Here we go again. If you would stay out of Macy's, you wouldn't feel cramped. We will move in due time."

"It's not like we don't have the money. Why are we remaining in this shoe box? This two-bedroom townhouse is no longer big enough for the both of us."

"Because it's important to save money."

'We can save money in a house," she pouted.

He kissed her forehead.

"I want to be able to get you the mansion you deserve. But first the wedding, right?"

Victoria pinned up her hair and grabbed her gym bag.

"This is stressing me out. I need a workout fix. You coming?"

Hill declined. "I've got some paperwork I need to prepare. Do a sit-up for me."

INEVITABLE

As she departed Hill heard his phone ringing upstairs.

He was hesitant about answering as he'd seen the unfamiliar number calling for the past few days.

"Hill Stokes?"

"Yes."

"Studied law and was on the debate team?"

"Yes, who is this?"

The voice on the other end gave a greasy chortle.

"Is this the *same* Hill Stokes that served me up at the orgy fest?"

"Who the fuck is this?"

"Don't worry about all of that. I got something you might want. Meet me at the food court inside Stoneridge Mall in 30 minutes. I'll be wearing a maroon and gray hoodie." The line went dead.

What in the fuck is going on, Hill thought as he got dressed.

As he anxiously looked around the food court, a fake thug-looking male approached him.

"Wassup blood, I'm Kevin."

"I'm not here for all that shit. What is this about?"

He took a seat and pulled out an envelope. He slid it across the table.

Hill's face flushed.

'Where'd you get these?"

Kevin smacked his lips.

"You know damn well where I got those. Don't tell me you don't remember that night?"

INEVITABLE

Hill was so high and drunk that he barely remembered anything from the post-Grammy Award festivities.

"In picture number one you are performing fellatio on me. In picture number two you are banging me doggy style. And in picture number three I'm eating your-"

Onlookers glanced as Hill pounded his fists against the table interrupting the man's allegations. "Why are you doing this to me? That was years ago."

"Because I can. Now, you will put $2,500 in this account on the first and fifteenth of every month." He pushed a piece of notebook paper across the table.

The numbers on the paper became blurry to Hill as he almost fainted. "What?! I don't have that kind of money."

Kevin slid closer to Hill. "Really? You mean to tell me that Mr. Big Timer doesn't have the money. Well, we both know that's a lie. If I don't get my money, the world will see these photos. And with Facebook poppin' the way it is, I am sure it won't take long to get around."

The man angrily jumped up, pushed his chair under the table and grabbed the envelope.

"Shit!" yelled Hill.

For the next several months Hill hid the payments to Kevin from Victoria. He knew that she was getting suspicious. When a credit card statement came in the mail, while he was out of town on business, she called and confronted him.

"What's going on, Hill?"

"What do you mean?"

"I just checked our P.O. Box and I see that you opened another credit card and you have a balance - you don't carry balances. And we haven't been out since God knows when. What's going on, Hill?" She breathed heavily into the phone while praying that he wasn't keeping a secret from her. "Baby, please talk to me."

"It's nothing really," he stammered. "I'm just paying off a little debt."

"I've seen your credit report. I thought you paid off all your debt."

"Well, this is kind of a personal debt."

Victoria swallowed hard and closed her eyes. "Do you have a child?"

Hill paused before answering. "No, no nothing like that."

"Well, then what?" she inquired.

"Several years ago, I took out a loan from a friend to jump start the firm and I never paid him back."

He recently contacted me and said he needed the money.

"Oh," she mumbled. "But everything is okay?"

"Everything is okay," he lied.

***

Hill had been watching his calendar and dreaded the fact that he had to dish out yet another payment.

No longer willing to jeopardize his relationship with Victoria, he decided he'd had enough. It was time to put an end to this foolishness. Hill didn't deposit the money into Kevin's account and awaited his call.

"Are you fucking crazy, nigga?!" he bellowed. "I told you I need my money on the 15th. It's the 16th. What the fuck is going on?"

"I can't drop five g's every month. It's disrupting my lifestyle. My fiancé is starting to notice."

"Let me take care of something and I'll call you back." Kevin hung up with no argument.

INEVITABLE

Hill let out a sigh of relief. He was hoping Kevin would compromise. *$5000 a month is a lot of dough*, he thought.

Hill didn't hear back from Kevin and decided to head into the office. He didn't expect to find Victoria sitting at the table when he returned home that evening.

"Hey baby, I thought you had a class to teach tonight?"

"I cancelled it."

"What?! You never cancel class!"

"Today I had reason to. She sat the familiar envelope on the table."

Hill froze in his steps.

"Let me explain."

"I gave you a chance to explain. You weren't man enough to explain so your friend had to explain for you."

"What are you talking about?"

"This guy named Kevin came up to me before class and informed me that he had some vital information to share with me. He also told me to tell you that if you don't get him his money, everyone will see this filth."

She stood in Hill's face. "So, are you going to tell me you're gay or is it *bi-sexual*? I'm all ears, Hill."

"I'm not gay or bisexual. I just had sex with men for money. That's it. It was a long time ago, Victoria. Please…"

"That's it?" she squawked as tears rolled down her eyes.

"You didn't think for one second that I deserved to know about this **before** we got involved?"

Hill was speechless.

"Answer me, Hill!"

"I don't know what to say! What do you want me to say?"

"I want you to say that this is not you in these photos!"

"That was my past. You have to understand that I was strapped for cash at the time."

"So, now what?? We're going to go broke paying this thug hush money? That's unfair to me. Not to mention that you are **the** Hill Stokes. What if this leaks to the media? My God!"

"It was my past, Vic. I don't do those things anymore. I never thought I would do them in the first place but it is what it is. You have to accept that the man in those photos is who I used to be."

Victoria grabbed her bag. "And you have to accept who I am now. Your fucking past."

She took off her Tiffany Soleste diamond ring and calmly placed it on the table. It was all she could do to not break down in front of him.

"I'll send for my things," she sniffed as she grabbed her keys and purse and fled through the door.

***

For the next eleven months Hill tried to get back in Victoria's good graces but was rejected at every attempt. She returned her key and moved back home with her parents. It was to no avail. She had made up her mind that it was over. For quite some time Hill fell into a deep depression. He closed himself off from the world. He had no social life and threw himself into his work. He even sought the help of a psychologist to help him cope. Hill became a hermit.

Hayden beat on the door but Hill refused to answer. He knew his sister meant well but she was becoming a nuisance stopping by every week.

"I know you are in there, Hill. Let me in! I'm not leaving until you do!"

Hill trudged past his bulldog, Sage, and unlocked the door.

INEVITABLE

She barged through the door. "What is wrong with you, Hill? Mom and dad are worried sick – especially since you didn't show up for Aunt Lorraine's retirement celebration last Saturday. That's not like you. I know you're going through some shit but this is ridiculous!"

Hill stroked Sage's nose as he reclined on his sofa.

"You wouldn't understand."

"Hill, it's been almost a year since you and Victoria split. I think it's time to move on big bro."

"I am moving along as fast as I can. It's more to it than you think."

"Well help me understand, because right now, I don't."

She opened up the blinds. "It smells like dirty clothes and sorrow in here. Get it together."

Hayden and Hill were close, but she was spoiled by their parents and known to stir up occasional drama in the family and amongst her friends. He wasn't sure if he could trust her but decided to open up anyway. After he explained everything that had happened he was surprised at her calm demeanor. Hayden wasn't as successful as her brother and Hill was unaware of her own financial troubles as a result of a failed marriage.

"Wow, that's a hell of a situation you've gotten yourself into."

"Tell me about it," he muttered.

"And all this time I believed that Victoria cheated on you. I knew that couldn't be the case. She just didn't seem like the type."

"I know," Hill huffed.

"Why don't you go to the police? I'm sure they can help."

"Hell no. That's going to make it worse. Look, I'm just going to continue to pay the man."

"Pay him for how long? The rest of your life?"

INEVITABLE

Hill suddenly thought about this. He couldn't imagine paying Kevin for the rest of his life.

"I'm ready for a change, sis."

"Well then, you know what Gandhi said!" she snapped. Hill knew his only sibling was right and planned on doing something about Kevin real soon.

***

Coincidentally, a few days after the conversation with his sister, Hill received a call that both humbled and encouraged him. When he saw the private number, he knew it had to be Kevin.

"What is it man? You just got a payment last week."

"Is this Hill Stokes?" asked the unfamiliar woman.

"Yes, who is this?!"

"This is Stephanie, Kevin's ex-wife."

"What? Why are you contacting me?"

"I'm contacting you to inform you that any debt you owed to Kevin is void."

"How? Why? What in the hell is going on?"

"Kevin recently found out that he has AIDS. I guess he's trying to get into Heaven or something. He was in a car accident a couple of years ago and had a blood transfusion. From what he told me, the doctors believe that's how he contracted it."

Hill was dumbfounded.

"Wait, how do I know this won't come back to haunt me?"

Stephanie smacked her lips.

"Look, I'm only trying to help him sort out his financial affairs as a courtesy. If you would like to continue paying up, I don't have a problem with you giving the money to me."

"No, I hear you loud and clear."

Hill hung up the phone and sat in complete shock. He wondered if it was true about Kevin's blood transfusion but quickly brushed it off. He felt bad that Kevin had contracted the disease but was glad he wouldn't be tapping his pockets anymore. He called and told Hayden the good news.

"Thank, God!" she sighed. Little did Hill know that Hayden would later use his past against him for her own selfish gain.

Hill immediately began planning his exit strategy to leave California. He had already flown to Texas and Atlanta to check out office spaces and finally decided that the latter would offer the most opportunity for his budding firm. He gradually came out of his slump and moved forward with life full speed. He was an attractive, successful Black man, and was determined to find love - no matter what. His sister even agreed to help him get settled in Atlanta. As Hill packed up his office he trolled the internet for the best lawyers in the city. He wanted to get a few networking contacts if need be. When he stumbled across Giselle's profile, he was in awe. He researched everything there was to know about her.

Now this is wifey material, he said to himself. *I've got to find out who this woman is.*

Hill was jolted from his thoughts as Giselle shook his arm.

19

"Hill, I can't believe you're ignoring me. Snap out of it and answer my question. Who was he?"

Giselle noticed two officers board the flight and move quickly towards Elicia.

"Gabriel Lowe. You're under arrest for the attempted murder of Nasir Harrison. We need to take you down to the station for questioning."

Elicia went into shock. "OH-MY-GOD!!" she yelled. "This has got to be a mistake! My husband is in a coma."

"Not as of last night. He was able to tell us who set the building on fire."

She looked at Gabe. "Gabe!" she sobbed. "What's going on? Please talk to me!"

He said nothing. The officers cuffed him and began to swiftly remove him from the plane.

He sadly glanced back at Elicia as they ushered him down the narrow aisle towards the gate. He didn't mean to be the newest source of Elicia's pain, but the Nasir situation had literally pushed him over the edge. As Gabe trudged through the airport, in handcuffs, he vaguely remembered what had taken place months ago. Passengers whispered to each other in the hopes of finding out what was going on. Some even came to the front of the plane and asked. The captain got on the PA system:

"We are preparing to depart Atlanta in approximately ten minutes everyone. No worries. We had a situation that is now under control. Please return to your seats. Sit back and relax as we prepare for takeoff."

Elicia began to hyperventilate while clutching her heaving chest. "I can't go…Jesus…what is happening…I have to know what's going on with Gabe." She grabbed her carry-on and rushed off the plane.

INEVITABLE

Giselle and Marley knew they couldn't leave their friend alone and followed. As they sped down the terminal, Giselle could not fathom what had transpired in such a short period of time.

"What in the hell is going on with you?" Marley asked as she studied Giselle's damp face.

Trey and Hill moved as quickly as they could with the heavy luggage to the car rental area.

Giselle suddenly came out of her trance. "I have...!" She sobbed as she grabbed her friend. Marley squeezed her tightly.

"Wh- what??? Look, hey, don't cry. We're going to get through this...whatever it is. Okay?" Marley chose to not press the issue as too much was going on and she was trying hard to not break down herself. All she could think about was her daughter.

While Giselle found her words to be comforting, it didn't alleviate the loneliness she felt. They waited in silence until Trey and Hill pulled up in a rental car.

Marley's phone buzzed as they were getting in. "Elicia texted and said she's decided to head to the hospital to be with Nasir. Let's go!"

Hill held Giselle's hand in the back seat as they raced to Atlanta Medical. They arrived to find Elicia in the waiting area on the third floor. Her eyes were red and she looked older than her 36 years.

"Are you okay? Can we get you anything?"

"No," she said as she stared off into space.

"Have you seen Nasir?"

"Not yet, they're changing his bandages before I go in. They said it'll be at least another half hour or so."

Giselle grabbed her hand.

INEVITABLE

"We're all here for you, sweetie. Know that." She glanced around the waiting area and noticed Hill in deep thought.

She walked over to him and tapped his shoulder. "What's wrong? You've been acting funny since we boarded that plane."

"I've just got a lot on my mind."

"Tell me about it," she lamented. She shook her head.

"We will get through this, **together**. But I do have something to say. With all this shit happening and the fact that I've fallen in love with you, I don't want us to go on any further with secrets."

She noticed his tone change and searched his eyes for answers.

"I'm not proud of some of the things I've done in my past. And before it surfaces in any kind of unpleasant way I want to tell you about it."

Giselle became uneasy. "Should we go somewhere private?" She was beginning to worry.

"Yes, we should."

They walked to the Emergency parking lot and settled inside the rental.

"So, what's this all about?" Giselle's heart rate was increasing with every breath she took.

Hill cleared his throat. "Before I tell you I just want you to know that I care a lot for you. More than my career. More than my material possessions. You mean everything to me and you make me better."

Giselle frowned. She felt her face getting hot.

"Many years ago, right after law school, I fell on hard times. I was broke, couldn't pay my bills and was looking for a quick way to make money. I worked my ass off as a paralegal until I was introduced to the world of escorting."

INEVITABLE

Giselle let go of his hand. "What? What are you talking about, Hill?"

He hung his head.

"Hill, answer me now. What are you talking about?"

"I used to sleep with people for money."

"You used to sleep with people for money?" she repeated as though she'd heard him wrong.

She shook her head in disgust. "How many?"

He rubbed his hands together. "Probably around thirty."

"You slept with thirty women? For money? I don't understand." The car suddenly felt extremely small to Giselle and she couldn't breathe comfortably.

He scratched his head. "Thirty encounters…with men."

At that very moment, time suspended and Giselle's entire world came crumbling down like a demolished building. Her vision became foggy and her head felt like two tons of weight. She could faintly hear Hill's voice in the distance, but couldn't respond. She tried to scream but suddenly everything became dark.

"Baby, please wake up! Wake up!" Hill immediately called Trey.

"Giselle has passed out. We're in the parking lot. Bring a doctor!"

In minutes, paramedics rolled out with a stretcher with Trey and Marley running close behind. Marley swung the car door open.

"Giselle! Giselle!" She grabbed her hand. "What the fuck is going on, Hill?" As paramedics moved Marley out the way and hoisted Giselle onto the stretcher, she began shoving Hill in his chest.

"What happened to her?! What did you do?!"

INEVITABLE

Trey grabbed Marley and placed her behind him. "Marley, you gotta chill out," he said firmly.

Hill brushed past them both to follow the paramedics.

Marley paced back and forth.

"He needs to tell me what happened to her! Now, Trey! She was just fine a few minutes ago!" Trey tried to keep up with Marley as she stormed into the hospital's emergency area. Once they'd found Giselle's temporary room she was already starting to come to. Hill stood over her, sobbing, as she tried to focus.

INEVITABLE

Shattered

INEVITABLE

20

Despite every obstacle, she had faced in her life, Giselle was somehow always able to bounce back. But this time was different. She couldn't seem to bear the weight of her friends' tumultuous relationships, her failing health and now the revelation of Hill's seedy past. She closed her eyes as tears started to well at the corners. In her bedroom, where she had been for the past eight days, she lay on her back resting...something she hadn't done in years. She reached for her VOSS water and a bottle of Imuran prescribed by her doctor to ease the Lupus flair ups. Cigarettes would no longer be enough to calm her unravelling nerves. She felt as though she'd lost complete control of her own happiness - the very thing she'd fought so hard to protect.

Giselle blocked Hill's number and tried to pretend like he never existed. The white walls were starting to close in on her as she was growing tired of the isolation. She longed for solace and a change of scenery. After showering and checking her stock pile of mail, she packed an overnight bag, fueled up, and jumped on Interstate 20. Taking a drive would be what she needed to clear her head. She lit a clove as Mary J. Blige glared from the speakers. After driving for three hours, she finally came upon familiar roads. She sighed as she unsuccessfully tried to dodge the potholes that masked the two-way streets. The shoddy neighborhood still looked the same. The peeling paint on the shotgun houses, messy yards with broken appliances and litter from weekend barbeques painted a picture Giselle knew all too well. She waved at the nosey neighbors who sat around drinking in the hot sun and pressed the gas harder as her Benz climbed the rocky pathway to her parent's trailer. Gerrod had shared that they were considering buying a three-bedroom ranch with the monthly stipend she'd been sending them for the past six years. *"Thank God,"* she muttered to herself. She sat in the car for fifteen minutes before walking up the rickety steps.

She wrinkled up her nose. The stench of musky beer and rotting flesh of dead rodents filled the air. Glancing at the back woods, she envisioned her childhood all too well. She tapped lightly on the screen door. Giselle watched her dad slowly trudge across the kitchen and through the front room. He had aged and his hair was near gone. She suddenly felt guilty for not keeping in better contact. He slowly opened the door.

"Ger...Giselle? What'chu doin' here?" His southern roots were evident in his drawl.

She half-heartedly gave her dad a hug and let herself in. She looked around the trailer and not much had changed. The same gold and green shabby furniture, that was covered in plastic, still was an eyesore. The lamps that Giselle and Gerrod constantly knocked over playing tag football in the house were taped up and sat like permanent statues on the end tables. She put her hands in her pockets and faced her father.

"You all say I never come home, so...here I am." She shrugged her shoulders.

He stared at her in disbelief. "I'm glad you here. It's been years."

"I know, Dad. I know. Look, where's mom?"

"She at work. She won't be home for another hour or so. Sit here. I'll warm you some tea."

She glanced around the double-wide trailer while he shuffled in the kitchen.

Giselle smiled. She remembered him doing this for her as a kid. He would always add just the right amount of sugar and honey to his special concoction. He adjusted the volume on the TV then handed her the same Transformers mug she used to drink out of at every meal.

As Giselle sipped her tea, her father looked her up and down. An awkward silence flooded the room.

"Ya...ya...look great," he stammered. "I like that car out there! I bet it feels real nice ridin' in somethin' that fancy."

"Thanks." Giselle was starting to feel lightheaded.

He glared at her again. This time as if he was staring right through her.

INEVITABLE

"You know ah, ah mean we, haven't seen ya since ya trip – only pictures that Gerrod sends us from time to time on these here *not-so-smart* phones." He chuckled to himself as he fumbled with the iPhone that Giselle had sent him two Christmases ago.

Giselle shook her head as she looked away.

"Seems life's been treating ya good."

"It has. It truly has."

"Yo' brother told us you finally made partner. I am so proud of the…ah I mean who you done become."

Giselle's obvious nervousness set in. "Do you mind if I go outside for a minute?"

Gerald grinned, showing his too-perfect dentures. "You can smoke in here if you like."

"No way! Not the way mom went off on me that time!"

They both exchanged a light-hearted laugh as she stepped outside on the front porch.

Giselle took three puffs and threw her head against the door as she tried to gather what she wanted to say. She rubbed her temples while the smoke swirled between her manicured fingertips. She stood there replaying the chain of events that had unfolded over the past couple of weeks. She wondered what Hill was doing at this very moment. Before she could get too lost in her thoughts, Grace pulled up in a 2002 Honda Civic. Her mother, much like her dad, looked very tired. She got out of the car and walked towards Giselle as though she was fixated in a trance. She stood at the bottom of the trailer steps and stared at Giselle.

"I can't believe it," she said as she almost dropped her grocery bags.

"I been asking God to send you this way for years. And today he answered my cries."

INEVITABLE

Giselle took another toke and put the cigarette out. She grabbed one of the bags from Grace.

"Still smokin' those nasty things, I see."

She rolled her eyes to the sky.

"Come on in. I'll fix you something to eat, baby." She gave her daughter a long, tight hug.

So many memories flooded Giselle's mind as she roamed the humble surroundings she'd grown up in. Her and Gerrod's room still had their twin beds situated with a small, wooden nightstand in the middle. A twinge of joy overcame her when she spotted the numerous accolades they'd won over the years for being high achievers. She ran her thumb across the engraved name on one of the trophies. Giselle flopped down on her bed and shut her eyes. As she let out a deep sigh she heard a quiet knock at the door.

"I warmed up some leftovers if you hungry. Fried chicken, greens, butter beans, yams and cornbread. Oh, and of course your favorite, vanilla ice-cream for dessert."

"No, thanks," she murmured. "I haven't eaten like that in years, ma."

She threw her dishtowel over her shoulder. "Oh, that's right, chile. You live in the big A-T-L now. Y'all be eatin' on them real fancy white plates with two string beans and a meatball on it. Now what kinda eatin' is that?!" She chuckled to herself.

Giselle cracked a smiled as the tension thickened. She sat on Gerrod's bed.

"So, what brings you all the way out here from the city? I raised you and I know you like the back of my hand. What's goin' on with you? Is something wrong?" Her mother stood inside the doorway with her hands on her hips.

She knew this might be the first and last time she'd bring the subject up, but she needed to understand her mother's reasoning all those years ago.

INEVITABLE

"How did you do it?"

"Do what?"

"Take Dad back after he slept with Miss Emma. I mean, she was your friend and was in this house almost every Sunday breaking bread with us and the whole time you didn't know what was going on between them. How? And then you forgave them in front of the whole church?" Giselle searched her mother's eyes for answers.

Grace reached down and adjusted her house shoe. "Because I loved your father. I still do."

"Well, I think it's crazy that you took him back after what he did."

"Giselle, it wasn't your decision to make." Her mother decided to rest on the bed next to her.

"He damn near destroyed our family. He hurt you! You didn't leave the house for two months because everybody was talking. And then the fighting…all I did was hear you cry yourself to sleep every night…" Her eyes began to well.

"And I prayed! I PRAYED! Remember that if you don't remember nothin' else about what happened between me and yo' father. When I shed those tears, I asked God to help me forgive him for his transgressions because, in my heart, I knew that he was a good man and provider. Yes, it took me a long while to cope with the messiness of it all…but I did. Everybody makes mistakes, and everybody has a past. Including you."

Giselle wiped the hot tears as they fell from her burning eyes and her mother's words stung her to the core.

"I know I never told you this, mom, but I admire you so much. I know you thought that Aunt Gigi was my world…and she was. But you? You are my universe. I will never be able to repay you enough. I send you the money because you deserve every bit of it." Giselle stiffened as she watched her father walk into the room and stand behind Grace.

INEVITABLE

"I'm sorry, Giselle. I'm sorry for what I did."

Giselle stared at the dark circles under his eyes. She shook her head as still couldn't bring herself to forgive him.

"Why daddy, why?" she passionately asked. "And with the pastor's wife? You embarrassed us. Why?!"

He shifted his hands in his overall pockets. "I was tryin' to deal with you the best way I could. Stress got da best of me."

"How dare you try to place blame??! You control what's in your pants. Not me!" she yelled.

Grace settled next to her on the bed and grabbed her hand. "Giselle, eventually your father and I sat down with Sister Emma and Pastor Norman."

Giselle stretched her neck in shock. "What?! Sat down for what? He cheats and you all decide to have a family reunion? She used to come over every Sunday and eat with us. I used to play with their daughter."

Grace knew that Giselle was upset but needed her to understand that true love requires forgiveness.

She shook her head in disgust. "And all the while she was fucking my father."

"Now you watch yo' mouf in this house! I made a mistake!" Her father's voice roared through the quiet trailer.

"What was I supposed to do? No, really, talk to me! What would you do if yo' child didn't know who dey wanted to be? And, my God, what that bastard William did to you was unforgiveable." He sighed and hung his head at the thought.

Giselle took a deep breath as a tear rolled down her cheek. She closed her eyes and opened them back up to the summer of **1991…**

INEVITABLE

21

Innocence Lost

"I want you to meet my honey, William." said Aunt Gigi as she sashayed around the room. William smiled bright and said, "the pleasure's all mines lil' fella," as he swigged on his whiskey. He stumbled and landed in the living room chair. Gerald stood in front of him and extended his hand.

William smiled sheepishly. "A man can tell a lot about you by the way you shake his hand." He tightly squeezed Gerald Junior's hand, and at that moment, he could hear his own father's voice reminding him to keep a firm grip and look every man he encounters square in the eyes. Gerald inhaled the older man's pungent scent of cigars and whiskey before looking away. He had never seen or met a man like William. He was a few inches taller than his dad and his cold, drunken stare somewhat frightened him. His stature was intimidating and the dark rings around his eyes and long fingers made Gerald take a few steps back from him. Yet, and still Gerald was curious to get to know him. As William turned the bottle up to his mouth again, he breathed harder with each swallow. His gold tooth shimmered with every swig. Gerald took a seat on the couch and turned on the television while watching his aunt out the corner of his eye.

Aunt Gigi re-adjusted her robe and sat on William's lap. He took his hand and squeezed her right breast, ignoring the fact that Gerald was in the room. Aunt Gigi tapped his hand. "Did you bring my catfish? I've been waiting to fry it all day. And where are my lottery tickets? Today might be my lucky day."

He grabbed the tickets out of his hip pocket. "You ain't won the lottery in all the time I've known you. Can't you see I'm trying to get to know the boy. The fish in the car. Go ahead and get it."

Gigi mumbled under her breath as she put on her house slippers.

William stared at Gerald as he watched Scooby Doo on television. It made Gerald uneasy and he was relieved when Gigi returned. The bin was so heavy she could only carry it to the door. She frowned upon opening the thermal container.

"And who's going to clean them? I said I'd cook them, not clean them."

INEVITABLE

"I'll clean them," Gerald volunteered.

"No, you won't," William blurted. "That's a woman's job," he sternly said. He staggered over to Gerald and got in his face.

"You ain't a woman, are ya?" he slurred.

"No, sir," he muttered.

William watched Gigi carry the fish bin over to the sink, struggling with every step. "Have you ever been fishing?"

Gerald shook his head.

"Well maybe I can take you one day. You got a fishing rod?"

Gerald shook his head again.

William reached for his wallet, almost spilling his whiskey. He handed Gerald sixty dollars.

"Head on over to Simmons to get you one and I'll take ya."

Gerald hadn't ever been fishing and wasn't sure he wanted to go with William.

"If he goes, you can't be taking this with you," said Gigi as she took the bottle out his hand.

He turned a cold stare on her. "Gimme my drank, woman. I'm not doing nothin' wrong."

"You've had enough William, save some for tomorrow."

As she twisted on the top, he snatched the bottle out of her hand.

"I told you I was fine."

Gigi didn't respond.

"Take the boy to get a fishing rod. I'll be back by tomorrow night." He stood up and headed to the door.

INEVITABLE

"What about dinner?" Gigi pleaded.

"I ain't hungry no more." He slammed the screen door as he left.

"Was he drunk?" asked Gerald as he stared at his aunt.

She sighed. "Not really. He's much worse when he's drunk."

He went and stood near the bin. "I can protect you from him, ya know."

She half laughed. "William wouldn't hurt a fly."

"Has he ever hurt you?" he asked in a concerned tone.

"Never, sweetie," she reassuringly answered. Gerald didn't know whether to believe her or not.

***

William came by the next day and the next. Gerald had been studying him carefully and decided that William wasn't that bad to be around. As long as he didn't drink, he was actually as cool as a cucumber.

"And where are you two going today? You've been spending quite a bit of time together. He's only here for a few more weeks."

"Hush up woman," William replied. "He's not supposed to be up under no woman all the time anyway."

Gigi sucked her teeth. "I'm not just any woman. I'm his favorite aunt."

Gerald noticed a hint of jealousy in her tone. He ran and locked arms with her.

"Don't be mad, Aunt Gigi. He kissed her on the cheek. I'll spend all day with you tomorrow."

She jokingly rolled her eyes. "Okay," she huffed.

"Let's go youngin," said William as he picked up his fishing rod. Gerald grabbed his newly purchased rod and trailed right behind him. Aunt Gigi was right. For the past few days William spent seemingly every moment of spare time he had with Gerald. Despite their first encounter, Gerald didn't mind. He was always used to competing with Gerrod for their dad's attention. Having someone to finally focus solely on him and not his brother was great. And while he'd only known him for a week, Gerald felt as if he had known him forever. Besides the fishing rod, William had given him $30 cash and bought him two games for his gaming system. Gerald had to admit that it felt good not to have to compete for attention. He, for once, felt accepted and wasn't constantly criticized for not taking an interest in sports and girls. He thought about his twin Gerrod in that moment and realized he hadn't talked to him since he'd been in Atlanta. He made a mental note to call him later to tell him about his fishing trip. He hopped in the green pick-up truck and fastened his seat belt.

"Where are we going besides fishing?"

"You'll see," said William as he turned up his radio. "Love will make you do wrong," he bellowed with the radio. Gerald shook his head at his off-pitch tone.

They made it to the local grocery store in record time. Unlike the country, everything was within a one-mile in proximity. William pushed a cart and had Gerald grab the things they would need.

He gave William a shady look once he picked up a twelve-pack of beer.

William shook his head. "You just like your aunt."

"That stuff's not good for you. You shouldn't drink it," he adamantly retorted.

William stopped the cart. "Have you ever had beer?"

Gerald shook his head. "You know Aunt Gigi would kill me."

"And your Aunt Gigi ain't here," he snapped back. Gerald dropped his head.

They drove for about 30 miles and Gerald was relieved to hear the incessant chatter about William's new job stop. They pulled up to the camping site and William punched in a code on the key pad. As the boom gate rose Gerald had a weird feeling come over him.

"We're going camping, too?" he asked as he began to read the signs.

INEVITABLE

"Of course, we going camping. That's what people do when they go fishing." They finally found a spot and William jumped out the truck.

He stood in the middle of the campsite and took in the scenery.

"God is something else, ain't he? Grab those two chairs out the back."

Gerald quickly made his way to the back of the truck and struggled to pull the lawn chairs out by himself. After setting them up, William removed the cooler, snacks, and portable television.

"It's hot out here, William. I need something to drink." It was 94 degrees out and Gerald's throat was dry and scratchy. His pants stuck to his thighs and he could feel the sweat slowly trickling down.

William wiped his brow. "Grab something to drink," he said.

Gerald opened the cooler. "Where's the water? Or juice?"

"Boy, those drinks are for sissies. Grab you a beer. You'll be fine." He pulled his whiskey flask from his pocket.

Gerald looked apprehensive. "No thanks." He sat down and stared at William.

William could see the sweat seeping through Gerald's pants.

"When are we going fishing? It's gonna be dark soon," he retorted. He was becoming irritated.

"Just relax, son."

"I can't relax!" he exclaimed. "It's hot as hell out here and you don't have any water. Like, what am I supposed to drink?"

William leaned forward in his chair. "Now you watch yo' mouth boy! I told you to grab a beer. We'll get water once we head over to the lake."

Gerald grabbed some ice cubes from the cooler, instead, and tossed them in his mouth. He sucked on them so fervently they disappeared in silence. William tossed him a bag of Lay's chips.

INEVITABLE

William removed his shoes and socks and wiggled his toes. "Ooh, ooh, that breeze feels good on my feet!" he exclaimed.

"What breeze?" Gerald muttered. He wondered if the sun was getting to William's head.

After watching baseball for about an hour or so, Gerald was ready to leave.

"William, I appreciate everything, but I'm ready to go. I'm hot and I'm getting tired, sir."

By this time William was clearly inebriated. He was slumped over in his chair. "You not enjoying this boy? We havin' a good time."

"No! You're having a good time. I'm hot, sticky, and hungry. I'm ready to go."

William leaned forward. "So, you'd rather be up under yo' aunt cooking and cleaning rather than doing what real men do?"

Gerald's eyes got wide. "No, sir."

"Yes you do. You'd rather spend yo' summer up under a woman than at football camp like your brother. I come along and show you what it's like to be a real man and you don't even appreciate it."

Gerald was furious. Several of his male classmates teased him constantly about the fact that he kept to himself and stayed in the library, even during lunch. Gerrod would always have to come to save him from potential fights.

He stood up and began to walk away from William.

"Where are you going, boy?"

"I'm going home. You make me sick."

He began to walk faster as tears streamed down his eyes. William called his name three times before he stopped.

"Come back here boy. I'm not going to chase you."

INEVITABLE

Gerald angrily spun around in the mixture of gravel and red clay in the road.

"NO!" he yelled and took off running.

William sprung up as fast as he could and ran after him. The ground was burning his bare feet as he trudged towards him. When he finally caught up he tackled Gerald to the ground.

"What..are..you..doing?" William panted. "It's too hot out here to be doing all this running."

He squirmed as he tried to loosen his grip.

"Get off of me! You're heavy!"

"Not until you get back down to the truck."

"Get off of me!" he yelled again.

William loosened his grip and picked him up. He threw him over his shoulders like a sack of potatoes. It happened so fast that Gerald didn't even have a chance to object. William trudged back to his truck and dropped Gerald in the chair.

His chest heaved up and down as he reached into the cooler and shoved a beer in his hand.

"Now, drink it." William demanded. Gerald popped the top and guzzled the bitter drink until he was done.

William grinned as he relaxed in his chair. "That's it. See, there's nothin' wrong with a little beer." He headed over to the back of the truck and grabbed a bucket of Kentucky Fried Chicken that he had hidden under a blanket.

"Man, William, you had food all this time and you didn't say anything?!"

"I'm trying to teach you how to be a man. You gotta tough it out sometimes, son. The world ain't gonna hand nothin' to you. You gotta be willing to work for it."

INEVITABLE

Gerald reached in and grabbed a wing. After a while he was feeling more relaxed and the sun didn't bother him. He laughed out loud as he licked his greasy fingers.

"This is good!" he exclaimed. He stood up and started dancing to a commercial on television.

William watched him, amused at the sight.

Gerald suddenly began to feel dizzy and collapsed in the chair.

"You alright?" asked William as he scuttled to grab a bottle of water from his hidden stash in the back of the truck.

Gerald shook his head in disbelief at receiving the water that William claimed not to have. "You're tough, William, but I love you."

William turned and faced him.

"What are you talking about boy?"

"I wish you were my dad. You don't judge me like he does.

In that moment William's demeanor changed.

"Are you serious, boy?"

"Yes. Yes, I am."

"Well, I guess I took a liking to you because you remind me of my nephew."

"I didn't know you had a nephew. Where is he?"

"He's with my sister. They stay over there in Hoover. Haven't seen him in about two years."

"Why?"

"Long story. My sister is angry with me still."

He stared off for a moment.

INEVITABLE

"You shouldn't ever fight with family. That's all you got."

"Yea. But it's a little deeper than that. Let's head on over to the lake. It's cooled off a bit now and I bet the fish are biting."

Gerald was still feeling a little buzzed but went along to prove to William that he could tough it out like a man.

Once they made it to the lake William showed Gerald how to bait his hook and cast his line. They waited for about 40 minutes and Gerald's line finally tugged. William immediately dropped his rod and stood behind Gerald as he helped him reel in his prize.

"I did it! I did it!" he screamed as they reeled it in.

"It's a big one boy!" yelled William. "I knew I was gon' have to help you. Looked like the fish was gonna pull you in the water!" He grabbed the fish by the tail as it flopped about wildly. They both howled as he tried to pull the hook out of the fish's lips. He then grabbed pliers and a disgorger to remove it. He high-fived Gerald and smiled with his gold tooth glistening in the sun.

As they rode home that night, Gerald felt proud of his big catch and couldn't wait to tell Gerrod. He was somewhat starting to feel like himself again accompanied by a pounding headache.

"Don't tell your aunt about today."

"I hadn't planned on it. Besides, she'd kill me if she knew."

Aunt Gigi wasn't home once they arrived, later that evening, so William let them in with his key. He found a note taped to the refrigerator. He balled it up after reading it.

"I don't know why she works herself to death. I told her I was going to take care of her once I got my settlement."

Gerald didn't understand what he meant and didn't ask. He headed to the spare bedroom, stripped down to his shorts, and climbed in the bed. William flopped on the couch and turned on the television. He decided to wait for Gigi. He needed his sexual desire to be appeased. He took off his boots and pants and stretched out comfortably on the couch. William replayed what Gerald told him over and over in his mind.

INEVITABLE

"He loves me," he said to himself as his hand made its way inside of his boxers. He stroked himself and stopped. He quickly sat up. William went to the refrigerator and grabbed a beer. He guzzled it and slammed the can down on the table. Before he knew it, he found himself at Gerald's door. He knocked softly but there was no response. He inched the door open and found Gerald lightly snoring with his back turned towards the door.

He stood in middle of the dark room. The walls began to cave in and there was a loud ringing in his ears. He turned to head back out the door. Before he left he glanced at Gerald again. All he could hear was Gerald telling him that he loved him. He put his hand on the door knob and slowly pulled it away. In an instant he found himself standing over Gerald watching him sleep again. He wiped the sweat from his brow. He pulled back the covers and laid behind him. Gerald tussled a bit but didn't wake up. William tried to control his heavy breathing. He heard the loud ringing in his ears again but chose to ignore it. Suddenly the front door slammed. William jumped out of the bed and pretended to come from the bathroom.

"Hey, my sweet lady," he cooed as he grabbed Gigi's bag. "Come sit down and let me rub your feet." Gigi was delirious and agreed. As William propped her feet on his lap, Gerald entered the room rubbing his eyes.

"Hey sweetie," Gigi said as she smiled weakly. "How was fishing today?"

Gerald looked at William then the ground. "It was fun. I caught a big catfish," he muttered.

He walked over and kissed Gigi on the cheek. William's eyes followed his every move. "Good night. I'm getting some water then going back to sleep."

William breathed a sigh of relief once he'd gotten a glass of water from the kitchen then disappeared. He continued to rub Gigi's feet and both relocated to her bedroom to fulfill his desires.

Over the next few weeks, Aunt Gigi noticed that Gerald's and William's relationship had become more and more mysterious.

INEVITABLE

Gerald seemed withdrawn. It was as if his personality changed overnight. His demeanor was strange and he didn't speak as much. She sensed that something was wrong and didn't like the uneasy feeling in her gut. She was determined to find out what was going on. Gerald bounced the ball through the kitchen as he made his way out the door to shoot hoops on his homemade basketball court.

Gigi stuck her head out the door.

"Come back in for a sec, sweetie. We need to catch up." Gerald squinted at his aunt, trying not to look directly at the sun.

He tried for another three and missed before entering the living room. He looked at her strange as he made his way to the couch. She tossed him a fruit roll up.

"So, what's been going on? You're leaving me tomorrow and I know that I've been working a lot lately. You haven't said hardly two words to me in over a week. What's going on?"

Gerald stared at the floor as he slowly unraveled the candy from the wrapping.

"What's going on?" she repeated, this time with more angst.

"Nothing," he mumbled.

She took a seat next to him on the couch and grabbed his face.

"I know you, Gerald. Now what's wrong."

In that instance, a single tear slowly streamed down his face. She wrapped her arms around him.

"You can tell me, sweetie," she said as she rocked him.

Gerald sobbed profusely and could barely catch his breath. She turned him towards her.

"Tell me what's going on, child." she demanded.

"Promise me you won't tell anyone," he whispered.

INEVITABLE

"I won't," she lied.

As Gerald told the harrowing story of how William stole his innocence, he watched his aunt's face go from concern to disgust.

"I'll kill him!" she screamed as she jumped up from the couch sobbing uncontrollably.

His aunt stormed into her bedroom and paced the floor while spewing profanity every ten seconds as she tried earnestly to keep from having a nervous breakdown in front of her nephew. She swooped Gerald up and squeezed him tight.

"I'm sorry! I'm sorry! I'm sorry!" she screamed over and over again. They sat in silence holding each other. Twenty minutes later, William pulled up in his truck.

"Wipe your face." She took a few dollars from her coin purse and gave it to him. "Go on and get some ice cream from the store. Go now!"

"No, Aunt Gigi! You can't tell him!" he pleaded as he held onto her waist.

"I won't!" she whispered harshly. "Now go on."

Gerald did as his aunt instructed and headed out the door. He watched William step out his truck and light a cigar before going inside.

"Hey boy," he uttered going up the steps. Gerald didn't respond.

He found Gigi on her couch, in deep, quiet thought.

"Hey, sweet cakes!" he said while kissing her on the cheek. She flinched away.

"What's wrong with you?"

"No, the question is, what in the hell is wrong with you?!" She stood in his face demanding an answer.

"How dare you fucking rape my nephew, William. How dare you!!" she screamed.

INEVITABLE

William cocked back his hand and knocked her to the ground striking her jaw with his diamond picky ring. "Don't you ever disrespect me like that another day in yo' life woman! I've done nothing to him!" He turned and lit a cigar again.

Stunned, Gigi licked the blood from the corner of her mouth and grabbed her cheek. Immediately she sprang from the floor and jumped on his back. She punched him in his face and continued to swing wildly until he knocked her to the floor.

"I told you I ain't touched that boy." William ran out to his truck and came back with a hammer. Gigi backed herself in a corner, scared for her life. Gerald heard the tussle from outside and ran in to find him hovered over her with the hammer. Gigi's eyes pleaded with her nephew. Gerald watched William attempt to strike her three times before she grabbed a knife and stabbed him in the shoulder with it. Once he fell to the ground, Gerald helped his aunt up and both ran out the door. He watched the blood trickle down her face as they scrambled across the lawn to the neighbor's house for help. It was that day that Gerald became a man.

For years Gerald unsuccessfully dealt with the trauma of his experience with William and witnessing his aunt almost being murdered over trying to protect him. He finally sought counseling, during his sophomore year in college, and accepted that he identified as a woman. Maybe it was his hatred for William or maybe his undying love for his aunt, but somehow that summer ultimately shaped him and his true identity. When Gerald confessed to his aunt, that he wanted to be a woman, she was neither shocked nor surprised.

"Some things are just inevitable, sweetie," she responded with tears of both sadness and joy streaming from her eyes.

***

The torn family held each other, in the tiny bedroom, releasing the anguish they'd all been harboring over the past twenty-something years. Giselle had never witnessed her father like this before and realized just how broken he had become over their troubled past.

INEVITABLE

"I think I'ma take a walk to calm my nerves," Gerald said as he exited the room.

Giselle's mother turned to her, "So, will we get to meet him?"

"Gerrod told you?" Giselle suddenly felt tired and realized she needed to take her medication.

"Chile, you know that boy can't hold nothin'. Yes, we know about Hill."

Giselle shifted her weight on the bed. "I don't think I can answer that question right now. I'm still trying to figure it all out myself. Here I was just living my life, not thinking that I would ever fall in love, and one night he calls me out of the blue saying that he'd been researching me. I was shocked but flattered at the same time. No one has ever pursued me like that. But, if he'd dug deep enough, we certainly wouldn't have gotten this far." She felt a hollowness in her chest.

"Well, baby, that's water under the bridge now. Do you love him?" her mother asked with compassion.

"I care for him deeply although I never imagined I'd feel this way about someone considering…"

"Then you know what to do. Take all the time you need, baby." Grace left the room, quietly, closing the door behind her.

Giselle walked to the dresser and picked up a photo of her and Gerrod wearing matching overalls and long-sleeved striped shirts – except Gerrod's was blue and green and hers was navy blue and purple. She was the older twin born at 7:43am with her brother entering the world shortly after at 7:47am. She went to the window and stared out into the yard at their old tire swing remembering the times they'd shared before her transition. Although she and her brother had always been close, her aunt was the first person to be introduced to "Giselle"…

INEVITABLE

22

The Reveal

Giselle's hands trembled with trepidation as she bent down to retrieve the spare key from under the mat and unsteadily let herself inside Aunt Gigi's apartment. Her long flight from Puerto Rico had given her jet lag. Her body was sore and she simply wanted to crawl into her aunt's bed and rest. She had promised that she would wait up for her until she got off work. After all, today was the day that she would finally be free. It had been a little over a year since she had seen her aunt and she was filled with angst and excitement as she wondered what reaction her new look would reveal. Giselle glanced at the clock and yawned. "Two more hours", she sighed as she headed to the bathroom to freshen up her new hair and makeup. After flipping through the channels for about thirty minutes, Giselle loosened her bra strap and lay down on the couch. The minute she closed her eyes she was awakened by the sound of keys jingling at the door. She jumped up.

"Don't come in yet! I have to give you the full presentation." Giselle made sure the chain lock was secure to keep her aunt from entering too soon.

"Once I unlock the door, wait ten seconds and then have a seat on the sofa."

Aunt Gigi sounded giddy on the other side of the door. "Okay, hurry up! I haven't seen my baby in forever!"

Giselle removed the door chain and rushed to the bedroom. Once she heard the door slam she prepared herself for her big reveal.

"Okay, I'm ready!" she said with great anticipation. Giselle took a deep breath and slowly entered the living room. Her aunt's eyes widened at the sight of her. She placed her hand over her mouth as she watched Giselle twirl in her purple sundress. She almost lost her balance in her stiletto heels but gained control before falling.

"So, what do you think?"

Aunt Gigi, holding her chest at this point, stared at her former nephew in amazement. I think you look amazing," she bellowed. She stood directly in front of her and carefully touched both sides of her face.

INEVITABLE

"Your makeup is gorgeous. And you have boobies." Giselle tried to contain her laughter as her aunt palmed her new breasts with both hands.

"Honey, turn around and let me see your butt."

Giselle slowly did a three-sixty. "Nice ass-ets," her aunt joked.

Giselle beamed.

"And this hair looks extremely expensive." She ran her hands through Giselle's golden tresses. "Everything looks so natural. You look... like...a woman. How do you feel?"

Giselle dropped her head to admire the new person standing in her aunt's living room. She slowly looked up and responded, "finally like myself."

Aunt Gigi grabbed her and embraced her with all her might.

"That's all I ever wanted you to be," she whispered.

"So, are you going to go by the name you originally picked out?"

"Yes."

Aunt Gigi looked her up and down. "I know you're not going to believe me, but you actually look like a Giselle!"

Giselle beamed from ear to ear. It was all the acceptance she needed.

"Now, come on in here while I fix us something to drink. I want to hear all about this procedure."

Giselle made her way to the kitchen after taking the stilettos off and slipping into some flip flops. This very moment made her cherish her aunt even more.

Giselle blew on her chamomile tea while Gigi continued to examine her.

Her aunt gasped. "Oh...my...goodness, you don't have an Adam's Apple anymore!" She rubbed her own throat. "Didn't that hurt?"

Giselle noticed the fading scar on the bottom of her aunt's jaw.

INEVITABLE

She began to explicitly tell her aunt about her transformation – the good, the bad, and the ugly. As she explained to her the few complications she had during and post-surgery, Aunt Gigi listened in awe. "I'm just glad everything went okay. You're one of the lucky ones, you know," she said while sipping on her tea.

Suddenly her aunt burst into tears, followed by excessive sobbing. This frightened Giselle, but she knew this day would cause her and her aunt to relive a painful past.

"I'm so, so, so, sorry, sweetie. I should have paid more attention to you!" Giselle hugged her aunt tightly as they rocked in each other's arms.

***

Since that fateful summer of 1991, Gigi was never the same and refused to allow another man to get close to her. Thirteen years later, ovarian cancer claimed her life, but Giselle knew that she had stopped living long before.

***

Since Hill's revelation, Giselle had gone through a number of emotions. From denial to rage to suicidal thoughts. She missed her aunt and wished she could advise her on this pivotal moment in her life. She'd returned to Alabama to finally embrace who she was and who she'd become. She realized that Gerald, Jr and Giselle were one and the same. For over two decades she'd allowed her past to define her present and she knew that in order for her to move forward, in completeness, she had to break her own cycle. She looked at her phone. The last text message she'd received from Hill had almost taken her over the edge..."*Baby, I am so sorry about what I did to you. My life is empty without you in it. I want to grow old with you. I want you to be the mother of my children. We don't have to spend a ton on a wedding. Let's elope. No friends. No family. Just me and you. Please forgive me.*"

She needed to share her truth with him. No one but her closest family knew her true identity. Gerrod was troubled when he first learned of her decision, but after five therapy sessions, he'd come to grips with who his brother wanted to be. He actually joked that he always wanted a "sister".

Giselle looked at her phone again and hesitated. She loved Hill and she knew that he loved her back. Forgiveness. That's what pulled her parents through the worst storm of their lives. Even though she had a successful career, beautiful home and loyal friends, what she longed for was true companionship. *What is the point in having it all without a life partner to share it with*, she thought. She placed the old photo of her and her twin brother to her chest and hit the call button. Hill answered on the first ring. "Giselle?"

She took a deep breath and closed her eyes. Her mouth was dry as sandpaper and her hand trembled uncontrollably.

"Hey, it's me. I have something to tell you…"

INEVITABLE

Book Discussion Questions

Hill Stokes & Giselle Mosely

Should Hill have disclosed his past to Giselle? Is this something she needed to know in order for them to have a healthy relationship?

How long do you believe Giselle should have waited before disclosing her past to Hill?

Whose secret was most likely to have the biggest impact on their relationship?

Do you believe that they will ultimately stay together? Why or why not?

Gabriel Lowe & Elicia Harris

Do you believe Elicia did everything she could to fight for her marriage?

Was allowing Gabe into her life, so soon after separating from her husband, the right thing to do?

Did Gabe allow his feelings for Elicia to send him over the edge?

Name some of the "red flags" demonstrated by Gabe throughout the novel.

Trey Roberts & Marley Cole

Why do you believe Marley put up so many walls around Trey?

Do you believe that based on Trey's lifestyle and actions in the book that he was a sex-addict?

Should Marley have taken better precaution to protect herself from Kahmin?

Gerrod Mosely & Eva Mosely

Was Eva wrong for seeking to have her tubes tied without first consulting with her husband?

INEVITABLE

Was Gerrod justified in how he reacted to Eva's concerns about raising a biracial son? Was there anything she could have done differently to stop him from cheating?

When you decide to take someone back after cheating, are you really able to forgive them?

Is it easier for women to be able to forgive their spouse/significant other for cheating if they claim there was never an emotional connection to the other woman?

Gerald Mosely & Grace Mosely

Do you believe that Grace truly forgave her husband?

Was Gerald justified in committing adultery once he found out what was going on with his son at the time? Do you believe Gerald blamed himself for what happened to him when he was 11 years old?

General Questions

Which character do you feel you identify with the most?

What do you think is inevitable in any relationship?

How involved should your friends be in your relationship?

What should you do when you love your partner but aren't happy in the relationship?

How do you define "loving" someone vs. being "in love" with them?

How important is it that your significant other support your dreams?

INEVITABLE

Acknowledgements

I am beyond appreciative for my twin, Avon, family and friends who have stood by me during this artistic process. Because of your knowledge, wisdom, and support, I am able to pen yet another masterpiece. You don't have to be named, individually, because your effect on my life is expressed throughout my daily walk. It is because of you I will continue to love my Black skin, create with my pen, and marvel in its beautiful blend.

To the marketing genius, N. Renee McFadden, I want to especially thank you for the role you played in helping to produce this best-seller! You are my sister in purpose and definitely one in a million!

Special thanks to my sister, Toi Baylor of the Baylor Youth Foundation for your contribution, as you have always been there to help pick up the pieces when needed.

If you have been a part of this project, in any aspect, please know that you are a blessing as a best-seller has been born!

About the Author

As she consistently strives to embody excellence, Bella Black (professionally known as Dr. Avis Foley) garners wisdom and direction from celebrated leaders who have come before her. She desires for others to use her own life as a blueprint to enable them to understand the power they possess to create effectual change.

Because she wholeheartedly believes that the educated never stop learning, Bella Black's passion lies in teaching through various mediums. An educator for over ten years, she has had the opportunity to serve as a mentor to hundreds of students, serve as Associate Editor of a magazine for young professionals, and publish her debut novel, *BLUE*, depicting the trials and triumphs of seven college friends. In her second novel, *Inevitable*, she explores the lives of three professional women on a quest for real love.

Bella Black's passion for enlightenment has enabled her to inspire many youth and adult learners to surpass their potential. She plans to continue her mission through an expanded platform to include public speaking and community outreach.

Follow Bella Black on Facebook, Twitter, Instagram and YouTube: @iambellablack

Website: www.inevitablethebook.com

Milton Keynes UK
Ingram Content Group UK Ltd.
UKHW051911300124
436988UK00011B/699